MW01139137

Sno-Isle

RESURRECTION IN MUDBUG

BY JANA DELEON

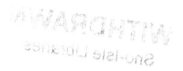

Copyright © 2013 Jana DeLeon

All rights reserved

All rights reserved. This copy is intended for the original purchaser of this book. No part of this book may be reproduced, scanned, or distributed in any printed or electronic form without prior written permission from the author except by reviewers who may quote brief excerpts in connection with a review. Please do not participate in or encourage piracy of copyrighted materials in violation of the author's rights. Purchase only authorized editions.

Chapter One

Maryse Robicheaux LeJeune polished off a truly excellent cinnamon roll and lifted her coffee to wash it down. She had just filled her mouth with the hot liquid when Helena Henry walked through the wall of the Mudbug Café and sat in the booth across from her. Before her mind could even process what she saw, her body reacted and she spit the coffee across the table, where it passed right through the smiling ghost.

"Are you all right?" the waitress asked.

Maryse nodded, attempting to look normal. "It just went down wrong."

"Looks to me," Helena said, "like it came *out* wrong."

Maryse waited until the waitress walked away and glanced around the café to ensure that no one was within hearing distance. Then she leaned across the table.

"This is not possible," she whispered. "You ascended a year ago. I saw you. We *all* saw you."

"I know what you saw. I was the one doing the ascending."

Maryse's mind raced with possibilities that might explain the ghost in front of her, but all of them were horrible.

"Is someone going to die?" Maryse asked.

"How should I know?"

"Then why are you here?"

"Because you weren't at home. I stopped there first hoping to get a glance of the sexy Luc in some state of undress, but you

1

were both already gone. So given the morning hour and knowing your lack of domestic abilities, I came here."

Maryse clenched her hands and willed herself not to jump across the table and attempt to strangle the ghost, who was deliberately misunderstanding her. "Why are you back on *earth*, Helena? Why aren't you in heaven?"

Helena shrugged. "It was boring, okay? And I might have done some things to make it more interesting."

Maryse sucked in a breath. "What things?"

"That's not the point."

"Really? Because it sounds like that's *exactly* the point."

Helena rolled her eyes. "Is it my fault that God doesn't have near the sense of humor you'd expect? I mean, he *did* put testicles on the outside."

Maryse closed her eyes and started counting. Maybe if she counted long enough, she'd open her eyes and Helena would be gone. Maybe if she wished it hard enough, this entire episode could be classified as a temporary mental break that she'd learn to live with.

Please God, don't do this to me.

"If you're asking God for help," Helena broke into her prayer, "I don't think he's going to comply if it means taking me back."

Then something Helena said clicked with Maryse and she opened her eyes, a trickle of fear running through her. "How do you know where I live? We built that house after you left."

Helena brightened. "Sometimes God let me watch you guys—you know, how parents plop their kids down in front of a movie to keep them out of their hair? Same concept."

Maryse sighed. If God couldn't handle Helena, she had no idea what he expected mere mortals to do. "I don't want you back, Helena, nor the trouble you bring with you. Everything has finally settled down here in Mudbug. People are happy and there hasn't been a single attempted murder since you left."

Helena took on her indignant pout. "I did not murder anyone."

"No, but everything seemed to center around you."

Helena threw her hands up in the air. "Well, I don't know what you expect me to do about it. I'm here and I have no choice in the matter."

Maryse downed the last of her coffee, wishing it were a shot of whiskey.

The peaceful existence she'd enjoyed for the last year was officially over.

Chapter Two

Jadyn St. James pressed the accelerator harder on her Jeep, causing her to bounce a good inch off the seat on the bumpy dirt road. It was her first official day as game warden and only her second day ever in the tiny town of Mudbug, Louisiana, but apparently, she had a crisis to handle before she'd even unpacked her bags. At least, that's how the sheriff's dispatcher referred to the situation when she'd made a frantic call to Jadyn for help earlier.

Jadyn attempted to find out exactly what she was driving into, but the distressed woman said she had to call the hospital and get a copter down there. Gripping the steering wheel with one hand, Jadyn looked at the rough map of the swamp that her cousin Maryse had drawn her the night before, and hoped she was headed in the right direction.

Tiny dirt roads snaked off in as many directions as the channels and inlets off the main bayou. One wrong turn and whatever crisis called for a helicopter might be over before she ever found the location. She took a hard right turn at a cypress tree split by lightning and hoped that she didn't have to deal with a fatality her first day on the job.

She'd only ever dealt with one fatality, and that one wasn't work-related. In the back of her mind, she'd always known that death would be part of the job someday, but she hadn't planned on facing her demons so quickly.

JANA DELEON

The dirt trail curved to the left and she rounded the corner, then slammed on her brakes, sliding to a halt right behind a truck with the sheriff department's logo on the side. A collection of people lined the bank of the bayou, all of them shouting in panic. Still unsure what she was facing, Jadyn grabbed her pistol from the glove compartment and hurried to the bank to see what was up.

It only took a glance to know this situation was way outside of her skill set.

The channel she'd been following ended in what could charitably be called a large pond. In the middle of the pond, half of a shrimp boat peeked up out of the murky water, but that wasn't the cause for alarm.

Around the shrimp boat bobbed floating plastic bags. From her spot on the bank, Jadyn couldn't see what was in the bags, but it must be something worth risking your life for. All around the edge of the pond, men jumped into the alligator-infested water, trying to grab a floating bag before one of the prehistoric monsters grabbed them.

Certain that Louisiana Wildlife and Fisheries had no protocol for this, Jadyn did the only thing she could think of and rushed up to the edge of the bank and yelled at the men closest to her to exit the water. She might as well have been yelling into a vacuum. The men didn't even acknowledge she was there, much less climb out. Instead, two men who'd grabbed the same bag started a fistfight.

She yelled, a tug-of-war ensued, and the bag split in two, sending money scattering into the air. She grabbed at one of the bills as it fluttered near her and almost passed out—a hundred-dollar bill! What in God's name was going on in this town?

She pulled out her pistol, prepared to take control, when a man's voice sounded behind her.

6

"Sweetheart, I need you to step back from the pond. I've got enough to deal with. I don't need you getting hurt trying to save your boyfriend or something equally as stupid."

Sweetheart?

She spun around to face the source of the voice and was momentarily silenced. The man before her was quite possibly the hottest guy she'd ever seen short of a movie screen. Even in jeans and T-shirt, she could see the size and flex of his muscles. His dark wavy hair was weeks past needing a cut, but somehow he made it look sexy instead of unkempt. He wore polarized sunglasses, so she couldn't see his eyes, but something deep inside of her hoped they were green.

He called you sweetheart.

She frowned as she crashed back to reality. "I'm not your sweetheart. I'm the game warden. As this is the game preserve, this is *my* business, not yours, so I'm going to go ahead and ask *you* to step back from the water."

"You've got to be kidding me."

She felt her back tighten. "Do I look like I'm kidding?"

He sighed. "Then you take one side of the bank and I'll take the other. Those gators are napping right now, but if we don't get these fools out of the water before lunchtime, it's not going to be pretty."

It wasn't that she thought his idea lacked merit. It was that she had no idea why he thought he could bark orders at her like she was some lackey.

"And why should I listen to you?"

"Because I'm right and I'm the sheriff—Sheriff Colt Bertrand. I'm the one who called you for help. Well, not you specifically, because if I'd known...anyway, take the side to the left and do something—hell, flash them if you have to, but get them out of the damned water!"

He stalked off down the right side of the bank and she

stared at him for a moment, before whirling around and heading the other direction. That was some condescending attitude. Clearly, the emergency in front of her rated her attention now, but as soon as this mess was handled, she would have a word with the sexist sheriff.

She walked up to the edge of the pond and yelled at some of the men to get out, even shouting her credentials, but they all pretended not to hear. Then she fired her weapon in the air, which got them to pause for a second, but as soon as she told them to get out of the water, they went right back to fighting and ignoring her.

Another man came running down the bank and she leveled her gun at him, threatening to shoot if he didn't stop. He ran right past her and bailed into the pond as if she were invisible. One glance at the back of the pond and her pulse spiked. The alligators were starting to stir. All of the thrashing about had gotten their attention and alerted them that an easy meal may be close by.

A rush of panic ran through her. If a significant portion of the Mudbug population were maimed or killed on her first day of work, it probably wouldn't reflect well on her. Even if they were all idiots who'd asked for it.

They weren't going to listen to reason. That much was obvious. And clearly, she wasn't about to resort to a flashing debacle, as suggested by the no-account Sheriff Bertrand, so she took the only other reasonable option and started shooting.

An introverted personality and a significant lack of trust for people in general had left her a lot of free time, and she'd spent much of it at the gun range. Not a single shot out of her first ten went awry. Every single floating bag she targeted popped, then rapidly sank beneath the slowly swirling water. She never stopped once to consider what Sheriff Bertrand would say. Quite frankly, she didn't care.

The men howled in horror and the fighting got more violent for the remaining bags, as she took out everything that wasn't already in someone's hand. The gators, who'd been contemplating an early snack, held their positions, either experience or some built-in defense letting them know that the sound of gunshots meant the possibility of a bad ending.

When she sank the last of the bags, she stuck her nine millimeter in her waistband and watched as the men started wading out of the water, not willing to risk diving into the murky depths after the money.

"Nice shooting," Sheriff Bertrand's voice sounded beside her.

She looked over to see him grinning, thumbs hooked over his jeans pockets.

"Are you going to arrest me now?" she asked.

"Why? You didn't shoot any residents."

"If they didn't get out of that pond, I was going to start."

The grin widened.

She stared at him and shook her head. How could someone appear so cocky and so relaxed at the same time? She'd expected him to be pissed at her choice; instead, he appeared amused. And that made her even madder.

"You could have helped," she pointed out.

"Why waste my own bullets? You had it under control, and I have a touch of a hangover from my day off. I figured it was okay to sit back and watch the show."

"I'm so glad I could provide you with some entertainment."

"You stupid bitch!" A man's voice sounded behind her.

She turned in time to see one of the swimmers running toward her, fist already cocked. Twenty years of martial arts training kicked in and she ducked before the hand could connect with her jaw, fully expecting the "moron" to tag Sheriff Bertrand.

But instead of hearing the sound of a fist connecting with a face, she heard a dull thud and rose up to see the sheriff holding the moron's fist in his hand, just an inch from his jaw.

Despite the instant disliking she'd taken to the sheriff, Jadyn was impressed.

In one fluid move, the sheriff twisted the man's arm behind his back and cuffed him. "That one buys you a night in jail, Junior."

"What for?" Junior protested. "I didn't even hit anyone."

"That's because you suck at fighting," the sheriff said. "Besides, you insulted our new game warden and if that's not against the law, it probably will be when the mayor lays eyes on her."

He pushed Junior up the bank. "The rest of you, get the hell out of here and leave everything you grabbed on the hood of my truck on the way out. If I see you here again or suspect you didn't turn over the money, I'm going to arrest you all and search your houses and boats. Anyone who buys a new toy will have it impounded because I know you're all broke. Are we clear?"

The men grumbled, but surprised Jadyn when they piled crumpled wet bills on the sheriff's truck. Clearly, they took Bertrand at his word, even Junior, who babbled about the cash in his overalls pocket.

"I'll get that when you strip at the jail," Sheriff Bertrand said as he pushed Junior down to sit on the bank. "The last thing in the world I'm going to do is dig in your pockets."

Jadyn hesitated on the bank, unsure what was expected of her in this situation. The men were already pulling away from the pond in boats, trucks, and ATVs, and surely her job description didn't include jumping into the pond and retrieving the remaining cash.

"So how do you want to handle this?" Sheriff Bertrand

asked.

She turned around to look at him, not understanding the question, so unable to formulate a decent answer. "What do you mean? Looks like you've got it all under control."

He raised his eyebrows at her. "Exactly how long have you been on the job?"

Her back tightened again. "If you mean here in Mudbug, today's my first day, but I've been the assistant game warden in Caddo Parish for the last five years."

"North Louisiana. That explains it."

Jadyn was certain she'd just been insulted, but couldn't figure out exactly what the insult was. "It explains what?"

"Why you don't see the bigger problem than those fools trying to kill themselves over a couple hundred dollars each."

Dumbass!

She'd been so focused on getting the men out of the pond before the alligators lined up for a buffet that she hadn't stopped to consider the ramifications of why they were willing to risk life and limb. She sucked in a breath.

"That's a shrimp boat, right?" she asked.

He nodded.

"I'm not overly familiar with the shrimping industry, but I'm going to go out on a limb and assume shrimpers don't usually carry around Baggies full of hundred-dollar bills."

"No, they do not."

"Shit."

He looked at the pond and sighed. "I couldn't have said it better myself."

11

Chapter Three

Colt thanked the tow truck driver and sent him down the narrow road, pulling what remained of the sunken shrimp boat on a flatbed trailer. With no other option but waiting on the state to send the proper equipment, Colt had called on the Mudbug residents for help extracting the boat.

By now, everyone in Mudbug knew what was in the pond, and he couldn't risk a drunken midnight parade from Pete's Bar, attempting to recover anything left in the boat. The new game warden agreed immediately to his plan, apparently having no trouble believing the men might come back drunk and attempt to resurrect the boat.

The whole event was a sketchy proposition but within a mere twelve hours, the one tow truck, six dualies, fourteen ATVs, and a horse finally managed to drag the boat out of the pond and onto the trailer.

"Marty Breaux owns the mechanic shop in town," Colt said to Jadyn as she walked up the bank, looking as exhausted as he felt. "He works on everything, so he's got stalls big enough for boats. I'll have him lock it up tonight, and you can decide what to do about it tomorrow."

Jadyn looked confused. "You're going to investigate, right? I assume that was drug money."

"Drug money is a good guess, but I'm not the one who should be guessing. See, that pond is in the game preserve, and I know how you game wardens are about your jurisdiction. This baby is all yours."

Her dismay was so apparent, it was almost cute. He clapped her on the back before walking toward his truck. "Welcome to Mudbug."

She was still standing on the bank, looking shell-shocked, when he climbed into his truck, but as he started to pull away, she came alive and stomped up the bank to her Jeep. Convinced she was safely leaving the scene of the crime, he took off down the dirt road back to town. He needed an hour-long shower and a six-pack of beer to erase the stench of the day.

He rolled his neck around, trying to release some of the tension, but it was useless. Even though he'd been accurate with his assessment that the boat and everything that came along with it was a problem for the game warden, there was no way he was leaving an investigation to the wide-eyed doe.

She was a top marksman, and she had completely surprised him—and Junior—with her martial arts ability, but no way was she qualified for a problem of this caliber. Problems like this one were often the precursor to a pileup of bodies. He'd seen it more than once working for the New Orleans Police Department. In fact, it was exactly this sort of problem that he'd been hoping to escape when he'd returned back home to Mudbug, a town with fewer people than New Orleans housed on a city block.

He sighed. All that running and the same problem had landed right back in his lap, but without the resources or experience he'd had at his disposal in New Orleans. Jadyn St. James was a hell of a good shot and she was way easier on the eyes than the previous game warden, who was three hundred pounds if he was an ounce and who'd had a perpetual case of exposed butt crack.

But she wasn't even remotely qualified to handle this kind

of criminal.

The question was—was he prepared to do it? And the even bigger question—was he qualified to handle Jadyn St. James?

One look at the fit, dark-headed beauty had sent his mind right back to Maria, and that was a place he never wanted to go. The truth was, he'd left New Orleans to get away from memories of Maria as much as he had the despicable criminals he'd been chasing. Every street, every building, every tourist...they all reminded him of her in some way. He'd thought returning to Mudbug would cause his childhood memories to return and eclipse his more recent ones. And so far it had worked pretty well.

Until today.

When Colt started his truck, Jadyn fought the overwhelming urge to scramble up the bank and run for her Jeep. The sun had already set, and it suddenly occurred to her that she might not be able to find her way back to town in the dark.

She forced herself to maintain a fast walk, but pushed her Jeep quicker than comfortable down the bumpy dirt road until she saw Colt's taillights rounding a corner about fifty feet in front of her. She slowed a bit and maintained that distance until they pulled onto the paved farm road that led back into Mudbug.

Colt turned off onto another dirt road about a mile outside of Mudbug—presumably to his house—waving at her as she drove past.

Jadyn gave a silent prayer of thanks that he lived off the main road and not buried somewhere back in the paths they'd just traversed. She didn't even want to imagine the humiliation she would have experienced if she'd quite literally followed the man to his front door. Lord only knows what he and everyone else in town would have made of that.

As she parked in front of the Mudbug Hotel, she felt some of the tension in her back and neck slip away. She'd call in a dinner order at Carolyn's Cajun Kitchen, then she'd take the hottest shower possible while waiting on her food to arrive and try not to think about the hundreds of daunting decisions she needed to make the next day.

Mildred, the hotel owner, was finishing up paperwork at the front desk when Jadyn walked in. The older woman looked up at her and gave her a sympathetic smile.

"I heard you had a pretty hard first day," Mildred said.

"It definitely wasn't what I expected."

Mildred shook her head. "It's not something we should ever expect in Mudbug. I was pretty floored, and very little surprises me anymore. I don't like to think that the kind of business that carries cash in Baggies is going on in my town."

"I don't blame you, but don't start worrying just yet. I'm hoping that storm yesterday blew the boat off-course. If that's the case, then the problem still exists, but maybe not in Mudbug."

Mildred brightened a bit. "That would be great…I mean, not for the other town, of course, but we had our share of trouble a little over a year ago. Things have settled down since, and I'd prefer they not get stirred up again."

Jadyn nodded. "I read a bit about that in the papers. Sounded like a nightmare."

"Oh, the reporters can't capture even the half of how horrible it was. I thought I was going to lose Maryse in that fray, then her friends. It was the worst months of my life."

"I'm sure this will turn out to be nothing," she reassured Mildred. "I'm going to think positive."

"Then I will too. By the way, the dispatcher called to let me know you were on your way back in. I figured you'd be starving, so I ordered you fish and chips and cobbler. Hurry up for a shower, and I'll bring the food up when it gets here."

Jadyn warmed at the older woman's words. Her own mother had been more interested in maintaining her marriage to her wealthy husband than raising Jadyn. It was nice having someone take care of her, even in a small way.

"I appreciate it. And yes, I'm starving. Thanks."

Jadyn hurried up the stairs to her room and turned the shower on full blast. She'd been a bit apprehensive about living in the hotel, but Mudbug had a limited supply of rental property and nothing would be available for another month. It was either stay at the hotel or pass on the job, and she wasn't about to pass on the job. Game warden positions in Louisiana weren't all that plentiful, and women had an even harder time getting the top nod.

Jadyn was certain the fact that Maryse owned the preserve had a lot to do with her gaining the position, and she wasn't about to let her cousin down, especially since Maryse had vouched for her without really knowing her. Given that Jadyn's mother thought Maryse's parents were beneath her social status, Jadyn had never really met her cousin until she came for the interview, but she'd taken an instant liking to her outdoorsy, down-to-earth manner and looked forward to getting to know her better.

The hot shower did wonders for her back, neck, and overall attitude, and she toweled off, her mouth already primed for the food she knew was on its way. As Mildred was the only person who would see her, she simply pulled her long wet hair back into a ponytail and threw on shorts and a T-shirt. She didn't even bother with shoes—a habit her mother loathed—but Jadyn was now her own woman with her own money and if she decided to go barefoot every day, by God she was going to enjoy every minute of it.

As she headed for the lobby, she forced all thoughts of her mother out of her mind. The game warden position and Mudbug were her big chance at a new, normal life.

And she was going to take it.

Maryse pushed open the door to the Mudbug Hotel with one hand and gripped the bag of food with the other, giving Mildred a wave as she walked across the lobby. She'd intended to visit the hotel owner earlier in the day, but work and other obligations had interfered and this was the first opportunity she'd gotten to fill Mildred in on the Helena situation. Mildred had raised Maryse after her mother died and was going to be unhappy and worried about this turn of events.

"Luc got a call in the middle of dinner and had to dash," Maryse said. "Sally was about to bring this over for Jadyn, so I told her I'd take it. I needed to talk to you anyway."

"Another dinner interruption for Luc?" Mildred frowned. "That's three nights in a row."

Maryse waved a hand in dismissal. "Occupational hazard. Apparently nothing interests the DEA until we're sitting down to eat. He'll be home late tonight and starving. I have the rest of his dinner in the truck."

"I don't know how I'm ever supposed to get a grandchild out of this arrangement if the man's never at home or exhausted from work when he is."

Maryse rolled her eyes. "Luc is never too exhausted for that, and bite your tongue—babies are not even on my radar right now. You'll just have to live vicariously through Lila."

Mildred smiled. "Can you believe Hank Henry is sober, employed, married, and having a baby? If you'd told me that a year ago, I would have laughed so hard I peed myself."

Maryse laughed, the thought of her previously irresponsible ex-husband now a productive citizen and future father still somewhat unbelievable. "You and me both, but it looks like he's really turned his life around. I'm glad. I really like Lila, and she's good for him."

"Well, if you didn't come to talk about my future as a grandmother, then what's got you playing delivery service?"

The smiled faded from Maryse's face as quickly as it had appeared, and she struggled to get out the words she'd been planning to say all day. No matter what combination she'd come up with, she hadn't found a good way to deliver the news to Mildred that Helena was back. She'd finally decided that blurting it out was probably the best way to go. After all, it wasn't just knowing that Helena was present that was painful. It was all the terror she'd no doubt bring with her.

"This morning—"

Maryse broke off as Jadyn ran down the stairs and into the lobby, giving her a wave as she jumped over the last two steps.

"I could smell hush puppies as soon as I opened my room door," Jadyn said. "Thanks for bringing this over. I am officially starving."

"You're welcome," Maryse said, feeling relieved that the Helena conversation had been pushed back a bit. "I heard you had a momentous first day. I didn't really expect the job to be this exciting when I recommended it. I hope you're not going to hold it against me."

Jadyn pulled a hush puppy out of the bag and took a bite. "Not at all," she said after she'd swallowed. "Sure, it's not what I expected, especially on my first day, but it's part of the job. The reality is, I could run into the same problem anywhere."

"All the same," Mildred said, "I still wish it hadn't happened here."

"It may not have," Jadyn said. "Think positive, remember?"

"What do you mean?" Maryse asked.

"Jadyn thinks the storm might have blown the boat off-course," Mildred explained, "and that it could have been bound for somewhere other than Mudbug."

"That would be great," Maryse said. "Not that I wish the problem on any other town, but I'd sorta prefer it if Mudbug wasn't the one-stop shop for trouble this year."

"Fingers crossed," Jadyn said. "Hey, who was that woman you were arguing with outside of the café this morning?"

Maryse clenched the counter with one hand as the blood drained from her face. "What woman?"

No way. No way was this happening. Not again.

"Sixties, overweight, wearing skinny jeans and shouldn't have been. I ask because she looked familiar and you looked really pissed."

"She's a relative," Maryse said, struggling to sound normal. "A really distant relative who lives out-of-state."

Mildred scrunched her brow and stared at Maryse, knowing full well that Maryse had precious few blood relatives left and she knew all of them. Maryse prayed that Mildred wouldn't chime in.

"I hope she doesn't visit often," Jadyn said, "because you sure didn't look happy to see her."

"She's a trial," Maryse said. "Fortunately, I don't see her often."

"Well, I hate to be rude," Jadyn said, "but if I don't eat, I'm going to pass out. Thanks for bringing this over, Maryse."

"No problem," Maryse managed as Jadyn grabbed the bag and headed upstairs. Maryse waited until she heard Jadyn's room door slam shut before she turned to Mildred.

"What's wrong?" Mildred asked. "It's all over your face. Something awful."

Maryse nodded. "Worse than awful."

Mildred clenched her hands together. "Spit it out. Then we can figure out what to do about it."

Maryse took a deep breath and steadied herself, knowing that even saying the words would make her weak.

"Helena is back."

"Oh, God!" Mildred clutched the counter and lowered herself onto the stool behind her. "I knew. Before you even said it, I knew. There was something about your expression—something I haven't seen since last year."

"It's probably an overwhelming look of doom."

"Yeah, that about describes it." Mildred ran one hand through her hair. "What did she say? Why is she back?"

Maryse relayed her conversation with Helena. Mildred made the sign of the cross when she got to the part about Helena pissing off God.

"That woman is going to bring the Revelation," Mildred said. "She's the rider on the pale horse."

Maryse nodded, unable to disagree.

"So where is she now?" Mildred asked.

"I don't know. I took off from the café and headed into the swamp for work. I haven't seen her since."

"Maybe she left again." The hopeful sound in Mildred's voice was clear.

Maryse shook her head. "Somehow, I don't think so."

"Have you told Sabine?"

"No. She and Beau don't get back from their cruise until next week. I figured it would be cruel to tell her they're returning to Mudbug complete with Helena Henry."

Mildred nodded. "You're right. Best wait. What about Raissa?"

"All I can get from her handler is that Raissa and Zach are deep undercover and can't be reached. I left a message for her to contact me, but that's all I can do."

"And Hank?"

"I left a message for him to call, but I haven't heard back yet."

"What are we going to do?" Mildred asked. "We can't have normal lives with Helena running around, especially now that she can stroll through locked doors."

"We've got an even bigger problem than the loss of sanity and privacy."

"What's that?"

"The woman Jadyn saw me arguing with outside of the café this morning—that was Helena."

Chapter Four

Despite her overly long and eventful first day, Jadyn was up early and out the door. She grabbed a quick breakfast at the café, then headed to the garage where the boat was stored. She figured the good sheriff would be at the garage first thing and didn't want to give him any ammunition to pull the case from her. It wasn't what she'd hoped for her first day on the job, but she was determined to prove she could handle anything the swamp could dish out.

She smiled when she saw the sheriff's truck pulling up to the garage just ahead of her. Perfect timing. He stepped out of his truck and waited on Jadyn to exit her Jeep before motioning to the end bay on the huge metal building.

"It's in the last stall," he said. "I don't suppose you thought to bring a camera, did you? I'm afraid ours met with a drunk and disorderly accident."

Jadyn held in a grin as she and lifted the camera bag from the backseat. Score number two. "Are you kidding? I'm not about to miss documenting this."

Colt nodded and started toward the stall. Jadyn fell into step behind him, her adrenaline starting to pump. At first, she'd been overwhelmed with the thought of such an investigation landing in her lap so soon. She had little knowledge of criminals beyond poachers, and aside from Maryse and Mildred, zero knowledge of Mudbug. It wasn't the best set of credentials for this level of

23

trouble.

But if it happened that the problem was Mudbug's, no way was she shirking her duty. In fact, the longer she'd thought about it, the more excited she became about the possibility of making a name for herself so soon. If she could solve this, she'd be golden. No more backhanded comments about women and quotas. No more sly up-and-down looks from men, making the insinuation that something besides her ability to do her job had gotten her the positions she'd gained.

It was an opportunity to cease being Jadyn the hot woman in hiking boots and become Jadyn the game warden. Period. At least, that's what she could hope for.

Colt unlocked the padlock on the door and rolled it up. Jadyn stepped inside and pulled the camera out, wanting to get some shots of the boat intact—well, as intact as it came out of the water—before she and Colt started tearing it apart.

"No name on the back," she commented as she worked her way around.

Colt, who was also doing a walk-around, nodded. "I'll bet there's no license, registration, or any other identifier. Whatever the owner was up to, it wasn't shrimping."

Jadyn froze and lowered the camera, an awful thought crossing her mind. "You don't think the owner is still…"

"In the boat? No. With the summer humidity, the smell would have hit us as soon as we got it out of the water."

Jadyn relaxed a bit. It wasn't the most pleasant of explanations, but he was right.

"So what do you think happened to him?" she asked.

Colt shook his head. "Could have bailed during the storm and swam for shore. Could have gotten pitched out during the storm and drowned. If it's the latter, we're unlikely to find a body."

"Not even this quickly? The boat couldn't have been there more than twelve hours, right?"

"Crabs alone will skin a body in a matter of a day or two. And they're not the only scavengers in these waters."

Jadyn frowned, thinking about the crab dinner she'd had at Carolyn's her first night in town. Maybe she'd cross crab off her list of acceptable dinner items.

"Had the crab at Carolyn's, didn't you?" Colt asked and grinned.

"Yes, but I don't see why you find that amusing," she said, irritated that he found her so transparent.

"No one's gone missing in the bayous here in years, so you don't have to worry about becoming a cannibal. Lots of people stop eating crab after big hurricanes, though."

Okay. Ick.

"You really know how to launch a great morning conversation, Bertrand."

He laughed. "You'll get used to it. I know you think you're a Louisiana native, but coming from north Louisiana, you may as well be a Yankee. Things are completely different in the bayous versus the piney woods."

"Yeah, I got that loud and clear, but you don't need to worry. I'm more than qualified to handle anything this town throws at me, Yankee or no."

He studied her a couple of seconds before replying. "Maybe. But if it's all the same, I'd like to keep my nose in things for a while. I have a vested interest in keeping this town safe. If something nasty is going on here, I want it gone."

She bristled a bit at his words and his scrutiny. He wasn't her boss or her employer. Who was he to sit in judgment of her abilities? For that matter, what of his own abilities if this had been going on under his nose? She could draw a line in the sand and tell him to back off her investigation, but for now, she'd keep quiet, a decision she'd probably end up regretting.

The sheriff was a little too good-looking, a little too smooth for her comfort. But he knew the town and the people, and for all she knew, might even have experience with this sort of thing. The stark reality was that she felt better knowing someone had her back, even if he might try to nudge her out of the way. Things here were too different...too strange for her to feel comfortable going it alone just yet, but damn if she was letting him take over. She could already hear the locals commenting on that one—"the pretty little girl couldn't handle the job so the big, bad sheriff had to rescue her."

No way was that happening.

"I appreciate the help," she said, deciding that sticking with the simplest sentiment was probably best.

He looked a bit surprised at the genuine tone in her voice.

"Not what you were expecting me to say?" she asked.

"It's usually not the response one law enforcement officer gets when they try to horn in on another officer's territory."

"I can appreciate that, but the thing you need to know about me is that I'm not stupid. And as I have no male ego to get in my way, I see the advantage of having help from someone who knows the people and the lay of the land. I plan to stay in Mudbug a long time. I want the locals to know they can count on me to keep their town safe."

He smiled. "It's going to be nice having a smart woman around. Sometimes it seems there's a shortage on brains all the way around in Mudbug."

Considering that it was only the day before that she'd watched a bunch of men jump into alligator-infested water for the chance to fight over plastic bags of money, Jadyn was inclined to agree with Colt's assessment.

"I am smart," she said. "I'm also in charge. I would

definitely appreciate your help, but it has to be my investigation and my terms. Is that all right with you?"

"It's all good," he said, but Jadyn got the impression that Colt had a completely different agenda. No way was the cocky young sheriff going to play second fiddle to a woman for long. She'd use him for the investigation, but if he stepped over the line, she'd cut him loose. It wasn't a balancing act she was completely comfortable with, but she'd make it work.

She didn't see another choice.

Colt studied Jadyn as she worked the boat, careful to go about his scrutiny unobserved. She was thorough—he had to give her that—documenting everything with the camera and voice-recorded notes before allowing a single item in the boat to be moved. She'd donned plastic gloves before boarding, but he doubted it was because she thought any prints remained. More likely, she was simply trying to minimize direct contact with the nasty mud and swamp foliage strewn all over the boat. Being a guy, Colt didn't have the same issues with dirty or stinky hands, so he went commando.

He'd been a little surprised when she'd accepted his offer to help so readily, but then he'd seen something in her eyes shift and she'd come back with the whole "but I'm in charge" statement. Apparently, the sexy game warden had something to prove. He'd been the same way when he'd made detective with the New Orleans PD. He could only imagine that the pressure for a woman in a traditionally male role would be even worse.

But all the same, how much he respected her desire to be in control depended on exactly where this whole mess was headed.

Even though they were thorough, it only took a couple of hours to determine that no identifiers existed on the boat. No registration, no license, no paperwork of any kind, except the Baggies of money that hadn't floated away. But that wasn't the thing that bothered Colt most. What worried him more was the fact that they still had no idea what the money was to be used for.

"I know this is a pointless question," Jadyn said, "but I have to ask if we can drag the pond?"

"A net wouldn't make it six inches before it hung on something it couldn't pick up. Not to mention, we'd probably snag some alligators in the mess."

"That's what I figured." She took a few final pictures of the outside of the boat, then packed her camera away in its bag. Leaning back against the metal wall of the garage, she stared at the boat and blew out a breath.

"So what do you think?" she asked.

"I think a lot of things, but none of them based on evidence, because we don't have much to speak of."

"I know. My mind's rolling through all the things a boatload of money might be used to fund, and each one is worse than the one before."

"Yep."

She looked over at him. "You know this area—these people—what's the most likely option?"

"With this area and these people specifically...none of them. I've known most everyone in town since I was a kid. I think I would have noticed if they were drug runners or something equally as despicable."

Jadyn frowned.

"What?" he asked. "You think I'm wrong?"

"Not necessarily."

"What then?"

"I think if someone has been conducting this level of business in Mudbug and not gotten on your radar, then it's something new or it's someone who's above reproach."

"That's a nasty thought."

"But not an inaccurate one. If this boat was headed for Mudbug, and if you really intend to help, you're going to have to let go of any assumptions you've made about the people here."

The implications bothered him far more than he'd like to admit. In New Orleans, he'd seen situations like this too many times to think she was dead wrong, but he didn't have to like it, and by God, he didn't. This kind of thing was one of the many reasons he'd left New Orleans. He'd wanted to deal with simple crime and simple criminals. Things that were obvious and clear.

This was everything but.

"Look," he said finally, "this is hardly my first rodeo. I spent ten years with the New Orleans PD, the last eight as a detective. I know all about the perp turning out to be the person you least suspect, or the person no one believed it could be. I've arrested too many of those 'no possible way' candidates for me to have much faith in humanity, in general."

"But?"

"But I'm not lying to you when I say I don't see any signs of major criminal activity here. No one is living beyond his means, except to the extent they're buying cigarettes and booze instead of paying the utility bill. No one is acting strangely. No one has had a sudden shift in behavior or taken up with new friends. No strangers have arrived in town recently except you and the normal round of traveling salesmen that visit the chemical plants and bunk at the hotel."

She considered his words, then nodded. "Maybe the storm blew the boat off-course and it was intended for another town. Maybe the problem isn't a Mudbug problem at all—and that's what I'm praying for. But I wouldn't be doing my job if I didn't turn over every rock and stump in the bayou looking for the answer."

"I agree," he said and sighed.

"How did the men find out about the money in the pond?" she asked.

He shrugged. "I asked everyone, but they all said another had called and told them. Most boats have CB radios."

"But someone had to find it first. Why call people at all? Why not take everything you could for yourself?"

He frowned. "Could be more than one fisherman headed to that cove. It's known for producing good-size bass. If it was only one or two men, they might agree to keep it a secret, but if you had three or more show up, then they probably got excited and started telling everyone in range."

"Or it could be that whoever lost control of the boat was attempting to collect all the cash when fisherman showed up. It would be helpful to know who was on-scene first."

Colt nodded. He'd already gotten around to that thought yesterday when he'd questioned all the men about how they'd been clued in to the money pond, but he was somewhat surprised that Jadyn had gotten there so quickly. She had a good mind for investigation. Maybe, just maybe, she wouldn't be as much of a liability as he'd originally figured.

"I'll ask again," he said. "They're more likely to tell me than you. If I get anything more out of them, I'll let you know."

She inclined her head and stared at him for a couple of seconds before speaking. "If there was going to be any bragging going on, where would it be?"

"Bill's Bar. But if you stroll in there flashing a game warden ID and asking questions, they'll sober up and clam up before you can get out the first question."

She grinned. "Who said I'd go in flashing a badge? Women flashing other things tend to get a lot more out of men at a bar. In fact, isn't that what you suggested yesterday as a means for me to get the men out of the pond?"

He felt a twinge of guilt as she threw his crass statement back at him. His mother would kill him if he knew he's said something like that. "Most women in authority don't want to run the risk of disrespect by playing that card."

"We're all given different assets, Bertrand. If it helps solve this problem quickly, I have zero qualms about using mine."

He shook his head, both surprised and amused by her take. Maybe Jadyn St. James wasn't as rigid as she seemed. "Do me a favor and stretch before you go. Some of those deflection moves you've got are probably going to come in handy."

He saw the blush creep up her neck and barely managed to hold in a smile. Jadyn was working hard at being tough, and on the outside, she looked the part. But she was rusty on the social side of things, which was charming compared to the barracudas he'd dated in New Orleans.

"Well," he said. "If we're done here, I'll make rounds and start questioning the men again. I hope you don't mind that I took the liberty of sending off some of the bills to the state laboratory last night. I don't expect to find prints, but I wanted to make sure the money wasn't counterfeit or stolen."

"That's great. Let me know when you hear from them."

"What are you going to do the rest of the day?"

"My job. Starting with getting to know the people of Mudbug from someone who probably knows all their dirty laundry and won't mind repeating it."

"Mildred." He nodded. "It's a good plan. She probably hears more dirt on Mudbug residents than the parish priest."

"Maybe I'll talk to him next." She swung the camera bag over her shoulder. "I'll catch up to you sometime this afternoon."

"Okay." As he watched her walk away, he decided that it was a great view. She was lean and toned, but not in an overdone way that made her sexless. Add in a curve to her hips and full breasts and Jadyn St. James might just be sporting one of the most perfect bodies he'd ever laid eyes on.

He sighed. All of which meant he better be at Bill's tonight in case she decided to flash her wares. A badge and handcuffs might come in handy.

He walked out of the garage and pulled down the door as she drove away, trying to clear the impression of her physical perfection from his mind. He told himself that he would have offered to help with the investigation even if the new game warden was a fifty-year-old balding man with a potbelly.

Now, he just had to convince himself that was true.

Chapter Five

"I'll move to Antarctica, I swear!" Despite a desperate attempt at control, Maryse's voice rose with her frustration level. "I can't live like this."

"Like I couldn't follow you to Antarctica," Helena said and rolled her eyes as she plopped down in a chair in front of Mildred's desk.

"You wouldn't dressed like that," Maryse said and waved her hands at Helena's disturbing lack of clothes that currently consisted of boy shorts, pasties, and thigh-high boots.

Mildred glanced over at the ghost and quickly looked away. Apparently, her breakfast hadn't settled enough to take in Helena in full view. Maryse couldn't blame her. She'd spit an entire mouthful of coffee on her new living room rug when Helena had walked through the wall that morning.

"You need to apologize to God," Maryse said, "and go home."

Helena crossed her arms, pushing her stomach rolls out even farther. "I am not going to apologize. *He* made me. How am I responsible for what he created?"

Mildred looked up at the ceiling, as if afraid lightning would bolt right into the room.

"Don't you dare put this off on God," Maryse said. "God didn't send you to my house at the crack of dawn this morning to try and catch a peek of Luc in the shower."

"Hail Mary full of grace..." Mildred mumbled and clutched the crucifix that hung around her neck.

Helena glared at Mildred. "Don't tell me it hasn't crossed your mind even once that it would be nice to catch a full nude of Maryse's sexy husband."

"He's practically my son-in-law," Mildred said, completely perturbed. "Do you know how awful that sounds?"

"Hmmmph," Helena huffed. "Keep lying to Maryse all you want, but as you aren't dead or blind, I know the truth."

Maryse waved a hand at Helena. "You can't just show up *in* people's houses, Helena. For Christ's sake, when you were alive, you would have had a stroke if someone showed up at your front door uninvited. Why on earth would you assume it's okay to walk into someone's bathroom when they're showering?"

Helena frowned. "Okay, maybe you have a point."

"Maybe?" Maryse struggled to maintain control, but the yoga lessons she'd been taking with Sabine were no match for Helena Henry.

"Okay," Mildred said, finally finding her voice for something besides prayer. "Let's talk this out like rational adults."

Maryse stared at her, certain at least one of them in the room was not rational or adult, and she wasn't referring to herself. Mildred caught her look and gave her the "mother stare." The one that said "shut up until I finish." Maryse clenched her jaw and flopped into a chair, exhausted already and it wasn't even 10:00 a.m.

"Now, Helena," Mildred began, "if you're going to be hanging around, then you have to respect our privacy just like you would have had to if you were alive. Unless they were on fire, Maryse wouldn't open her front door for anyone first thing in the morning, and she definitely wouldn't let someone in the bathroom to see her husband showering."

Helena sighed. "So you're saying anything I couldn't do in physical form, I'm not allowed to do in spirit form?"

"Exactly."

"That blows," Helena ranted. "I mean, what's the use of being a ghost if I can't use any of my special powers?"

"You can use them all you want," Mildred said in her most placating voice. "Just not on me, Maryse, Sabine, Raissa, or Hank."

Helena scrunched her brow for a moment, then pouted a bit before speaking. "I guess that's fair. It's not near as much fun, but I suppose I shouldn't piss off the only people I can have a conversation with."

"Is that okay by you, Maryse?" Mildred asked.

"If that's the best we can do," Maryse conceded, "but what about drop-ins? It's Helena we're talking about. She might not pop through a wall, but that won't stop her from standing on my doorstep and ringing the doorbell for an hour."

Immediately, Helena looked guilty and Maryse knew she'd clued in to her next stage of attack.

"No drop-ins," Mildred said.

"But how am I supposed to schedule a visit?" Helena protested.

You're not, was the first thought that passed through Maryse's head, but she knew she wouldn't get away with a "you can never visit" policy. And given that Lila was pregnant with Helena's grandchild, she knew it would be impossible to make her stay away once the baby was born.

"You can touch things now, right?" Maryse asked. "I mean, consistently?"

"Sure," Helena said. "Well, mostly. I mean, occasionally, I have an issue, but I'm probably 90 percent."

Maryse tried not to think about what happened during that 10 percent fail rate. "Then we'll get you a prepaid cell phone.

You can call if you want to visit. But you cannot keep calling. And if we say no, it's no. We have lives here, Helena."

"Fine," Helena said, "but I just want to say that you people are as uptight as ever. I thought you'd loosen up a bit after I left, but I guess there's no hope."

Maryse looked at Mildred and sighed.

"No hope" was far too accurate.

Jadyn's spirits lifted a bit when she saw Maryse's truck parked in front of the hotel. The two people she wanted to speak to in one convenient place. If anyone could give her some insight to the inner workings of Mudbug and its residents, it would be Mildred and Maryse. And given that they were the only two people in Mudbug she knew well enough to trust, her options were limited.

Mildred wasn't at the front counter, but Jadyn could hear angry voices down the hall where Mildred's office was located. She hesitated for a second before starting down the hall. It probably wasn't the best time to interrupt, but she wanted to catch Maryse before she hurried into the swamp to work. And if she were being honest, Jadyn couldn't imagine what would cause Mildred and Maryse—two of the most practical women she'd ever met—to argue that way, and she had to admit to a morbid curiosity.

The door to Mildred's office was halfway open, so she had a clear view of the scene inside. The woman Maryse had been arguing with the day before sat in a chair next to Maryse, and it appeared as if Mildred was trying to work out whatever problem the two of them had. Given that the woman was dressed completely inappropriately for her age, size, and the Bible belt,

Jadyn had no problem understanding why Maryse was upset when she visited.

Jadyn rapped on the door and stuck her head in.

"I'm sorry to interrupt," she said. "I needed to talk to Mildred and Maryse about a game warden matter."

She approached Maryse's relative and stuck out her hand. "I'm Jadyn St. James, Maryse's cousin and the new game warden."

The older woman's eyes widened and her jaw dropped. She looked frantically from Mildred to Maryse, but both of them were oddly frozen in place with panicked looks on their faces.

Whatever the problem was, good Southern upbringing must have finally won out, and the woman hesitantly stuck her hand out. "I'm Helena. It's nice to meet you."

Jadyn reached for the woman's hand and then the strangest thing she'd ever seen happened—her hand passed right through the other woman's, as if it wasn't even there.

"What the hell...?" Jadyn reached for her hand again, but only cool air brushed her hand.

She looked at Maryse and Mildred. "Is this some kind of joke?"

"God, I wish," Maryse said, looking absolutely miserable.

Helena glared at Maryse. "There's no cause to get rude."

"Really?" Maryse asked. "Because I think there's plenty of cause."

Maryse rose from her chair and took a deep breath, letting it slowly out before looking Jadyn directly in the eyes. "This is going to sound ridiculous, and impossible, but you need to believe what I'm telling you."

"Okay," Jadyn replied, an uneasy feeling sweeping over every inch of her body.

"This is Helena Henry," Maryse said. "My former mother-in-law...who was murdered a year ago."

Jadyn stared at Maryse, certain she'd lost her mind, then

looked over at Mildred, but the hotel owner looked completely serious and very miserable.

"You're joking," Jadyn said finally.

"I wish I was," Maryse said.

"Rude again," Helena piped in.

Jadyn looked at Helena again, then back at Maryse. "You want me to believe that I'm standing here talking to a ghost?"

Maryse shrugged. "Ghost…Angel of Death…"

"Okay," Helena ranted, "that's just downright insulting."

"And accurate," Mildred finally chimed in.

Helena waved a hand in dismissal. "That's not the point."

"That's exactly the point," Maryse said. She turned back to face Jadyn. "Look, I know this is hard to wrap your mind around, but after Helena was murdered, she started appearing to different people, and every time she appeared, their life was in danger. So I've been nervous ever since you told me you saw her yesterday. Seeing Helena doesn't usually bode well for people."

Jadyn's mind whirled as she tried to make sense of what Maryse said, but she simply couldn't understand why the most practical woman she'd ever met would assume she'd believe such crap. "You're telling me I'm going to die?"

"No," Maryse said. "I'm saying that someone will probably try to kill you. So far, no one we care about has died, but they've all come close."

Chapter Six

Jadyn felt a rush of blood run up her face. "Look, I don't know what kind of joke you're trying to pull, but it's not funny. I didn't think the two of you stooped to this kind of childish behavior."

Jadyn turned to leave, disgusted that the only two people she had trusted turned out to be crazy as loons.

"Wait!" Mildred shouted.

Jadyn stopped, respect for her elders still overriding her indignation. She turned back to face the hotel owner.

Mildred pulled a newspaper out of her desk drawer and handed it to Jadyn. "Look at the front page."

Jadyn took the newspaper and read the headline: "The Truth Comes Out: Helena Henry Was Murdered."

Then she saw the picture below the headline and her breath caught in her throat. She looked at the woman in the chair. "It's not possible."

"Put on something decent, Helena," Maryse said. "You're making this harder."

Helena sighed and waved a hand. Instantly, she was clothed in the same outfit she wore in the newspaper photo. Even her hair had altered to match the picture.

The blood that had rushed into Jadyn's head earlier left faster than it arrived. She felt herself sway as dizziness washed over her. Maryse grabbed her shoulders to steady her and guided her into the empty chair.

Her hands still clutched the newspaper as she looked over at the woman…ghost, one more time. Every cell in her mind screamed that it wasn't possible, but if the woman wasn't a ghost, what other explanation was there?

"This can't be happening," Jadyn said. "I must be dreaming. Or I'm still hungover from the beers last night."

But even as she said the words out loud, she knew neither was true. It took far more than two beers to create a hangover that had one hallucinating and besides, she'd just spent the past couple of hours working with Colt. He probably would have commented if she were sleepwalking or drunk.

She looked at Mildred and Maryse, who both stared at her, wearing worried expressions. Then she looked at Helena once more. She just looked bored.

Get it together, St. James.

She took a deep breath and slowly blew it out, trying to force her mind to focus on one thing at a time. "Okay, the truth is, I've always thought ghosts existed, but I never figured on meeting one, much less sitting in a hotel office and talking it over like she was a real person."

"I am a real person," Helena protested.

Mildred gave Helena the stink-eye and she clammed back up.

"But I'm shocked," Jadyn said, "and that feels awful because things rarely surprise me. I think it's going to take some time to put this into perspective."

Maryse bit her lip and looked over at Mildred, who frowned.

"The thing is," Maryse said, "you may not have time to dwell on this."

Jadyn sucked in a breath as she remembered Maryse's earlier comment and then thought about how she'd spent her morning.

"You really think I'm in danger?"

"I don't know," Maryse said, clearly miserable, "but everyone who's seen Helena has been. Granted, that was last year when we were still trying to solve her murder so she could ascend, and her visit this time is for completely different reasons, but until we can be certain, we have to assume you're at risk."

"Okay," Jadyn said. "How can we be certain?"

"You don't die," Helena piped in.

"Not helping," Mildred admonished the ghost before turning to Jadyn. "We don't know how to be certain. I don't know how much time would have to pass before Maryse and I would feel comfortable saying you're in the clear. As long as you can see Helena, we probably never will."

The overwhelming desire to pack her duffel bag and haul ass out of Mudbug as fast as possible washed over her. She'd barely started her job and hadn't signed a lease. Nothing or no one could force her to remain here.

Running from life again, Jadyn?

Her mother's words echoed in her mind, and she felt her back tighten. Marissa St. James was a former Miss USA runner-up who'd dallied with Jadyn's handsome electrician father but had married a short, balding attorney, twenty years her senior, who was now a state senator. She'd expected Jadyn to follow her path of using her looks to snag a wealthy, successful husband, and had never missed an opportunity to insult Jadyn for the choices she made—personal and professional.

Jadyn's hand clenched involuntarily and she felt a blush creep up her chest and onto her neck. No way would she give her mother the satisfaction of leaving Mudbug after less than a week on the job.

Even if it killed her.

"So if we assume the death bell tolled," Jadyn said, trying to look at the situation logically, "then what do I do next?"

Some of the tension disappeared from Mildred's and Maryse's expressions and Maryse sat on the edge of Mildred's desk.

"First off," Maryse said, "you are not in this alone, so the correct question is what do *we* do next?"

Mildred nodded.

A trickle of unfamiliar warmth formed in Jadyn's belly. She had no doubt the two women were absolutely serious about helping her, and it was a strange feeling. She'd never really had friends—women tended to look sideways at her because of her looks, and men tended to look all ways at her, which only caused more problems with women.

At first, Jadyn hadn't understood the unsolicited animosity. She'd never considered herself a beauty like her mother and certainly took no care to appear as such. But there was no denying when she looked in the mirror that her mother's excellent bone structure and wide-set amber eyes were stamped clearly on her face.

But now, these two women—whom she'd only known less than three days—wanted to protect her from potential death. It was both touching and overwhelming at the same time.

"Okay," she said and gave them a small smile. "Then what do *we* do?"

Maryse glanced over at Helena and sighed. "As much as I hate to do this to you, having Helena around can help to keep you safe. You spend a lot of time in the bayou, which makes it really easy for someone to pick you off with a rifle."

Jadyn glanced at the ghost, who'd reverted back to her pasties and boy shorts, and frowned. "I don't understand. How does having her around help protect me? If other people could see her, their eyes might bleed, but from where I sit, I see only the downside."

Helena glared. "Doesn't take a genius to see you two are related. You're both the same flavor of rude."

"Helena can stand guard," Maryse explained. "Since no one can see her, she can be on constant patrol and lookout for anyone who might want to harm you."

Jadyn glanced over at the ghost and struggled to keep from blanching. "I'm not arguing with you in theory, but as you already pointed out, I'm in the swamp all day. A crack shot with a rifle—and I'm guessing Mudbug has more than one—could easily get me from a hundred yards away, probably more. Helena doesn't look like she can cover a hundred yards in every direction, even if I was sitting still."

Helena threw her hands up in the air. "I'm so sorry. If I'd known I'd have the role of security detail in death, I would have done Weight Watchers and the elliptical before I died. But as I didn't get a say in dying, either, this is what you get. That whole 'you get a new perfect body when you die' thing is bunk."

Then Helena jumped up from the chair and walked through the wall.

Jadyn blinked and stared at the wall for several seconds before looking back at Maryse and Mildred, who didn't seem fazed with Helena's fit.

"Don't worry," Maryse said. "She'll be back."

Jadyn nodded, not entirely sure she wanted the ghost back. "I'm not convinced that death would be worse."

Maryse smiled and Mildred let out a guffaw.

"Welcome to our world," Maryse said. "Here's what you need to know to deal with Helena. One, she was rich and spoiled in life and she is used to getting everything her way, but she's also a bully. So if you tell her directly to do something, she'll usually back down. Two, even though she'll never admit it, you can guilt her into doing things your way by telling her it's her fault your life is in danger."

Mildred nodded. "It may sound a bit mean on the surface, but trust me, after you've dealt with Helena for a couple of days, you'll grasp at any relief."

"So true," Maryse said.

"I'll give her the room next to you," Mildred said, "so that she's not sitting on top of you all the time."

"If she gets to be too much and you get desperate," Maryse said, "then tell her that Sabine will perform an exorcism on her."

Jadyn stared. "Who's Sabine?"

"She's my best friend and owns the psychic shop in town."

"And she performs exorcisms?" Jadyn asked, a trickle of worry running through her. "Is there a large need for that around here?"

"Hmmm," Maryse said, and scrunched her brow, making Jadyn worry even more.

"I don't suppose there's a need for exorcisms," Maryse said, "unless they can fix stupidity. And Sabine has no idea how to do one anyway. But Helena finds Sabine just odd enough to worry her, so I use that to my advantage."

Jadyn blew out a breath. "So I have a ghost as a bodyguard, which doesn't sound like a huge advantage as she can't shoot a gun."

Maryse's eyes widened and she looked back at Mildred.

"Shit," Maryse said. "If Helena has gotten adept at touching things, she *can* fire a gun, but her accuracy would be highly suspect."

Mildred shook her head in dismay. "Let's just hope she doesn't figure that out anytime soon. No way that would turn out well."

Maryse nodded in agreement before turning back to Jadyn. "Mildred and I were just discussing getting Helena a prepaid cell phone before you showed up. You won't get signal in most of the swamp, but at least when signal's available, she can call for help if you run into trouble."

"She can use a cell phone?" Jadyn asked.

Maryse shrugged. "We're assuming so. She can touch things and God knows, Mildred and I can hear her. She couldn't call 911, but Mildred and I assume we could hear her over a cell. We're going to give it a try, anyway."

Jadyn struggled to wrap her mind around a ghost with a cell phone, but simply couldn't make the stretch. It was too bizarre to register as real. "So that's it? On my side, I have an out-of-shape, cell-phone-toting ghost with a bad attitude against an unknown enemy who probably wants to kill me. It doesn't sound like the best of odds."

"It's not," Maryse said. "Trust me, I know that firsthand, and one evening I will bring over catfish and a case of beer and Mildred and I will tell you all about our Helena-laden past. But Helena is not the only advantage we have."

"What else is there?" Jadyn asked.

"You're on alert," Maryse said. "It's harder to get at someone who's expecting you because you'll be more careful...more observant. And the one thing they definitely won't count on is you coming for them."

"What?" Jadyn stared at Maryse, more confused than ever.

"Part two of the plan is figuring out who wants to kill you," Maryse said. "You have more of an advantage than I did. You're a trained investigator. Being a lab rat, I was at a total disadvantage."

Jadyn considered this for a moment and decided that while completely ludicrous on the surface, what Maryse suggested made sense.

"Well, given that I've only been here a couple of days," Jadyn said, "there's only one thing I could think of that might be the source, and that's what I was here to talk to you about."

Mildred's eyes widened. "The boatload of money. Damn it. I hadn't even put the two together. You know what this means?"

Maryse frowned. "That someone we know is involved in something really dirty."

"And he'll try to kill me," Jadyn said as she slumped back in her chair.

This was not at all what she'd signed up for.

Chapter Seven

"I don't like this idea," Mildred said as she paced Jadyn's hotel room.

"Me, either," Maryse agreed, plopping down on the end of the bed.

"It's too risky," Mildred continued. "What if the bad guy is there and figures out what you're up to?"

Jadyn lowered her mascara and looked over at the two clearly worried women. "How would he do that?"

"Because you're in a bar, hitting on men," Mildred said. "I can't imagine that's your normal scene, although I'll admit, you look the part."

Jadyn smiled. "It's definitely not my normal scene, but the thing is, no one in Mudbug knows that except you two. For all the rest of the residents know, I could be a game warden by day and floozy by night. May as well use that advantage now while I still can."

"She's got a point," Maryse said.

Mildred stopped pacing and looked down at Maryse. "Why don't you go with her?"

Maryse laughed. "Because then everyone in Mudbug would *definitely* know something was up. I don't 'do' the club look, and besides, I haven't set foot in that bar since...you know. It might stand out if I show up now."

Jadyn picked up on something bad in Maryse's tone and

looked over at her. "Is the bar dangerous?"

"No," Maryse said. "The bar owner was. He was the man who tried to kill me."

Mildred patted Maryse's shoulder. "He was her father's best friend and had always been like an uncle to Maryse. It was a harsh blow."

"Wow," Jadyn said as a flood of emotion washed over her. She'd spent most of the afternoon going over the locals with Maryse and Mildred, but no one had stood out to any of them as a potential for this level of criminal activity. Hearing that Maryse had almost been killed by her dad's best friend was a sobering thought. Clearly, the man's psychotic nature had gone undetected by everyone who knew him. Why wasn't it possible that someone else had managed the same thing?

Jadyn held in a sigh. She'd already imagined it would be hard on Mildred and Maryse to find out that someone they knew was involved in something so sordid, especially since she'd spent the afternoon on her laptop, reading every online news report about all the happenings in Mudbug the year before. But the reports didn't mention any of those kind of awful details—like the fact that the killer was so close to Maryse.

What if the person tied up with the money was someone else they'd known their entire lives? Someone else they liked and respected?

"I'm really sorry," Jadyn said. "I spent most of the afternoon reading online news reports because I didn't want to ask you and Mildred to revisit bad times, but they didn't mention anything like that."

Mildred nodded. "Everyone tried to keep the worst of the details out of the news. There was already too much focus on the town, and Maryse had enough to deal with. It's one of those times you're really happy to be part of a small community that still has that desire to insulate their own."

Jadyn checked her face and hair and dropped the mascara into her makeup bag. When she'd read the articles, she hadn't considered the small-town workings that would come into play. That people would hedge the truth to protect what was left of their reputation or to provide a tiny amount of relief for the person who'd taken the brunt of it all.

From a personal standpoint, it was nice to know people would close ranks to protect you. From an investigative standpoint, it meant Jadyn was going to have to ask Maryse and Mildred to relive everything that had happened the year before. Somewhere in that complicated mess may be a clue to what was happening now. Asking these two nice women to relive the most horrifying time of their life was the last thing in the world Jadyn wanted to do, but given what Mildred had just revealed, she didn't see another option.

She fluffed her hair and pushed all thoughts of what would have to come out of her mind. It didn't have to be dealt with now. Tonight already held enough challenges. She grabbed her shoes and began the lengthy process of winding the straps around her ankles.

"What do you think?" Jadyn asked as she strolled into the bedroom, then did a model turn.

Maryse whistled and Mildred beamed.

"I would totally hit on you," Maryse said. "In fact, please don't ever dress like that around my husband."

Mildred laughed. "Luc is totally devoted to you and you know it."

"I know," Maryse said, "but I don't want him to get any ideas about how I should dress. You know I wouldn't make it across the room in those shoes without breaking an ankle."

"There is that," Mildred agreed.

"Don't worry," Jadyn said. "This is hardly going to become

a habit, and it's the only hooker outfit I own."

Maryse scrunched her brow. "You look great but I have to ask—why do you have even one hooker outfit?"

Jadyn smiled. "Because men are already halfway to foolish just existing, but they get all the way there around a hot woman. If anyone at that bar knows something about the cash, they'll be falling all over each other to tell me about it before the night is out. It's worked before."

"Even though you're the game warden?" Maryse asked.

Mildred patted Maryse's shoulder and gave her a motherly look. "Honey, they won't be thinking about her profession—just what other abilities she may possess."

Maryse brightened. "I get it. Like how I walk around the house naked to get out of doing laundry. Luc never complains that it takes me weeks when I say I have to be naked because I have nothing to wear."

Jadyn grinned. With a little effort, her cousin could be quite a looker herself, but Maryse was every bit the nerdy scientist she claimed to be, spending most of her day in jeans and rubber boots. Even so, Jadyn could clearly see what had captured Luc's attention.

"Now you're catching on," Jadyn said. "Well, if you have no last-minute advice, I'm going to go get this over with."

"Helena!" Maryse jumped up from the bed and banged on the wall of the adjoining room. "Hurry up. It's time to get this show on the road."

Jadyn held back a frown, still not completely adjusted to having a ghostly bodyguard, but Maryse and Mildred had insisted. Given Maryse's past with the original bar owner, Jadyn now understood why it would look strange for her to go into the bar, and Mildred, who preferred to drink in close proximity of her own bed, couldn't remember the last time she'd been in the bar for socializing purposes. That left Helena as the logical choice. At least if Jadyn ran into trouble, the ghost could fetch Maryse and Mildred to help.

"I'm coming!" Helena yelled back. "You can't rush perfection."

"She waves a hand and changes clothes," Jadyn said. "Why does it take her longer to get ready than me?"

"Helena's wardrobe doesn't always cooperate," Mildred said, "but she's getting better at it."

"Unfortunately," Maryse chimed in, "I'd bet a year's salary that Helena's delay has nothing to do with a wardrobe malfunction and everything to do with a wardrobe miscalculation."

"There is nothing miscalculated about my appearance," Helena said as she stepped through the wall. "I look hot."

"God help us," Maryse said as Mildred's hand flew over her mouth.

Jadyn turned around to look at the ghost and almost fell off her heels.

Helena was clad head to toe in bright pink spandex, except for the random—and extraordinarily ill-placed—holes covered with lime-green lace. Her shoes matched the lace and were at least an inch taller than Jadyn's. Her hair was bright pink to match her spandex, and looked like it had been blown out around huge rollers. Fake diamonds glittered across the top of her eyes.

She looked like an old, fat, even skankier Peggy Bundy.

"You are not wearing that," Jadyn said.

"Yes, I am. It's not like anyone can see me."

"I can see you. That's bad enough."

Maryse, who'd clenched her eyes shut as soon as Helena entered the room, nodded. "I may never be able to look at pink again without blanching."

Mildred's face wrinkled up as though she'd smelled shrimp rotting in the hot summer sun. "This is absolutely the second-worst thing I have ever seen you wear."

Jadyn stared at Mildred. "What was the first?"

"There was this *Boogie Nights* theme—"

Before her mind exploded, Jadyn waved a hand to stop her. "I've changed my mind. I don't want to know."

Helena put her hands on her hips. "You get me like this or not at all."

Maryse bit her lower lip and glanced over at Mildred, who looked as conflicted about the options as Jadyn felt. Death or the Helena the Hippo Hooker. On the surface, it seemed like such an easy choice, but when faced with the spandex wall of doom, things got blurry.

Apparently sensing her quandary, Maryse rose from the bed, still looking sideways at Helena, as if afraid she'd turn into a pillar of salt if she took in the entire spectacle. "Here's the problem, Helena. You have no place to hold a cell phone. You can't carry it. A floating cell phone will attract the wrong kind of attention and is certain to clear out the bar."

"Hmmm." Helena scrunched her brow for a moment. "You have the phone?"

Maryse pulled the prepaid cell phone from her pocket and handed it to Helena. She attempted to take it but it fell to the floor.

"Damn it!" Helena ranted then reached for the phone, her hand swiping through it every time. Finally, her fingers latched on and the phone came up in Helena's hand.

"The phone isn't going to do any good if you can't be consistent with touching things," Maryse said. "Concentrate like you did earlier today."

"You think I'm trying to fail?" Helena asked. "I assure you, failure is not something I'm fond of."

"Well, maybe," Maryse shot back, "if you spent more time practicing touching things and less time trying to cross MTV with porno, you'd be better at it."

Helena glared at Maryse, then shoved the phone down the spandex in between her breasts. Jadyn covered her mouth with her hand and hoped that if the time came for Helena to get help, she could locate the phone in all that smashed-together flesh.

"Well, if you all are done complaining," Helena said, "we have a bar to work."

Helena walked through the wall and into the hallway. Mildred rose from the bed and patted Jadyn on the back. "Don't worry. Maryse and I will be downstairs in the lobby. If anything looks odd, we'll head over."

"Something already looks odd," Jadyn pointed out.

"Heard that!" Helena shouted from the hall.

Maryse sighed. "Just concentrate on your investigation and try not to look at her. Helena and alcohol are not a great mix."

Famous last words.

As Jadyn had expected, Bill's was nothing special to look at. A solid wood bar stretched in a U shape on one side, a row of kegs and shelves full of whiskey bottles spanning the back wall. Scarred metal tables covered the remaining floor space, and the cracked, vinyl-cushioned chairs completed the seating areas. The floor was constructed of rough wooden planks, definitely not Jadyn's first choice for a heel-walking surface.

The lighting was dim, but not dim enough that Jadyn couldn't assess her prospects. It was especially easy as all conversation had ceased and every man in the bar had turned to stare when she'd walked inside. For a split second, she pictured how different the scene in front of her would look if they could all see Helena stomping in behind her, and she held in a laugh.

She recognized a man at the south end of the bar as Junior, the one who had taken a swing at her. He was the only one scowling, so probably not a good place to start. Two men at the north end of the bar looked familiar, so she'd start with them. As she made her way over, a flash of pink crossed in her periphery and she figured Helena was going to eavesdrop on the table-sitters as they'd discussed before leaving the hotel.

Jadyn perched on a barstool and crossed her legs, well aware that the tight black dress she wore slid up past her mid-thigh. At one of the tables to her left, she heard an intake of breath and held in a smile.

The bartender, an older man with silver hair and a stocky build, lumbered across and gave her the once-over. "Get you something?"

"Beer, please. Whatever you have on tap."

He gave her a single nod and turned around to pour a mug of beer from the keg. When he pushed the mug across the counter, he studied her again.

"You're not from around here," he said.

"Not until a couple of days ago," she agreed. "I'm Jadyn."

His eyes widened and he started to grin. "The new game warden? The one that shot up bags of money?"

She nodded. "I see my reputation precedes me."

"It's not preceding. It's running ahead of you yelling. Hell, that's the funniest and saddest story I've ever heard. Figures they all left out the part where you're a looker. First beer's on me. A woman who looks good and can fire a weapon shouldn't have to pay for drinks in this town."

He gave her a wink and headed to the south end of the bar where Junior was waving his beer mug and grumbling.

"That was a pretty smooth move yesterday" the guy to her right said. "When you ducked Junior's punch."

She turned to look at the man and smiled. "Thanks."

He was probably in his midthirties, but summers out in the hot Louisiana sun tended to age people more than their chronological years. His buddy was around the same age and neither looked like they worked desk jobs. Their shoulders and forearms were rippled and scarred, indicating a lot of regular manual labor.

"I'm Bart," the first man said, "and this is Tyler."

"I'm Jadyn. It's nice to meet you."

Bart nodded. "Where'd you learn to fight that way?"

"Martial arts training. Sometimes the best way to win a fight is to avoid it altogether."

Tyler laughed. "Hell, what's the fun in that?"

Jadyn laughed too and glanced around the bar before looking back at Bart and Tyler. "Are you guys going to catch crap for talking to me? Some of the other patrons don't look very happy."

Bart waved a hand in dismissal. "Piss on 'em. At least ten of them assholes claim to be my friends, but not a one put out a CB call to us about that money. If Tyler and I hadn't been headed to the pond already, we'd never have known."

"Really? Then how did the rest of them find out? Don't tell me you were all headed to the same fishing hole?"

"No. Some of 'em didn't even have fishing tackle. My guess is Junior sent out the call on his channel, and Junior and I are the opposite of friends. But you'd think one of my buddies on Junior's channel would have switched over and filled us in."

"That seems the polite thing to do," Jadyn said. "Explain this channel thing to me—who decides which channel to use?"

"There's only a handful of channels that get decent reception in the swamp. Law enforcement uses one of them, and those of us that's been here forever have divvied them up based on the type of fishing we like to do. If you're into largemouth bass, you don't care if speckled trout are biting."

"I see. So someone on Junior's channel found the money first, but no one bothered to broadcast it to other channels."

"Exactly. Greedy bastards."

"Makes you wonder if the first guy out there told everyone not to. Because I can't imagine that many people making the independent decision to keep quiet."

Bart frowned. "You've got a point there."

Seeing her opening, Jadyn moved in for the kill. "Then I guess you just have to figure out who was first and that's the guy who tried to cut the rest of you out."

Bart looked back at Tyler, whose expression moved from relaxed to perturbed. Obviously, Bart had a clear idea of who had tried to cut him out.

"Excuse me for a minute," Bart said and jumped off his stool before strolling across the bar to where Junior sat.

Tyler slid off his stool but remained standing next to Jadyn. "If Junior's the one who called for silence, this isn't going to be pretty. He and Bart have a long-standing feud—the Hatfields and McCoys kind."

"Really?" Jadyn perked up, feeling only slightly guilty that the prospect of the seemingly affable Bart stomping the clearly disturbed Junior into the floor until it splintered caused her a bit of excitement.

"Yep," Tyler said. "Junior's mom wasn't exactly the kind of stuff housewives were made of. She set her sights on Bart's dad almost as soon as Junior's dad dragged her to Mudbug. One weekend, both of them disappeared and ain't no one heard from either of them since."

"Okay, that just sucks," Jadyn said, feeling bad for Bart,

trying to feel bad for Junior. After all, it wasn't his fault his mom had turned out to be a husband-stealing slut. His obvious anger issues with women made a lot more sense now.

"Yeah, it was one of the shittiest things I ever seen, and I seen a lot of shitty things."

Suddenly, the guilt that had been pushed aside came creeping in, reminding Jadyn that she *was* a law enforcement officer, even if her authority didn't extend to the bar.

"Maybe I shouldn't have said anything," she said.

"It would have happened eventually, anyway. Bart may not get around to things as quickly as you do, but sooner or later, that same thought would have struck him. Besides, the ambulance can get to them easier here than in the swamp."

Tyler downed a big gulp of beer, a smile hovering on his lips, and Jadyn realized he hadn't stood up because he was worried he'd need to intervene—he was waiting for the first blows so that he could jump into the fight.

The voices at the end of the bar grew louder and Jadyn hopped off her stool. She'd started this mess and needed to end it before things got out of hand. As she walked toward the two yelling men, something pink moved in the corner of her eye. Apparently figuring something was up, Helena had left her corner to move toward the bar. With the way she teetered on the ridiculous heels she wore, Jadyn doubted she'd make it halfway across the bar before falling.

"I don't like what you're accusing me of," Junior said. He puffed his chest out, but it still didn't reach farther than his stomach.

Bart didn't appear any more impressed than Jadyn. "You don't like it because I caught you being the sneaky bastard you are. Guess it's in your genes."

Junior turned beet red and clenched his fists. "I done told you it wasn't me, and even if it was, what are you gonna do about it?"

"Gentlemen," Jadyn said, even though she was fairly sure the moniker wasn't applicable. "I can't let you start a fight in here, so I'm going to ask you both to cool it."

Junior snorted. "That's big words considering you ain't got the sheriff here to protect you this time."

"The way I remember it, I didn't need him last time."

"You troublemaking bitch. All this is your fault." Junior shoved Bart to the side and launched at Jadyn, who neatly sidestepped out of his path and sent him crashing into a table.

Junior struggled to get up from the floor, glaring at her the entire time. She had no doubt that as soon as he got upright, he was going for tackle number two. Jadyn shifted her weight to the left, ready to spin out of his way, but her right foot remained fixed in place. She glanced down and her pulse spiked.

Holy crap!

Her heel was caught in one of the wide cracks in the plank floor and it wasn't budging. If she'd been wearing pumps, she would have simply stepped out of them and completed her move, but the leather laces were wrapped firmly up her calf, keeping her foot firmly affixed to the shoe.

So not good.

Chapter Eight

The door to the bar swung open and someone walked in, but Jadyn was too busy trying to work her heel out of the floorboard to worry about who was witnessing the spectacle. Helena had made it halfway across the bar and was huffing like a train. Of even more concern, she was picking up speed.

Junior had made it up from the floor, and even worse, had seen Jadyn's shoe caught in the crack. "You're not getting away with it this time," he said.

Bart and Tyler, who'd moved to stand on each side of Junior, both grabbed an arm to prevent him from charging, but the angry man's adrenaline and hatred outweighed the two lighter men trying to hold him back. He shook them both off like rag dolls, lowered his head, and charged.

"Stop or I'll shoot!" Jadyn heard Colt's voice sound from the doorway, but Junior didn't hear anything but his own rage.

"Knife!" Jadyn yelled at the bartender, who pulled a pocketknife from his jeans and tossed it to her. She opened the knife, sliced the laces from her ankles, and dived to the left side just in time to miss the charging Junior.

Colt stepped forward at the same time, probably in an attempt to stop the charge, and ended up in the worst place possible. Helena, who'd long since lost control of her legs or her momentum, ran full speed toward Colt. Jadyn expected her to pass right through, but instead, the ghost hit the sheriff with a thud and launched him forward, right into Junior's path.

Junior ran square into Colt, knocking him to the ground and flinging the handcuffs he'd been holding in one hand into the air. Junior dove for the handcuffs, completely flattening Helena as he went, then rolled over and attempted to handcuff the sheriff with his own cuffs. Unfortunately, Helena was still in the middle of the mix and although Jadyn was certain neither man could see her, she still held some sort of solid form. Invisible, but solid.

Junior slapped the cuffs at what he thought was Colt's wrist, but instead, the cuff clicked into place on Helena. The ghost managed to wriggle out from under the fighting men and jumped up from the floor.

"What the hell?" Junior stared at the handcuffs dangling in front of him and Jadyn jumped in front of Colt to block his view. All around her, men fled the bar, not wanting to be any part of a fight involving the sheriff. Helena ran right out the front door along with them.

So much for security detail.

Mildred and Maryse were on their second round of gin rummy when they heard yelling across the street. They both jumped up to peek out the front window of the hotel, and stared as men came running out of the bar and tore away in their vehicles. At the end of the pack came a burst of pink, racing right past the hotel. The shoes were gone, but the spandex was still intact…with an addition.

A pair of handcuffs dangled from Helena's wrist.

Maryse looked over at Mildred. "This can't be good."

Colt took advantage of Junior's momentary loss of concentration and clocked him square in the jaw. Between Colt's punch and the amount of beer Junior had consumed, the troublemaker fell straight back onto the hardwood floor and didn't move so much as a finger.

"Nice punch," Jadyn said and tossed the pocketknife back to the bartender. "Thanks."

The bartender nodded and put two beers on the counter. "I figure you both earned these, even though you cleared out my customers."

Colt looked over at the bartender. "Damn it, Bill, why didn't you break that up before it got out of control?"

The bartender grinned and shrugged. "'Cause Junior Thibodeaux's an asshole who needs a butt-whooping."

Colt sighed, but Jadyn noticed he didn't argue. He glanced around the floor, then threw his hands up in the air. "Where the hell are my handcuffs?"

"They must have gotten taken in the stampede," Jadyn said.

"I don't even have spares on me. I was planning on having a beer, not breaking up a bar fight."

"Here ya go." Bill tossed Colt a piece of rope. "It'll rub his wrists something awful if he starts struggling, but I figure that's a plus."

Colt flipped the lifeless Junior over and secured his hands behind his back. He was just finishing up when Maryse and Mildred burst into the bar. Jadyn took one look at them and couldn't hold in a laugh.

Maryse had a purple lamp from the hotel lobby and held it over her shoulder like a batter ready to swing. Mildred clutched a phone book.

"Is everything okay?" Maryse asked, scanning the bar.

61

Colt took one look at them and grinned. "And if it wasn't, what the heck did you two plan on doing—illuminating the fight and calling for pizza?"

Maryse lowered the lamp and Mildred dropped the phone book on a table. "We were playing cards over at the hotel when we heard the commotion," Mildred explained. "We were afraid Jadyn might be in trouble so we grabbed the nearest items and hauled it over here."

Colt raised one eyebrow. "And why would you automatically assume Jadyn was mixed up in that mess?"

"Because we saw how she was dressed when she left the hotel," Maryse said.

Bill starting laughing. "God love you, Maryse. You have a way of seeing the gem in the shit. You should come in more often."

Suddenly Maryse froze and the lamp slipped from her hand and crashed to the floor. Her eyes widened and all the color rushed from her face.

"Oh no," Mildred wrapped her arm to steady her. "Take a deep breath, honey. It's just a building."

Maryse blew out the breath with a whoosh and sucked another in so rapidly Jadyn was afraid she'd hyperventilate.

"Oh man," Bill said and hurried from behind the bar over to Maryse. "I'm so sorry. I didn't even think about...look, I ain't got no words for what my cousin did 'cause there ain't none that makes sense of it, but I ain't him and I aim to turn this bar into something useful again."

Maryse nodded as she took a deep breath and slowly blew it out. "I know, Bill. I didn't mean to make you feel bad."

"Hell, don't apologize to me. You ain't got nothing to apologize for."

"I think I better go," Maryse said.

Bill squeezed her shoulder. "The bar's closed on Sundays, but I'm here doing the books. If you want to come in and sit with it all for a spell, just knock on the door. My granny always said everything could be fixed by sitting with it."

"Thanks," Maryse said and gave Jadyn a nod before allowing Mildred to guide her out of the bar.

Colt watched them leave, then downed a big gulp of beer. "Am I to assume you started this mess?" he asked Jadyn.

Jadyn took in his somewhat aggrieved expression and felt her irritation grow. "I did nothing of the sort. All I wanted to do was have a beer and relax, maybe get the local gossip."

Colt shook his head. "You were flashing your goods at the locals and trying to find out who got to that pond first."

"I was doing nothing of the sort," she said, not sounding the least bit convincing.

"You can't do this kind of thing in Mudbug," Colt continued, completely ignoring her denial. "The men here aren't used to this kind of play. You'll end up causing a fight every time, and likely leave with nothing but a wasted night and a few more enemies in the end."

"Maybe a few fans," Bill said and winked at Jadyn. "Why didn't you tell me you were looking for information on the pond? I could have told you anything that's been passed around the bar."

"Because I don't know you?" Jadyn suggested.

Bill stroked his chin. "I guess there is that, but I bet Colt here was coming in to do the same thing, despite all his claims of peaceful beer-drinking."

Jadyn narrowed her eyes at him. "I see. So it's okay for you to come in here and ask questions but not for me to do so, even though I'm in charge."

Bill whistled and leaned back against the bar, ready for the show.

"Look," Colt said, "it's not about who's in charge. It's about how things get done in small towns. Men in places like Mudbug are not ready for women in charge who look like you—especially not dressed like that. It clouds their minds and then they do stupid things."

"Ha," Jadyn said. "I'll bet a million dollars Junior has been doing stupid things since birth. The way I'm dressed didn't have a thing to do with it."

"She's got a point," Bill said.

Colt glared at the bar owner. "Whose side are you on?"

Bill grinned. "Do you have to ask?"

Colt threw his hands in the air. "Fine, keep dressing like you're going to a city club and stirring up the locals, but the next time, I'm not wading into the fray."

"Who asked you to?" Jadyn shot back. "I was doing fine on my own."

"Didn't look like it from where I stood. Speaking of which, who pushed me into that freight train Junior?"

Jadyn shrugged. "Someone with a warrant? Got to be a few of those in this town."

Bill nodded. "More than a few, I'd imagine. Anyway, if the two of you would stop running your mouth for a minute, I'll tell you what you came for. Might as well shut down early and watch *Saturday Night Live* since you ran off all my customers."

Jadyn and Colt took seats at the bar in front of Bill, and Jadyn took a drink of her beer. "So you know who was first to find the money in the pond?"

"Maybe."

Jadyn snapped her fingers. "*SNL* is waiting. Talk."

Bill grinned. "Bossy. I like that." He leaned forward and placed his hands on the bar. "It wasn't Junior that found the money. He broadcast to his friends, but I could hear people yelling in the background when he sent out the call. I figure they was already at the pond."

"So how did Junior find out?" Jadyn asked.

"He says a call went out on Marty's channel that bass was biting big at the pond."

"Marty?" Colt shook his head. "That can't be right."

Jadyn stared. "Marty, as in the guy who owns the garage? The garage where we left the boat last night? The same boat that had no evidence as to origin or ownership when we searched it this morning?"

Colt frowned. "Marty was at the garage yesterday morning. I bought a set of spark plugs from him. He couldn't have transmitted from the pond and if he'd known about the money, he would have closed the garage and been in the middle of the fray with them."

Bill shrugged. "I just know what I heard and that is that word came down the pipe from Marty."

"I don't understand," Jadyn said.

"I don't either," Colt said. "But I don't like it."

Colt adjusted his rearview mirror and watched Jadyn cross the street to the hotel. It was a particularly great view, and if he hadn't been so troubled, he would have enjoyed it a lot more. He waited until Jadyn's truly impressive form disappeared into the hotel, then backed his truck up and headed for the sheriff's department.

What Bill said didn't make sense, but Colt had no reason to suspect Bill was being untruthful. Except for the time he served in the army, the bar owner had always lived in Mudbug and had never been trouble—at least, not anything outside of the ordinary Mudbug kind. If someone had told Colt they'd seen Bill poaching deer, he would have believed that wholeheartedly, but involved in whatever prompted tons of unmarked bills in Baggies…he just didn't see it.

When his cousin Johnny had been killed the year before while attempting to murder Maryse, Bill had been quick to step to Maryse's defense and disavow his cousin's actions. He'd been the sole heir to Johnny's estate, such as it was, and had inherited the bar. Out of respect for Maryse, he'd left it closed for almost six months, and changed the name and facade before reopening.

The week before he reopened the bar, Bill sold his shrimp boat and all his equipment, claiming he and his bad knees were officially retiring from all that manual labor. And to the best of Colt's knowledge, the man didn't even fish. Colt always assumed he was burned out.

He pulled in front of the sheriff's department and glanced back at Junior, who was snoring on his backseat. All that ruminating over Bill hadn't gotten him one inch closer to a solution to the current problem.

Nor did it make you forget how Jadyn looked in that dress.

He gripped the steering wheel and blew out a breath. Sometimes one's subconscious was a real son of a bitch—letting things out into the consciousness that were better off buried.

He'd heard the ruckus before he ever opened the door to the bar and knew right then that the likelihood of sipping a beer in peace and quiet had just flown right out the window. What he hadn't expected was to see Jadyn in the middle of a brawl, and certainly not looking hotter than any woman had the right to.

Sure, he'd noticed her looks and her body at the pond and again this morning, going through the boat, but when she enhanced all that natural beauty and stopped hiding her body in jeans and T-shirts, it was a sight to behold. Jadyn St. James was quite frankly the most gorgeous woman he'd ever laid eyes on.

And he'd bet a year's salary that she knew it.

The hair and makeup…that dress…all carefully calculated to get the local population wagging tongues. And it probably would have worked quite well if Junior hadn't gotten sideways.

Speaking of which.

Before his thoughts trailed off into places they never belonged, he jumped out of his truck and hauled Junior out of the backseat. The big man was still drunk and would be sporting a heck of a shiner the next day, but he didn't protest as Colt led him inside and locked him up in the corner cell.

"Problems at the bar?" Eugenia, the night dispatcher, asked as he walked back into the main office area.

"The male ego sort. When he sobers up, cut him loose. I'm not interested in doing the paperwork."

"You got it, boss."

He headed into his office at the back of the building and closed the door.

As he sat down at his desk, Jadyn's words came back to him.

"…or it's someone who's above reproach."

He turned on his computer and sighed. Maybe it was time to dig a little deeper into Bill and Marty.

Maybe it was time to dig a little deeper into everyone.

Chapter Nine

"You've got to get these off of me."

As she hurried downstairs in her normal nighttime outfit of yoga pants and T-shirt, Jadyn heard Helena whine for at least the hundredth time.

"I'm trying." A clearly frustrated Maryse poked at the hole in the cuffs with a bent paper clip. "I'm not a criminal, Helena. This isn't in my skill set."

Maryse looked up at Jadyn as she stepped into the lobby. "I don't suppose you have any at your office?" Maryse asked, sounding a little desperate.

"No, sorry," Jadyn said. "If I'd known the state wasn't going to have my equipment here when I arrived, I would have bought some supplies of my own and brought them with me."

"Cut it off," Helena said.

Maryse sighed. "I'm not even sure what kind of saw it would take to cut that cuff off, but I'm certain I don't have one. Give me a minute."

Maryse pulled out her cell phone and tried again to reach Luc. She'd made several attempts before Jadyn had gone upstairs to change, but they'd all gone straight to voice mail. Jadyn was surprised when Maryse actually started talking.

"Do you have your handcuff key on you?" Maryse asked.

There was a slight pause, then Maryse blushed a bit. "No, it's not that kind of night. Actually, I need you to stop by the hotel on your way home. I'll explain when you get here."

Maryse slipped her cell phone back into her jeans pocket.

"He should be here in a couple of minutes," Maryse said.

Jadyn looked from Helena to Maryse and bit her lip. "What are you going to tell him...I mean to get the key without showing him what's going on?"

"Hiding all this mess isn't necessary," Mildred said as she walked into the lobby with a tray of coffee. "Luc knows all about Helena."

Jadyn's stared. "Seriously?"

Maryse nodded. "Luc's Native American. When we first met, he shocked me by admitting he could see her, then for a couple of weeks, he saw more than he ever wanted to. After he shot Johnny, she disappeared...to him anyway. When she ascended last year, Luc hoped it was permanent. Although he hasn't had the pleasure of sharing the same space with her again, he's not happy she's back."

"So you think he's going to be pissed about the handcuffs?" Jadyn asked as Maryse paced the hotel lobby.

"He's not going to be pleased," Maryse said.

Jadyn sighed, wishing her cousin wasn't in this situation. "I wouldn't be, either."

"That's rude," Helena complained, "since I'm wearing these cuffs because I was protecting you."

Jadyn shook her head. "That idiot Junior would never have touched me. The only thing you accomplished was assaulting the sheriff and stealing his handcuffs. I hope Junior was the only one who saw them floating. At least Colt will dismiss that as a drunken hallucination."

Helena crossed her arms and huffed. "See if I try helping again."

"Why didn't you call, Helena?" Maryse asked. "That was the

whole point of the cell phone. Not only did you forget all about the phone, you went running off down the street, leaving Mildred and me with no idea what we were walking into."

"I guess you think a floating cell phone wouldn't have looked out of place."

Maryse threw her arms in the air. "Then go into the storeroom or a bathroom stall or step outside behind the bar. You've got more options for avoiding detection than a human ever could, but you refuse to take them into consideration when making these half-assed decisions."

Helena clammed shut and went into pout mode, which meant she knew Maryse was right but wasn't about to admit it. Apparently, over a year of being a ghost still hadn't seeped into Helena's decision-making process.

Maryse's narrowed her eyes at Helena. "Do you even still have the phone?"

Helena looked at the floor. "It might have fallen out of my cleavage at some point."

A red flush started on Maryse's neck, but when she started to respond, headlights flashed across the front of the hotel. Maryse shot Mildred a worried look before she hurried to the front door. "He's here," Maryse said.

Jadyn inched over to stand beside Mildred, a little antsy about meeting Maryse's mysterious husband. She'd hoped for happier and more casual circumstances, but very little about her life in Mudbug had been happy or casual since the moment she'd set foot in the town.

Maryse opened the door and kissed a man before standing aside and allowing him to enter. Jadyn had to admit, her cousin had chosen well. Luc LeJeune had perfectly chiseled features, long black hair drawn back into a ponytail, and dark skin. But even more attractive was the smile he wore as he looked at his wife.

Then he looked over at Jadyn and Mildred and the smile slipped away, replaced with a look of horror and disgust. For a split second, Jadyn was confused, thinking he was looking at her, then Maryse sucked in a breath and it all made sense.

"Holy Mother of God," Luc said.

"You can see her," Maryse whispered.

"Hell yeah, I can see her. Astronauts on the moon can probably see her glowing right through the roof of the hotel."

"Good to see you too, Luc," Helena huffed.

Luc crossed the lobby and stood in front of the ghost. "The feeling is decidedly not mutual. Maryse told me about your falling out with God, and I'm not amused. I don't care how bad you hate it, you need to apologize and get back to the afterlife where you belong."

"You're not nearly as good-looking as I remember," Helena said. "I don't know why I tried to see you naked."

Maryse groaned as Luc took one step closer to Helena and put his finger directly in her face. "Understand this, I catch you anywhere near me when I'm missing so much as a shoe, and I'll have you banished into a mason jar."

"You can't do that." Helena sounded anything but certain.

"I can't, but my tribal elders can."

Jadyn saw the fear pass over Helena's expression as she waved one hand in the air. "Fine. I never would have found you attractive in the first place if I'd know you were this uptight. Maryse must be rubbing off on you."

"Unbelievable." Luc shook his head. "You're insulting the only two people who can free you from those handcuffs." Luc looked over at Maryse. "Do I even want to know how this happened?"

"Probably not," Maryse said, "but I'll tell you on the way home, anyway. Let's just say that Helena was trying to help Jadyn and things didn't go quite as planned."

"How was I supposed to know I'd get solid?" Helena asked. "You people act like I intended to assault the sheriff."

Luc closed his eyes for a moment and shook his head. "Like that time at the hospital?" he asked Maryse.

Maryse nodded, then looked over at Jadyn. "The night Helena and I broke into the hospital, she had a solid moment and ran over a nurse."

Jadyn inwardly cringed, wondering just how much more there was to learn about Helena, the invisible-but-not-always-ethereal disaster. Based on Luc's expression, she'd guess a lot, but figured now wasn't the time to ask.

Luc pulled a handcuff key from his pocket and unlocked Helena. Then he handed the handcuffs to Mildred, mumbling something about "the responsible one" and turned his attention to Jadyn.

"You must be Maryse's cousin," he said and extended his hand.

"Yes, I'm Jadyn," she said and shook his hand.

He glanced back then gave her a smile. "I'm sorry we didn't meet under better circumstances, and I'm more sorry than you'll ever know that you've been cast into this drama. If you run into any problems—with anything—let me know."

He pulled a business card from his wallet and handed it to her. "I'm not always the easiest person to get a hold of, but if you're in a pinch, it never hurts to try."

"Thanks." Jadyn stuck the card in her pocket. "I really appreciate everything you, Maryse, and Mildred are doing for me."

He nodded. "If only we didn't have to." He looked over at Maryse. "Are you ready? I can drop you off at the café in the morning if you want to leave your truck here."

Maryse grabbed her purse off the counter. "Sounds good to me. Jadyn, we'll catch up tomorrow."

Luc headed toward the front door as Maryse gave Mildred a hug, then dashed behind him. Jadyn watched as he walked out of the hotel and looked over at Helena.

"For the record," she said, "I can't really blame you for wanting to see him naked."

Maryse poked her head back inside and winked before shutting the door behind her.

Jadyn and Mildred both laughed. Helena, who was apparently over her crush on Luc, didn't even crack a smile.

"If you're all done complaining about me," Helena said, "I'm going to bed."

Jadyn watched as the ghost stomped up the stairs, then turned to Mildred. "What do you think it means...that Luc can see her again?"

Mildred frowned and shook her head. "I don't know. I don't even have a guess. It's not something I expected at all. First thing in the morning, we need to sit down with Maryse and try to make some sense of this."

"Speaking of which, do ghosts sleep?"

"With Helena, Lord only knows." Mildred patted Jadyn on the arm. "You should try to get some rest. It's been an eventful night, and morning will be here sooner than you think."

Jadyn started toward the stairs, then paused and looked back at Mildred. "They look good together—Luc and Maryse."

Mildred smiled. "Yes, they do. They fit in a way that's rare to see."

Jadyn nodded. "I've only seen it a time or two, and never even come close to experiencing it."

"You've got time. And who knows, your perfect match could be right here in Mudbug." She gave Jadyn a sly look. "You and the sheriff looked pretty good standing there together in Bill's Bar."

"Oh no." Jadyn shook her head. "Colt seems nice enough on the surface, but I get the impression he thinks I'm incapable of handling my job and has every intention of taking it over."

"He's always had a bit of the white-knight complex, but he's no fool. He'll figure it out."

"Not my problem," Jadyn said and gave Mildred a wave before hurrying upstairs.

Jadyn was no fool, either. She hadn't missed how Colt had looked at her in the bar. She'd seen that appreciative look on the face of plenty of men looking at her and even more looking at her mother. Then she'd gotten old enough to buck her mother's rules and advice on appearance, and the looks had lessened, but not disappeared.

Still, this was the first time in years that she'd donned that kind of getup to attract the attention of a man. The last time had been such a disaster, she hadn't felt like revisiting it. Come to think of it, tonight hadn't exactly been a roaring success.

She turned on the television, shrugged off her yoga pants and climbed into bed. A feature on wildlife was playing, which normally would have interested her, but for some reason, she couldn't get into the program.

Finally, she clicked the television off and sighed. Colt wasn't the only one who'd paid attention to how other people looked. With his worn jeans, T-shirt, and hiking boots, Colt had clearly been dressing for comfort, but even his obvious aggravation with his ruined night didn't deduct from how sexy he looked. He had a slow, smooth way about him—like everything was under control—that made him even more attractive.

Like James Bond on the bayou.

She shook her head. Good God, she needed to get a life, and some hobbies, or hobbies and a life. Whatever. But the one thing she would not do was sit in her bedroom for the next fifty years, turning regular small-town sheriffs into action heroes.

Sighing, she sank down into the bed and pulled the covers over her shoulders.

More than anything, she wished she'd gotten to finish her beer.

It was 6:00 a.m. and Colt hadn't even poured his first cup of coffee when Eugenia yelled at him from the front desk. He put down the coffee mug and hustled to the front of the building where Eugenia sat perched in her office chair, one hand on her headset and one pressing the mute button on the receiver.

"It's Leroy Pendarvis, and he's in a bad way. Best I can figure, something bad happened at Duke Leger's house. Leroy's been wailing and mumbling. I've tried to calm him down so I can understand better, but nothing's getting through to him."

"Shit." Colt shoved his pistol in his waistband and grabbed his truck keys. "Call for an ambulance…just in case."

Eugenia gave him a nod and he hurried out the door and tore off down Main Street. Colt had known Leroy since he was a boy. Leroy was a lot of things…a poacher, a cheater, and a liar, but the one thing he wasn't was weak. If something had upset Leroy to the extent Eugenia described, then it was bad.

Duke's residence, which could charitably be referred to as a shack, rested on a thin strip of land between two channels. Colt pushed his truck down the narrow, bumpy dirt path as quickly as possible, growing more and more tense with each passing mile. Mudbug wasn't New Orleans, and he'd had his share of panicked calls from dispatch, but this one felt different.

This time, he had a really bad feeling.

He made the drive to Duke's house in twenty minutes flat, which was probably a record of some sort. He wasn't sure what he expected to find, maybe Leroy standing out front waving a knife or a pistol or maybe even a semiautomatic weapon—he'd seen both before. But instead, he found something he never expected.

Leroy sat on the front porch steps, staring at him as he climbed out of his truck. The older shrimper didn't move, not even so much as a blink. Colt walked up to him and shook his shoulder, then waved his hand in front of Leroy's face, but the other man never gave any indication that he was aware Colt was there.

He's in shock.

Colt looked past Leroy to the cabin. The front door stood open but he didn't see any movement inside. He pulled out his pistol anyway and started up the steps. He paused at the doorway and peered inside.

His hand dropped to his side and he had to force himself to grip the pistol before it slid out of his hand and onto the rotted wooden porch. He clutched the doorway with his other hand and closed his eyes, trying to push away the dizziness and nausea that coursed through him.

Of all the things he'd seen during his time with the New Orleans Police Department, he'd come all the way back home to see the worst.

Chapter Ten

The sound of screeching woke Jadyn up at dawn. She bolted upright, momentarily startled with the unfamiliar surroundings. It took a moment for her to remember she was in the Mudbug Hotel, but that didn't explain the racket. It took her a while to realize the howling had a pattern and a failed attempt at carrying a tune. Then she placed the loud, tenor voice as Helena. A second later, she realized the shower was running in Helena's room.

How the hell did a ghost take a shower?

Since sleep was obviously a thing of the past, she threw the covers back and tossed on jeans, a T-shirt, and tennis shoes before heading downstairs. If there was a God, Mildred would be up and have a pot of that paint-stripping coffee of hers brewing.

The strong aroma of Mildred's special brew hit her as soon as she started down the stairs and she smiled. Mildred was in the small kitchen in the back room of the hotel and had just lifted the pot from the coffeemaker when Jadyn walked in.

"I'll give you a year's salary for a cup of that," Jadyn said.

"As I know what you make, I have to say, you're not offering much." Mildred smiled and grabbed two mugs from the shelf above the coffeepot.

Jadyn gratefully took the mug of steaming coffee from Mildred and sat at the small table in the corner. She held the container of sugar over her cup, and then the sound of Helena's screeching blared through the air registry above her. She dumped twice as much sugar into her coffee as usual, but figured at this point, it didn't matter. The morning was already ruined.

Mildred looked up at the ceiling and scowled. "What in the world is she doing up there?"

"I think she's singing in the shower. Is that even possible?"

Mildred shook her head and took a seat across from Jadyn. "Heck if I know. Helena didn't exactly come with an instruction manual."

"I never really thought much about ghosts and the like before. I mean, I guess I always figured it was possible, but I never thought about what actually happened after the transition. It would have never occurred to me that a ghost wouldn't know how to do ghost things. Does that make sense?"

"Sure, and that's the entire rub. Even though Helena and her shenanigans make me want to up and move to Canada, or worse, a part of me still feels a little sorry for her."

"Why is that? Not to be rude, but based on what I've seen, she doesn't seem like the kind of person that would inspire much empathy."

"Oh, don't get me wrong. When she was alive, Helena Henry was the biggest bitch that ever walked the sidewalks of Mudbug. I suppose she had her reasons, although I'd like to think I wouldn't have chosen the same path had it been me in her shoes."

Mildred sighed. "Regardless, she didn't deserve to be murdered, and she had no choice in getting stuck in some kind of limbo with no idea how to navigate it. Helena was born into money and had people serving her everything she needed her entire life. Then she died and no one could help her, even though we wanted to."

The full force of Helena's predicament slammed into Jadyn,

and she tried to imagine the confusion, hurt, and bewilderment the woman must have felt when she awakened into some sort of nonliving nightmare.

"That must have been awful," Jadyn said. "What about her immediate family? I mean, why appear to Maryse, when she's only related by marriage? Is that why you think she appears to those in danger?"

"That's part of it," Mildred said. "Helena didn't have any family to speak of except her husband, who tried to kill both her and Maryse but was too stupid to get it right. And back then, Hank was hardly the stuff good sons were made of. Helena's parents both died when she was a child, but they never loved her. They never loved anything but money."

Jadyn's heart clenched at Mildred's words. She understood that situation far too well for comfort. "I can't imagine carrying all that around. It's like something out of a bad horror movie."

"It is, although she managed to hide it all behind insults and bad choices, which we tolerated then, given the situation. But this time is a little different."

"How's that?"

"This time she brought it on herself—claims she pissed off God and got thrown out of heaven. Now, I ask you, what kind of person finds something so wrong with the ever-after that they get banished?"

Jadyn shook her head. "It sorta boggles the mind."

"Most things with Helena do." Mildred took a sip of her coffee, then studied Jadyn for several seconds. "I have to say, though, you're taking this a lot better than Maryse and I expected."

Jadyn shrugged. "What are my options? Don't get me wrong, my first inclination was to throw my duffel bag in my truck and leave."

"Then why didn't you? If your seeing Helena has anything

to do with the mess with the boat full of money, that problem would disappear for you if you left Mudbug."

Jadyn paused before answering, trying to come up with something that was truthful but didn't delve into her issues with her mother.

"You may be right," she said finally, "but who's to say I wouldn't run into the same or an even bigger problem at my next job? What if I'm simply scheduled to face something like this? Here, I have the advantage of you and Maryse and a ghost that assaults sheriffs and steals handcuffs."

Mildred smiled. "Well, I don't know how much of an advantage some of us are, but I'm certain we're all doing our best."

"Maybe it would be better if Helena did a bit less than her best."

Mildred laughed. "Definitely."

Jadyn heard the bells jangling on the front door of the hotel, and seconds later, Maryse strolled into the kitchen, looking every bit the woman who'd spent a satisfying night with a hot man. A ripple of jealousy ran through Jadyn and she squashed it down. She was genuinely happy for her cousin, but part of her knew that what Maryse had with Luc was rare. Even if Jadyn lowered her guard enough to allow a man in, her chances of finding a match as Maryse had were slim to none.

"Good morning," Maryse said, fairly singing out the words as she poured herself a cup of coffee.

"Hmmpff." Mildred raised one eyebrow. "Apparently, everyone's morning isn't as good as yours."

Maryse grinned and took a seat at the table. "I have no complaints."

Helena's voice boomed through the air registry and Maryse cringed.

"Until now," Maryse said. "What is she doing up there—killing cats?"

Jadyn shook her head. "Best I can figure, singing in the shower."

"I don't even want to know." Maryse took a sip of coffee. "I have a ton of work to get to, but I wanted to see if there's anything I can help with first."

Maryse reached into the back waistband of her jeans, pulled out a container of Mace and placed it on the table in front of Jadyn. "And I wanted to bring this. I know the game warden office has a set of shotguns and rifles, but I figured you could use something smaller and less deadly given the propensity of the locals to take a swing at you."

Jadyn picked up the Mace and smiled. "So you want me to start spraying men like Junior with Mace?"

"Heck yeah. In fact, I can provide you with a list of targets if you're interested."

"I don't think I'll have any trouble finding my own."

"Probably not," Maryse agreed. "That shoots a hard, steady stream. I carry the same one."

Jadyn smiled. "Yet you came to rescue me at the bar holding a lamp."

"I panic in those sort of situations, which is exactly why I carry Mace and not a pistol. A rifle gives me time to think about what I'm doing."

"That makes sense. Thanks."

"I know it's a lot to ask," Maryse said, "but if possible, take Helena with you if you leave downtown today. She's a horrible pain, but she will try to help." Maryse glanced up at the ceiling. "I'd never let her hear me say this or she'd use it against me forever, but the truth is, she saved my life. If she hadn't sent Luc after me, I would have died in the alley right behind this hotel."

Jadyn felt her heart tug at everything that had happened to

her cousin. The news reports didn't even scratch the surface of the real horror she'd lived through. "If I leave downtown, I promise to take her with me—assuming she will go. But I will not listen to her singing the whole time."

"No argument there," Maryse said.

Jadyn's cell phone rang and she frowned. As it was Sunday, technically, she was off from work, and her mother never rose before 10:00 a.m., insisting on her beauty sleep. One glance at the display and she felt her pulse tick up a notch.

The sheriff's department.

"Ms. St. James?" the dispatcher asked.

"Speaking."

"Sheriff Bertrand has a situation at Duke Leger's house, and he's requesting you for backup."

Jadyn clenched the phone. The last time Colt had requested help with a "situation," a bunch of fools were jumping in alligator-infested water to steal questionable money. But this time, the dispatcher's tone wasn't frantic like it was two days earlier.

This time, the woman sounded scared.

The dispatcher's directions led Jadyn down a narrow trail into the swamp. Giant cypress trees ran along each side of the road, their limbs so large that they formed a canopy over the dirt path that served as a road. Normally, Jadyn wasn't subject to flights of fancy, but the dim pathway felt ominous, as if the darkness were closing in around her.

Clearly bored, Helena sat in the passenger seat, drumming her fingers on the armrest and driving Jadyn to the brink of insanity. Despite at least twenty minutes of showering, Helena popped downstairs completely dry when Mildred summoned her.

Unfortunately, she was wearing a plaid pleated miniskirt, vest sans undershirt, and high-topped, bright purple tennis shoes. She even had gray pigtails. Helena claimed it was a Britney Spears homage, but Jadyn was fairly certain if the real Britney got a glimpse of her, she'd ask Helena to skip the tribute.

Jadyn had taken one look at Helena and claimed she didn't need protection detail for this jaunt. After all, she was on her way to meet the sheriff. But Mildred had looked so worried that Jadyn had finally acquiesced to the older woman. It seemed a small price to pay to give the hotel owner a little peace of mind.

At least, it had seemed a small price to pay when Jadyn agreed. After ten minutes of humming, and now another five of finger-tapping, Jadyn regretted her decision. Next time, Mildred would just have to worry.

"Tell me about this guy—Duke," Jadyn said, figuring if Helena was along for the ride, she might as well be useful.

Helena stopped the finger-tapping and shrugged. "He's a shrimper, in his fifties. Very little in the way of manners, and not someone you'd want to tangle with in a bar fight."

"How is that?"

"He's former military and my understanding is he was some sort of boxing champion while he was in. Has a big scar across his right cheek that he claims he got while being held hostage during his service."

"Married?"

"Not hardly. Duke's the kind of man that has little to no use for women. His mom was the town whore. Ran out on him and his daddy when Duke was just a baby. Don't think I've ever seen him with a woman except the kind that take cash only, if you know what I mean."

Then he'll love me.

Jadyn sighed. "Has he been in any trouble with the law?"

Helena snorted. "Most every male and a good portion of

the females in Mudbug have been in trouble with the law in one form or another—bar fights, poaching, drunk and disorderly, hunting out of season—it's standard fare for this kind of town. But nobody thinks much of it."

"So you're saying he hasn't had anything but the ordinary sort of trouble."

"Exactly."

Jadyn turned her truck around the final corner to Duke's house, hoping the current trouble consisted of one of the fairly benign things Helena had mentioned that would fall under her purview. But deep down, she already knew that Colt hadn't called her out into the swamp at the crack of dawn over poaching.

She pulled around an ambulance in front of the cabin and parked beside it. The paramedics helped a man into the back, and gave Jadyn a nod before closing the back doors and pulling away. The man stared vacantly past her, as if he were stoned. He didn't have a scar, so Jadyn assumed he wasn't Duke.

"That's Leroy Pendarvis," Helena said. "A buddy of Duke's. Looks like crap."

Jadyn didn't want to consider what had Leroy looking that shaken. It was best to see firsthand than guess. Her imagination would probably dream up far worse things than the truth.

"Don't wander off too far," she told Helena. "I can't exactly call or go looking for you when it's time to leave."

Helena waved a hand in dismissal. "Nothing here I want to see."

Jadyn exited her Jeep and walked toward the cabin. Colt came out the front door as she walked up the steps and onto the porch. "I assume Duke is inside?" she asked.

"You could say that." Colt's voice was grim. "But I need to warn you before you go in. It's one of the worst things I've ever seen, and I've seen my share of horrors. I wouldn't even think about letting you in there if it wasn't necessary."

Jadyn glanced past Colt to the open doorway then looked back at him. His expression was a mixture of disgust, concern, and sadness. The vacant look she'd seen on Leroy's face flashed across her mind. She took a deep breath and slowly blew it out.

Was she ready for this?

Ultimately, the answer was irrelevant. If Colt needed her here in a professional capacity then she had no other option. She said a silent prayer that she wouldn't embarrass herself and gave Colt a nod. "I'm ready."

He didn't look even remotely convinced, but he turned around and motioned for her to follow him. Jadyn forced one foot in front of the other and stepped inside the cabin. The scent of blood and death assaulted her before she'd taken even one step forward. Colt stopped and turned to the right, and she turned to the right as well to see where Colt had focused his attention.

She staggered backward and one hand flew involuntarily over her mouth, in a failed attempt to stifle a cry. She had been dead wrong—her imagination could never have come up with something this horrible.

Colt immediately moved beside her, his hands on her shoulders to steady her. She clenched her eyes shut, unable to look at the horror in front of her for another second, and a wave of dizziness flooded her. Her knees weakened and she felt Colt slip his arm underneath hers to keep her from falling.

"I'll get you outside," he said.

"No." She forced herself to take another breath, careful to breathe through her mouth and not her nose. "I can do this."

"You're sure?"

She nodded and locked her knees into place before opening her eyes.

The scene in front of her was no less horrific now than it had been seconds before, but the shock was fading away. Her mind slowly turned to professional mode and started locking onto the details.

What was left of Duke hung from rope stretched from roof beams on each side of the room and tied around his wrists. She took a step closer and forced herself to study his center mass, where the bulk of the damage occurred.

"It looks as if...as if someone field-dressed him...like a deer."

Colt gave her a single nod. "That was my assessment."

She leaned over and studied the entrails on the cabin floor. "I see signs of predation. Smaller animals mostly, based on the tracks in the blood. Was the door left open?"

"The back door was, and look at this." Colt turned around and pointed to a trail of blood that led from the living room through the kitchen and out the back door. "There's a cup with blood in it on the kitchen counter."

Jadyn's stomach rolled and she clamped it down once more. "The killer wanted to lure the animals inside."

"You understand what that means?"

Jadyn nodded. "He was still alive when the creatures started to feed."

Chapter Eleven

Jadyn struggled to breathe normally. "What in the world could this man have done to justify such a horrible death?"

Colt pulled a wad of plastic bags out of his pocket. "I found these in the kitchen trash. They're all clean as a whistle. He wasn't storing food in them."

She stared at the plastic bags, a million thoughts—each one more horrible than the next—running through her mind. "But no sign of the money?"

"No, but I don't think it's a leap."

"I don't remember seeing Duke at the pond yesterday."

"That's because he wasn't there."

Jadyn blew out a breath, considering the implications, but they all came back to the same thing.

"These bags are the reason I called you here," Colt said. "I wouldn't have if there had been another choice. No one should have to see this."

"No one should have to live this. No matter what he did." Jadyn shook her head. "Do you think the killer was trying to make him talk?"

"Unless whoever did this is simply a sadistic bastard, that seems the most likely choice."

"The man who left in the ambulance...I assume he's the one who called this in?"

Colt nodded. "Yeah. Leroy's been friends with Duke since

they were kids. He was in shock when I got here, then he totally freaked. The paramedics sedated him."

"Did he tell you anything before the sedation?"

"No. He was just rambling. They're taking him to the hospital up the highway from Mudbug. They promised me he'd be held overnight. It will take several hours to document and secure the crime scene, and then I'll head to the hospital and question him."

She blew out a breath. "Where do you want to start?"

He looked over at her, a hint of appreciation in his expression. "You're one tough broad, and I mean that as a compliment."

She gave him a small smile. "Because I can see that's true, I'll let the broad comment pass."

He nodded. "I have gloves and plastic aprons in my truck. The coroner is on his way. I've asked the paramedics to return after they drop Duke off at the hospital because I don't expect the coroner to have the supplies to handle this type of body transport."

"I'll grab my camera."

Jadyn hurried out to her Jeep. She reached for the camera bag in the backseat and spoke to Helena while the driver's seat hid her from Colt's view.

"I'm going to be here awhile, I'm afraid," Jadyn said.

"Is Duke dead?"

"Yes, and Colt found empty plastic bags like those on the boat, so it's my gig."

"Maybe I should come in and help. I might notice something you don't."

Jadyn froze. "I wouldn't advise that. Duke was, uh…gutted."

She would never have considered the possibility that a ghost could lose all color, but that's exactly what Helena did.

"Like an animal?" Helena whispered.

Jadyn nodded.

"Oh my God. I thought when all that stuff happened last year—well, it was the worst thing this town had ever seen. I can't believe something like this is happening here. I don't even want to."

"I understand the sentiment, but unfortunately, that's not reality. Trust me, I don't like it any more than you, especially with your appearing to me factoring into the mix."

Jadyn was momentarily surprised to find that Helena looked guilty and even more surprised that she felt a little tug of sympathy for the woman. It couldn't be easy living in limbo, even if you brought it on yourself and even if you could change clothes by waving your hand.

"Look," Jadyn said, "this isn't your fault. Whatever is going on here started long before I got here or you returned."

Helena gave her a small smile. "I know you're right, but you'll excuse me if I feel sorry for myself for a minute."

Jadyn pulled the camera from the bag and hung it around her neck. "Take all the time you need. I'm going to be a while."

"I think I will wander around the outside. Maybe I'll find something. If you get ready to leave and don't see me, just honk the horn."

Helena exited through the passenger door and strolled off into the swamp. Jadyn shook her head. Yeah, because honking the horn wouldn't appear remotely odd.

She took pictures of Duke before the coroner arrived, trying not to look too closely at the body as she clicked. Then she got shots of the blood trail leading out the back door and the animal prints in the blood spatter. When she was done with the obvious items, she began snapping pictures of the rest of the cabin, making sure she covered everything in the open front rooms before moving into the bedroom, where Colt was searching the closet.

"Anything?" she asked.

"Just these," he said and pointed to three rifles, two shotguns, and four pistols on the bed. "I'd already done a good sweep of the cabin while I was waiting on you to get here. Those were already out on the bed. Other than that, there's not much to find."

Jadyn stared at the pile of weapons and frowned. "Was there forced entry?"

"No."

"So he had an arsenal on his bed, but didn't fire. So either the killer found the guns but didn't want them, or Duke had them out for God knows what reason but didn't have them ready because he knew his attacker."

"Which narrows it down to everyone in Mudbug and anyone he knew outside of town."

"Look on the bright side—unless he's a great actor, we can cross Leroy off the list. One down, couple thousand to go."

He nodded. "I don't think they'll be of any use, but can you take some shots in here? There's not much to this shack, and Duke didn't have much in the way of possessions."

"No sign of the money that came out of the Baggies?"

"I found a cubbyhole in the closet floor. The board covering it was already lifted and the space was empty. Maybe the money was in there."

"Maybe that's what they were trying to get out of him."

Colt frowned. "Maybe."

"But you don't think so?"

He stared at the closet floor for a moment, then looked back at her. "It wasn't all that great of a hiding place. That board doesn't even fit flat when it's down. A six-year-old could have found that cubbyhole."

"Maybe they were looking for something else. But what?"

"I have no idea."

"The bigger question is, did they get what they came for?"

He shook his head. "Part of me hopes they didn't, because then Duke got in the last blow, of sorts."

"And the other part?"

"Is afraid that if they didn't get what they wanted here, there could be a repeat performance."

She sucked in a breath as the validity of his fear overwhelmed her. "You said Leroy was Duke's best friend, right? If Duke was mixed up in something, wouldn't he be the logical person to know about it...or even be mixed up in it with him?"

"Yeah." He pulled his phone from his jeans pocket. "I'm going to send the state police over to the hospital to guard Leroy's room—at least until we can sort some of this out."

The sound of a car engine and tires crunching on gravel caught Jadyn's attention and she looked out the bedroom window along with Colt. A balding man, probably in his fifties, climbed out of a late-model sedan.

"The coroner?" Jadyn asked.

Colt nodded and started out of the room. "I need to prepare him before he walks in here."

"Okay. I'm going to poke around outside," she said as Colt hurried away.

She took a few shots of the bedroom, then went out the back door, careful to avoid the trail of blood as she exited the cabin. The backyard, if it could even be called such, was in even worse shape than the inside of the cabin.

An area about fifteen feet long had been cleared, leaving a line of cypress trees running the length of the cabin and beyond. Although the area was free of trees, it was not free from weeds, vines, and brush that reached several feet in height in most places. Two rusty lawn chairs sat against the cabin wall, a cracked ice chest between them and a pile of beer cans in between one of the chairs and the steps to the cabin.

What a dismal existence.

Jadyn lifted the camera and started taking some shots of the back area, even though she had no idea what their usefulness could be. The animal tracks disappeared into the overgrown lawn as soon as the steps ended, making tracking impossible except for a professional. Mudbug probably had more than its share of hunters capable of performing such a task, but Jadyn couldn't see the point of chasing scavengers into the brush. It wouldn't put them any closer to a solution than they were now, and would waste time and resources to boot.

"Did you find any clues?"

Helena's voice sounded behind her and Jadyn spun around.

"Sorry," Helena said, looking a bit chagrined. "I didn't mean to startle you. I guess you couldn't hear me coming."

"No, which all things considered, is a good thing. Unfortunately, we didn't find much of use."

"What did you think you'd find?"

Jadyn blew out a breath, trying to come up with a less gory version of the truth. "We think whoever killed Duke was trying to get information out of him—like the location of an object perhaps. But we didn't find anything inside that seemed to warrant his actions."

Helena nodded. "So either he got what he came for or it's still hidden somewhere."

"Yeah, but I have no idea where. It's a tiny cabin and Colt was thorough."

"He wouldn't have hid anything in the cabin."

Jadyn frowned. "Why not?"

"Because that's the first place anyone would look—there or his boat."

"So where would he hide something then?"

Helena shrugged. "If he was as dumb as my husband, Harold, he would have buried it in the backyard. I found a whole box of porn one year when I was putting in new rose bushes. Try explaining that to the gardener."

"Seeing as I'll probably never be able to afford a yard that rates a gardener, I doubt I'll need a backup plan for that situation. But I get your point. So was it like the pirate movies—ten paces from the coconut tree, then five paces right—that sort of thing?"

"Good Lord, no! Harold would have forgotten those sorts of instructions by the time grass grew over the hole. He just stuck a birdbath on top of it."

Jadyn scanned the weeds for a sign of something that would serve as a marker. "So if I were Duke, what would I mark the spot with that I'd be certain not to forget?"

Helena laughed. "This one is so obvious it hurts." She pointed to the stack of beer cans. "Look how faded the cans are. They've been out here a while."

"Having been inside the house, a mess *outside* hardly seems out of line."

"Fine then. I'll look myself." Helena stomped over to the stack of cans and reached down to pick one up, but her hands kept passing right through it. "Damn it!"

Jadyn held in a sigh and removed the camera from her neck, placing it on the dilapidated cooler. As she bent over to push the beer cans out of the way, a bloodcurdling shriek followed by a loud thud boomed from inside the cabin. Helena barreled straight through the cans, scattering them everywhere and flattening Jadyn in the process.

"Someone's being killed!" Helena shouted as she ran across the weed-infested backyard for the swamp.

Colt rushed out the back door and hurried over to Jadyn, extending his hand to help her up. "What happened? Did something attack you?" He whirled around to face the swamp, where Jadyn could hear Helena plowing through the brush. "I hear it. Stay here."

Before Jadyn could utter a word, Colt tore off into the swamp.

"Help!" Helena's voice boomed. "He's going to shoot me!"

Jadyn hesitated for a moment before running into the swamp after Colt. Apparently, Helena had "pulled a solid" and Colt was running after the sound. Helena, being a half-wit when under pressure, was making matters worse by continuing to thrash through the brush like a psychotic moose.

Fortunately, Helena's energy ran out in a matter of minutes and Jadyn slid to a stop beside Colt and he scanned the foliage, looking right past the glowing purple high-tops. Helena was doubled over and wheezing so hard Jadyn wondered if her chest would explode. If this was her better body in death, Jadyn did not want to know what the live one was like.

"I thought I had it," Colt said, clearly frustrated. "And then it just disappeared."

Because that's sorta what had actually happened, Jadyn just nodded. "Did you see what it was?"

"No." Colt studied the ground and frowned. "The ground cover is too thick to leave prints, but it must have been something big, based on the size of the trail. Maybe a bear."

Helena rose up and glared at Colt. "Did he just call me fat as a bear?"

Jadyn rubbed her nose to mask the tiny smile that crept out.

Colt turned to look at her. "You didn't see it? I thought you'd been attacked."

"No. I tripped over something in the yard and lost my balance," she said. It wasn't exactly a lie. She had tripped or had been tripped by Helena.

"That place is a tetanus shot waiting to happen." He shoved his pistol back into his jeans and started walking back to the cabin. Jadyn gestured at Helena to stay put—the last thing they needed was a repeat—then dropped into step behind him.

"Was that the coroner who screamed?" she asked.

"Yeah. I tried to explain the situation before he entered the cabin, but he insisted he'd seen it all and didn't need someone young enough to be his son trying to tell him how to do his job."

Jadyn shook her head. "I'd have been tempted to let him walk in there without a warning."

"That's exactly what I did. Hence the scream right before he passed completely out."

Suddenly, the timing of everything hit Jadyn and she held in a smile. "So he's still there crumpled on the floor?"

"Unless he woke up or the paramedics got there, I suppose he is. I guess next time he'll listen."

This time, Jadyn didn't bother to hold in her smile. It wasn't polite, but she would have wanted to do the same thing. The difference was, she probably wouldn't have gone through with it. The fact that Colt had not only followed through but had no regrets about his decision scored a point in his favor and got the know-it-all coroner a deduction.

As they stepped out of the swamp and into the makeshift backyard, Colt sighed. "I don't hear the paramedics, so I guess I better go scrape him up off the floor. Try not to trip over anything else. We've only got one set of paramedics on call."

And with that comment, his point earned for the coroner episode faded away.

Jadyn watched as he stepped back into the cabin and shook her head. Colt was just like every other man she'd ever known—convinced that she was incapable of making it through life unscathed without the support of a strong man. To hell with him and his archaic attitude.

She walked back over to the cooler to collect her camera and get the hell out of there. She'd fulfilled her obligation and nothing more could be gained hanging around. In fact, hanging around with Helena in tow could cause more trouble than it was worth.

"I can't believe he called me a bear," Helena groused as she barreled out of the swamp.

"Stop stomping," Jadyn whispered. "We don't know if Colt can still hear you. And why in the world were you running? You're already dead. What the hell could he possibly do to you?"

Helena crossed her arms. "You're just like Maryse—always pointing out that I'm already dead. Well, my mind hasn't latched onto that yet, so when a man with a gun starts chasing me, I run."

"It's been a year, Helena. How long should it take you to get a grip?"

"I don't know. I'll let you know when it happens."

Jadyn shook her head. "That's not good enough. You could have hurt me when you tore out like that. This entire place is one big germ. Even a cut could cause a problem. You have got to start considering your circumstances for more things than your wardrobe."

"Whatever."

Jadyn held in a sigh. It was no wonder Maryse resorted to threatening her with exorcism. The woman was exhausting and quite possibly even more self-centered than her mother, which Jadyn hadn't thought possible.

"We need to get out of here," Jadyn said, "and you and I need to spend a little time apart."

"Fine by me, Your Rudeness."

As Jadyn started to turn, she glanced at the spot where the beer cans had rested before Helena had shoved her into them, and stopped in her tracks. The ground underneath was loose as if it had been recently turned, which was in direct opposition to the thought that the beer cans had been sitting there fading for weeks.

She picked up a piece of rotted wood from the ground and started scraping the dirt to the side. On her fourth pass, something hard and black came out of the hole with the dirt.

"Did you find something?" Helena asked.

Jadyn picked up the object and looked up at Helena, who was leaning over her.

"A key," Helena said. "A really old key."

Jadyn nodded. The black iron key was heavy and larger than those used for contemporary locks. This one reminded Jadyn of the keys carried by spooky caretakers used to open huge wrought iron gates that kept haunted mansions secluded from prying eyes.

"What's it to?" Helena asked.

"How the heck should I know?"

"Hmmpff. You're the investigator."

"Neither my university degree nor my on-the-job training included a course on identifying old keys."

"Whatever. I told you something was hidden under the beer cans. I should at least get credit for that. In fact, if I hadn't shoved you into them, you may not have noticed the dirt."

Jadyn stared. Helena truly was a piece of work. "Fine, you get credit for the idea, but it still doesn't outweigh you running me over or your hysterical dash into the swamp."

"If you're going to hold grudges, I don't know that I'm interested in protecting you."

"If you're going to wear ridiculous clothes and do stupid things, I'm not sure I want to live."

"You doing all right out here?" Colt's voice sounded from the back doorway.

"Yeah, fine."

He glanced across the back yard and frowned. "I thought I

heard you talking."

"I was—to myself. Occupational hazard from being alone so much, I guess," she explained, hoping she didn't sound completely ridiculous.

He raised one eyebrow. "I see. What's that you're holding?"

"A key. It was buried beneath the beer cans. I guess it's a good thing I fell or I wouldn't have noticed the freshly dug hole underneath."

She extended the key to Colt, who walked down the stairs to take it.

"Do you have any idea what it might unlock?" she asked.

"None whatsoever. But it must be important if Duke buried it under a stack of beer cans."

"Important enough for someone to kill him over?"

Colt shook his head. "I guess that's the question." He slipped the key into a plastic Baggie and shoved it in his jeans pocket. "I'll show it to a couple of people. See if I can figure out what it goes to."

Jadyn felt her back tighten at his presumptuous decision. "But I found it. This is my case, remember?"

"Not anymore. Duke's murder is my jurisdiction, and murder trumps a bunch of floating cash."

Jadyn felt a blush rush up her face. No way was she just handing him her first case. "You *know* they're related."

"Probably so, and that's why I'm going to let you keep investigating with me, but from here on out, I'm calling the shots."

"I've finished my work in here." The coroner poked his head out the back door. "Is there anything else you need from me before I leave?"

"No, thank you," Colt said. "James Calvis—this is Jadyn St. James, our new game warden. James is the coroner."

James stepped outside and reached down to shake Jadyn's hand. She noticed that his face was still pale and his hand shook a bit as he extended it. "It's a pleasure, ma'am, although I would have preferred better circumstances."

"Me too," Jadyn agreed.

He pulled a card from his pocket and handed it to her. "That's my information. I hope you don't need my services anytime soon, but just in case."

"Thanks," Jadyn said and stuck the card in her pocket as James ducked back inside the house.

"If you're done taking pictures," Colt said, "I'm ready to seal this location."

"Yeah, I'm all done," Jadyn said, trying not to dwell on the duplicity of her statement. Without so much as a good-bye, she slung her camera over her shoulder and headed around the corner of the house to the front. Helena, apparently sensing that now was not the time for conversation, climbed into the passenger seat and sat completely silent as she pulled away from Duke's cabin.

The silence lasted all of five minutes.

"I take it you're mad that Colt took over?" Helena asked.

"What do you think?"

"Definitely mad." Helena stared at her for a couple of seconds, an uncertain look on her face. Finally, she spoke again. "Look, I've always been a control freak, and I get and totally support the whole feminist movement, so I can see why you're offended. But do you really think you're more qualified to handle a murder investigation than the sheriff?"

Jadyn clenched the steering wheel and stared straight ahead, trying to control her frustration. Of course Colt was more qualified to conduct a murder investigation. She wasn't even trying to argue the fact, but he didn't have to take the key and then summarily dismiss her as if she had no value to the investigation. He wouldn't even have the key if it hadn't been for her.

And Helena, although she'd never admit that to the ghost.

"I don't like being put on a shelf like a pretty little art object," Jadyn said finally. "I may not be a cop, but I can help with the investigation."

Helena nodded. "I believe you. But I'm not the one you have to convince."

Jadyn blew out a breath and concentrated on the narrow, dirt road. She knew exactly whom she had to convince.

She just didn't know how.

The man shook his head as she drove away. What was the world coming to when females were allowed to hold positions like game warden? From his vantage point, he'd seen her pilfering around behind the cabin, and wondered what in the world she could possibly hope to accomplish in what was essentially an overgrown dumping ground.

The sheriff had talked to her for some time before she left, but he hadn't been close enough to hear the conversation. Whatever was said, the woman didn't look happy about it. As soon as he had an opportunity, he took a peek at the back yard.

One look at the freshly dug hole next to the stairs and he immediately knew what it implied. That stupid son of a bitch was the one who'd stolen his key, and he'd hidden the access to half a million dollars' worth of product in a three-inch deep hole. This is what he got for working with fools and amateurs. He should have done the job himself, instead of trusting it to a local.

In her poking around, the woman must have found the key, and he was sure she understood the significance given the manner in which it was hidden. The question was how long would it take her to figure out what the key opened, and could he find the location before she did? The sheriff wasn't cause for concern as the Mudbug native would never suspect him, but the woman was a problem. She wasn't a local. To her, everyone would be suspect.

That meant the woman had to go...soon.

He had to make this right with his associates. No way was he going to end up like Duke.

Chapter Twelve

Jadyn had planned to head straight back to the hotel, dump Helena, then ask Mildred about the mysterious key, but as she drove into Mudbug, her cell phone rang.

"Ms. St. James? This is the sheriff's department dispatch."

Jadyn clenched her phone, praying that a second crime scene hadn't been uncovered. "Yes, this is Jadyn."

"We got a call saying two men are poaching alligator in Johnson's Bayou."

"Who was the call from?"

"I don't know. The reception wasn't good and the call dropped altogether before I could ask any questions."

"Well, then I guess I better check it out."

"Thank you, ma'am."

Jadyn disconnected the call and looked over at Helena. "Do you know where Johnson's Bayou is?"

"Of course. It's the big one that shoots off Mudbug Bayou, just west of town."

"I don't suppose there's a road that follows it."

Helena raised her eyebrows.

"Never mind." Jadyn swung her Jeep around and parked on Main Street. "I left my boat docked behind the sheriff's department."

Helena climbed out of the Jeep and followed Jadyn around back to the dock. "Why are you going to Johnson's Bayou?"

"To catch some poachers."

"Is that really a priority?"

"Given that I'm the game warden, I'm going to go with 'Yes, it's a priority.'"

Helena shook her head as Jadyn untied the flat-bottom aluminum boat. "You and Maryse both have the same annoying addiction to doing your job."

"I have an addiction to eating and having a roof over my head. That's why I do my job." Jadyn tossed the rope into the boat and jumped in after it. "Are you coming or not?"

"If I don't, I'll never hear the end of it from Mildred and Maryse. Those two could win an Olympic event in nagging." She plopped down on the bench at the front of the boat, then turned around as Jadyn pushed the boat away from the dock. "But for the record, you poor people and your jobs are exhausting."

Jadyn threw the accelerator down and the boat launched away from the dock, sending Helena tumbling backward into the bottom of the boat. Unfortunately, her plaid skirt was up around her neck and Jadyn could clearly see her giant white granny panties, so the joy she'd hoped to feel at her spiteful prank was considerably diminished.

Helena flopped around like a fish for a bit before getting herself upright. She climbed back onto the bench, this time facing backward, and glared at Jadyn. "You did that on purpose."

Jadyn shook her head. "I'm not used to this boat yet. It's got a sensitive throttle."

Helena didn't look completely convinced. "Well, stop manhandling everything. You're a woman, for Christ's sake. Try a little finesse." She hefted her large legs over the bench and whirled around to face the front.

Jadyn held in a laugh. Finesse advice? From Helena Henry? Maryse and Mildred would get a huge laugh out of that one.

"That way," Helena said, pointing to a left fork in the bayou.

Jadyn guided the boat to the left into the smaller channel and continued down it at a decent clip. At about fifty feet wide, the bayou was larger than most, but she could easily scan both sides for signs of the poachers without drastically reducing her speed.

"How far out will a cell phone get reception in this channel?" she asked Helena.

"How the hell should I know? Do I look like someone who fishes?"

Since she looked like a hooker long past retirement, Jadyn elected to remain silent. Instead, she pulled her cell phone from her pocket and checked service—two bars. Whoever called may have been farther out, assuming his service company was the same as or similar to Jadyn's. But if he had worse service, he could have been standing on Main Street and still had bad reception.

She slipped the phone back in her pocket and pushed on down the bayou. Cypress trees lined both sides, sometimes leaving a little space for a muddy bank, but most often creating walls of gnarled roots. Periodically, they passed a fisherman or two, but all of them had shallow boats and none of them were loaded down with alligators.

As she rounded a sharp left turn, a loud ping rang out.

It took a second bullet whizzing only inches from her face before Jadyn realized someone was shooting at her.

She dropped to the bottom of the boat and pulled out her nine. Helena looked completely shocked and confused, but hesitated only a second before leaping onto the bottom of the boat beside her.

"Someone's shooting at me," Jadyn whispered.

Helena's eyes widened. "Where is he?"

"That bank," Jadyn said and pointed to the left side of the

boat. Taking a deep breath, she peered over the edge of the boat, but couldn't see any sign of movement in the dense foliage.

"I can't die again, right?" Helena asked.

"How the heck should I know? I'm a little more worried about me dying the first time than the possibility that you can die twice."

"Then I'll go look," Helena said.

"You're going to swim to the bank?"

Helena grinned. "I can walk on water. Didn't they tell you?"

Jadyn couldn't even formulate a thought, much less a response before Helena popped up from the bottom of the boat. Despite her attempt to sound confident, Jadyn could tell she was nervous. She froze for several seconds, staring at the bank, as if waiting to see if the shooter would fire at her. She must have decided she was invisible because she climbed over the side of the boat and onto the bayou.

Jadyn's jaw dropped as Helena did exactly as she'd claimed and started walking across the bayou. Unfortunately, the tide was coming in and it swept her too far upstream. She changed to a jog and worked at a diagonal until she reached the bank, then climbed up the bank and disappeared into the trees.

Every second ticked away like an eternity as Jadyn kept her gaze locked on the bank. Finally, she saw Helena emerge from the swamp and scamper back down to the bayou. When she got to the water level, she gripped a tree root with one hand and waved the other at Jadyn.

"Come pick me up!" she yelled. "I'm exhausted."

"Is it clear?"

"I walked along the bank a good half mile each way. No one's there."

Jadyn inched across the boat and crouched behind the driver's column. She started the engine and directed the boat toward the bank, trying to keep as low as possible behind the column. When she got to the bank, Helena climbed over the side and collapsed in the bottom of the boat.

"Are you all right?" Jadyn asked. This was the second time in one morning that Helena had made a mad dash, and Jadyn was starting to wonder if all that exercise couldn't be detrimental to the ghost. It seemed a ridiculous thought, but then nothing about Helena was logical.

"I'll be fine when I get my breath back—you know, in a year or two." She pushed herself off the bottom of the boat and sat on the bench. "I didn't see a sign of anyone. Maybe he left."

Jadyn frowned. "Maybe," she said, but it didn't make sense. Why would he leave without finishing the job?

"Do you think it was a hunter who made a bad shot?" Helena asked. "He might not have been shooting at you."

"Did you hear a gunshot?"

Helena scrunched her brow. "Now that you mention it…"

"Exactly. I didn't either. Do most hunters in Mudbug use a silencer?"

"Oh, I get it. Damn."

Exactly that. Damn.

"Let's get out of here," Jadyn said. She pushed the boat away from the bank and reached for the accelerator, but before her hand could grip the control, a bullet tore right through the dashboard.

Jadyn dove to the front of the boat and tucked herself in front of the driver's column.

"Drive!" she yelled at Helena, who was staring at her as if she'd lost her mind. "He's shooting at me. Get the hell out of here!"

Helena bolted up from the bench and ran to the driver's seat. "How do I make it go?"

"The throttle is that lever on the right. Push it down."

The boat leaped away from the bank and Jadyn heard Helena scream, then crash to the bottom. The ninety-degree turn was straight ahead and the boat barreled toward it, complete out of control.

"Helena, the bank!"

Jadyn's pulse spiked so high her head ached. She braced herself against the bench in front of her and watched in horror as they flew toward the bank of cypress roots.

This is it. I'm going to die.

She clenched her eyes shut, not wanting to see the impact, but instead of the expected crash, she found herself flung across the boat as it made a hard right turn. She opened her eyes and saw Helena clutching the steering wheel with both hands, looking as panicked as Jadyn felt.

"Slow down—what the hell!"

Jadyn heard someone yell from a boat as they sped by at top speed and could only imagine what the fisherman thought. From his point of view, it looked like an empty boat was careering down the bayou.

One look at Helena's face and Jadyn knew the ghost had completely checked out.

She checked behind them, trying to gauge the amount of distance they'd covered and was pleased with the progress. Unless the shooter could run like a cheetah, she should be in the clear. Before she could change her mind, she crawled around the driver's column and yelled at Helena to move.

Helena remained frozen at the steering wheel, so Jadyn finally reached through her and pulled the throttle up until the boat slowed to a manageable pace. A chill ran up Jadyn's arm and she yanked it back from the throttle, more than a little creeped out.

"Helena, move out of the way."

The ghost didn't even flinch.

"If we stay here, people might start shooting again."

She released the steering wheel as if it were on fire and bolted from the driver's seat. "I've never driven a boat," she said.

"You don't say?"

"You don't have to be so pissy about it. I saved your butt, didn't I?"

Because that statement was reasonably accurate, Jadyn decided to let the whole thing drop. "Fine, but you and I are going to have a boat training session at first opportunity—just in case I need you to drive again."

Helena plopped down on the bench at the front of the boat. "Being dead is exhausting."

"Oh yeah? Try staying alive."

"Hmppffff." Helena crossed her arms and stared at the bottom of the boat, apparently out of valid comments.

"Are you all right?" A man's voice sounded behind Jadyn and she whirled around to see a boat coasting beside her.

The man in the boat was Bart, the guy who'd started the fight with Junior in the bar the night before.

"I'm fine," Jadyn replied, forcing her voice to normal.

Bart frowned. "I saw your boat tearing down the bayou, but I didn't see you in it. I thought it was a runaway."

"It was," Jadyn said, latching onto a potential explanation. "The throttle was stuck and no matter how far up I pulled it, it hung at top speed. I was crouched down trying to fix it. That's probably why you couldn't see me."

Bart shook his head. "You came awful close to nailing that bank head-on. It probably would have been smarter to bail."

"Yes, I suppose it would have been, but I thought I could fix it."

"Did you?"

"It seems to be working fine now, but I'll have a mechanic

give it a once-over before I take it out again. Was that you who yelled when I went by?"

"No. That was Old Man Broussard. He's a real grouch about this sort of thing. Don't be surprised if he asks the sheriff to arrest you." Bart grinned.

She forced a smile. "Something to look forward to. Hey, I was out this way because I got a report that someone was poaching alligators on this bayou. Did you see anything like that?"

Bart shook his head. "You'd have to be pretty stupid to poach on Johnson's Bayou in the broad daylight. Besides Mudbug Bayou, this is the busiest channel in the swamp. Maybe your call-in gave you the wrong channel."

Jadyn nodded. "Dispatch said the reception wasn't good. She may have misunderstood. Well, I need to get back to the office. Thanks for stopping and for the information."

"Anytime. If you're ever interested in finishing that beer, let me know. I'd be happy to buy you another." He flashed a smile at her and backed his boat away.

"Looks like you've got a boyfriend," Helena said.

"Not hardly. A man is the last thing I need. I've already got enough trouble. Speaking of which, I thought you said no one was on that bank—so who the hell was shooting at me?"

Helena shook her head. "I swear, I didn't see anyone. I looked all up and down the bank. No one was there."

"Clearly, you're wrong, unless you're not the only ghost in Mudbug and the other one carries a gun and wants to kill me."

"I guess it's more likely that I didn't see him, huh?"

Jadyn sighed. This whole ghostly bodyguard thing wasn't working out as well as Maryse and Mildred had hoped.

"I think we have a problem," Helena said.

"You're just now cluing in to that?"

Helena rolled her eyes. "The boat is sinking."

JANA DELEON

Jadyn looked down and realized she was standing in two inches of water. What the hell?

"Grab a seat behind me," Jadyn said as she reached for the throttle. "I need to get this boat on top of the water if we're going to have any chance of making it all the way back to the dock."

Helena plopped down on the bench across the back of the boat.

"Do you see that plug at the bottom of the bench?" Jadyn pointed. "When I take off, the water is going to come rushing back toward you. As soon as you feel the boat settle on top of the water, pull that plug so that it will drain."

"Hey, wait a minute—what do you mean the water will come rushing back toward me?"

"Hold on tight!" Jadyn yelled, no time to humor Helena and her fifty questions.

She paused only long enough to see Helena's eyes widen as she grabbed the edge of the bench before she shoved the throttle down, forcing the waterlogged boat to jump forward.

It lagged for a couple of seconds, then the momentum got the better of the additional weight and it popped up on top of the bayou. The water, which had increased to several inches by that time, came rushing from the front of the boat to the rear, crashing into Helena like a tidal wave. Helena responded, of course, by screaming as if someone was killing her.

"Pull the plug!" Jadyn yelled. With the speed she had to maintain to keep the boat on top of the water in the curvy bayou, she couldn't even afford a backward glance or she may clip the bank, a stump, or even worse, a fisherman.

"It's stuck," Helena cried.

Jadyn felt the boat slow and checked the gauges. The additional water weight was straining the engine. "Unstick it or we're going to sink."

113

She turned onto a long straight stretch and was just about to tell Helena to take the wheel while she removed the plug when the boat's speed increased. She glanced back to see a drenched Helena holding the plug and glaring at her.

Her tiny gray pigtails were plastered flat on her head, which oddly enough, was almost an improvement. Unfortunately, her soaked vest and skirt now clung to every bulge on her body and that was an awful lot of bulging.

Jadyn couldn't begin to fathom the reasons the ghost would be soaked, and she didn't even try. She'd stood in a shower for a good twenty minutes that morning and come out completely dry. The entire thing boggled the mind.

But the bottom of the boat was now empty of water, and that was all that mattered. "Put the plug back in," she said and slowed the speed to a more manageable level while still maintaining the hydroplane.

"Pull the plug out. Put the plug in," Helena complained. "I didn't sign up for this kind of abuse. This outfit is ruined."

Jadyn looked back at Helena. "I didn't sign up for being shot at, and according to Maryse, that wouldn't be happening if you weren't here."

Helena crossed her arms and stuck out her lip, like a petulant child.

Jadyn whipped around before Helena could see the smile that forced its way through. Maryse definitely had Helena's number with that guilt thing. She just hoped it was enough to keep her in line. She really didn't want to play the exorcism card unless things were dire.

It took about ten minutes to get back to the dock, and she made a wide swing out before directing the boat straight at the muddy bank just to the side of the concrete launch.

"Hold on," she told Helena as she increased speed and ran

the boat straight up the sloping bank.

The boat hit the bank at a good clip, and Jadyn almost lost her grip on the steering wheel. She heard Helena scream followed by a splash. The boat lurched to a halt and she looked back to see a bedraggled Helena pulling herself up from the bayou behind the boat. She glared at Jadyn, then stomped up the bank, trampling the marsh grass as she went, her shoes squeaking.

"You could have let me off at the pier," Helena complained.

"The boat would have sunk before I could get the trailer and get it out. I need to figure out what happened."

Helena threw her arms in the air. "Someone shot at you. How much more explanation do you need?"

"We can start with why the boat was sinking."

"The Mudbug city councilmen are the cheapest bastards in the world. Do you know I gave this city millions' worth of real estate and all they did was have some horrible sculptor make a statue of me that they erected in town square? To add insult to injury, the sculptor made me fat. I am not fat."

"What does any of that have to do with the boat?" Jadyn wasn't about to touch the issue of the statue. She'd seen the artwork, and now that she'd seen the real thing, she knew the artist had been kind with the trim work.

"I'm just saying they wouldn't pay for the best equipment, not even for their own law enforcement, and they probably don't contribute enough money to keep things properly maintained. The light at the end of Main Street was out for two months— two months, I tell you, before they finally got it changed, and they're all too dim."

"Maybe they were busy with more important things."

"Not even. They said it cost too much to bring a truck out with an extension bucket that could reach the light. I said one of them should shimmy up the damned thing if they were that worried about money, because the rest of us were more worried about being mugged."

Helena's tirade only half registered with Jadyn as she scanned the bottom of the boat, trying to locate the source of the leak. It didn't take her long to discover the hole in the bottom of the boat, but the location was a surprise. She'd suspected the bullet had traveled through the aluminum somewhere on the side, allowing the water to seep in, but the clear round hole was directly in the bottom of the boat.

"This doesn't make sense," she said.

"Tell me about it. I told them that if they didn't want to pay for lightbulb changes, they should have bought shorter light poles—"

"Not that." Jadyn waved a hand in dismissal. "The bullet hole. It's in the bottom of the boat."

Helena stomped over to the edge of the boat and stared down at the hole. "Makes sense to me—they shot a hole in the boat and we were sinking. Even a six-year-old could figure that one out."

"They couldn't shoot a hole in the center of the boat from the elevation of the bank. They weren't high enough." She sucked in a breath. "He was in a tree. That's why you couldn't see him, and why he could get a bullet down into the boat."

Helena's eyes widened. "Then why didn't he pick you off when you pulled up to the bank? Wouldn't that have been even easier?"

"He must have been farther up the bank and didn't have a clear shot through the trees. Think about it—he didn't fire another shot until I pushed away from the bank."

"Holy shit. You're right."

"I suspected this already, but the tree thing confirms it." Jadyn looked at Helena. "You know what this means, right?"

Helena shook her head.

"That call to dispatch was to lure me into the bayou. Unless you think someone who wants me dead just happened to be sitting in a tree with a rifle and a silencer hoping I would pass by."

"Who made the call?"

Jadyn glanced back at the sheriff's department and frowned. "I don't know. But I'm going to find out."

Chapter Thirteen

Colt left the morgue and headed to the elevators. Leroy was in a room on the second floor, and Colt had just received a call from the nurse that the man was out of shock and rambling on to anyone who'd listen. Colt figured after what Leroy had seen that day, there were only a handful of people who had the stomach to hear what Leroy had to say, and he was one of them.

The coroner had still been passed out cold when Colt had returned to the cabin from the chase in the swamp. It had taken a cup of cold water dumped square in his face to jolt the man back into consciousness. He'd bolted upright, sputtering and scattering the water everywhere, then taken one look at Duke and probably would have passed out again if Colt hadn't grabbed his shoulders and shaken him.

It wasn't the nicest thing he could have done, but the paramedics hadn't arrived and Colt was out of patience. They all had a job to do, and he figured if the new game warden managed to not only stomach the scene but process it from an investigative standpoint, then the least James could do was stay awake and do his job, especially as he'd already pointed out to Colt how competent he was.

He could hear Leroy ranting as soon as he stepped off the elevator. A harried nurse came from the direction of Leroy's room and hurried over.

"Sheriff Bertrand?"

"Yes."

"Thank God. He's disturbing the other patients, but we can't get him to quiet down. Dr. Henning said we couldn't sedate him until you spoke to him, so we've been trying to manage, but I have to tell you, it's not working out well."

He fell into step beside her as she motioned him down the hall in the direction she'd come from. "I take it he's completely lucid?"

"He's plenty lucid. Unfortunately, I can't vouch for sane. Some of what he's saying…he didn't really see that, did he?"

"I'm not sure what you heard, but if it was the most awful thing imaginable, then yeah, that's exactly what he saw."

The nurse's hand flew over her mouth and she paled a bit. "Oh! I feel bad for complaining, given the circumstances."

Colt gave her an encouraging smile. "Your job is to take care of all the patients. Regardless of how valid the reasons, you don't need one upsetting everyone."

They stopped in front of the door to Leroy's room. He'd gone strangely silent as they approached and Colt wasn't sure which was more unnerving—the man's yelling or his silence.

"I will make this as fast as possible," Colt said, "and as soon as I'm done, you can give him elephant tranquilizers for all I care. He'll probably appreciate it."

"Thank you so much, Sheriff." The nurse's relief was apparent.

Colt said a silent prayer that Leroy could give him some answers, then pushed open the door and entered the room.

"About damned time you got here!" Leroy bolted up straight in his bed and glared at Colt. "What the hell are we paying all those tax dollars for if you're not going to do your job?"

A litany of answers sprung to Colt's mind, but it wasn't worth stating them. Leroy was worked up and determined that someone else would take the blame for it.

"I'm sorry it took so long for me to get here," Colt said, "but I had to handle things at the cabin and arrange for transport of the body. I know you want things taken care of correctly so that there can be a proper funeral."

Leroy looked a bit mollified. "I suppose a situation like that would take more time than usual."

Colt nodded, knowing it was the closest he would get to an apology or an acknowledgment that he was doing his job. "The sooner I get started on this investigation, the more likely I can catch the perpetrator. I know I'm asking you to do something really hard, but if you could tell me exactly what happened this morning, it would be a big help."

"Duke's been my friend as long as I've been on this earth. Doesn't matter how hard it is. I want that bastard caught— unless you get the opportunity to shoot him outright."

"I promise, if the killer gives me any reason, I will definitely shoot him outright."

Leroy gave him a single nod. "We was supposed to go fishing early this morning. Snapper are biting right after dawn over at Vernon's Point, and we wanted to get the good spot by the cattails. I went to pick him up, just like we'd agreed."

"Did you see anyone at his cabin when you pulled up?"

"Not a soul. His front door was standing wide open, but I didn't think anything of it at the time. Duke is…" Leroy choked a bit and coughed. "…was a tough old bastard. Didn't have AC. He wouldn't have thought twice about leaving his doors and windows wide open."

Colt nodded, patiently waiting for Leroy to get to what he needed to know, and hoping that if he let the older man process it at his own pace, he'd be more thorough with his description and less inclined to get off-balance again.

"I honked the horn," Leroy continued, "but he never came

out. I figured maybe he was changing out his tackle so I headed to the house to see if I could hurry him up." He took a deep breath and blew it out. "The smell hit me as soon as I stepped onto the porch. I got a nose like a prize bloodhound. Usually, it comes in handy, but today, I would have given anything to have a cold."

"You showed a lot of bravery, going in there," Colt said.

Leroy shrugged. "He was my friend. What else was I gonna do?" He looked out the window, then down at the blanket that covered his legs. "I stepped inside, already figuring I was gonna see something bad, like Duke had accidentally shot himself while cleaning one of his guns. But I never thought...I ain't never..."

He looked up at Colt, his expression haunting. "Whoever did that ain't human. Ain't no way a normal man could do such things."

"I agree, and you don't know how sorry I am you had to find Duke that way."

Leroy nodded. "It didn't take but a glance to know he was gone—had been for a while. I got dizzy and grabbed the doorjamb, trying to keep my balance, then as soon as I could move, I stumbled back outside. It was all I could do to get to my truck and call the sheriff's department. My chest hurt and my vision blurred. No matter how much I breathed, I couldn't catch my breath. You ever had that happen?"

Colt nodded. "Yeah, I have."

A look of relief passed over Leroy's face. "I managed to call dispatch and as soon as Eugenia answered, I panicked. My heart was beating so hard, I thought it would pop my chest. I started yelling and crying and damned if I'm going to feel bad about either."

"You have nothing to feel bad about."

"I stumbled around the front yard while I was talking and

finally collapsed on the steps to the cabin. Then it's like my whole body went numb and I got real cold. Didn't even notice when you drove up. Didn't even know you'd been there at all until the paramedics told me on the ride to the hospital."

"You were in shock."

"I gotta tell you, it feels like shit. I don't ever want to see something so bad it puts me in shock again."

"I don't either."

"Did it put you in shock…seeing Duke?"

"No, but it was hard to maintain control, even with all the training I have and all the things I've seen working in New Orleans."

"Then I guess I ain't doing too bad, given that I ain't had no training and such."

"You're doing great. Is there anything else you can think of to tell me about this morning?"

"No. That's all I seen and all I know."

Colt studied the man's face closely and decided he was telling the truth—at least about this morning. The question was, did he know more?

"I found some plastic bags in the cabin," Colt said. "They look like the bags holding money that sank on that shrimp boat. You heard about that, right?"

Leroy's eyes widened. "I heard about it all right, but I don't know nothing about it. I went to New Orleans the day before and spent all night at the blackjack tables. Heard about the whole mess at Bill's that night."

"Did Duke go with you to New Orleans?"

"Nah. He said thirty-count shrimp was running in deep water and he wanted to cash in."

Colt nodded. "Count" referred to how many shrimp it took to make a pound. At only thirty shrimp to a pound, the size of the shrimp was extra-large and highly desired by the finer restaurants. The shrimp house paid a premium for thirty-count shrimp and larger. The only problem was, Colt had been listening to the local fisherman complain for over a month now that they couldn't find any large shrimp left in the area. So either Duke had found the only pocket of large shrimp or he'd lied to Leroy.

"Duke wasn't one of the guys that went after the money yesterday. Do you have any idea why he would have some of it?"

"No," Leroy said, but Colt could tell he was lying.

"You're sure? Because there's a good chance that money is what got Duke killed. Are you willing to risk the same fate yourself?"

Leroy paled and he clutched the edge of the blanket. "I swear, I don't know why he had the money or what he was doing with it."

"But you know something?"

"About a week ago, Duke told me he'd come across some side work that was going to make him a mess of money. I figured he was doing some carpentry. He hates it, but he's good at it. But he said it was way better than that and paid enough for him to retire."

"You didn't ask him what he was doing?"

"Of course I did. Hell, if Duke was making enough money to retire, I figured there might be some more to go around."

"So what did he tell you?"

"Told me he couldn't say anything about it or they wouldn't work with him, but he'd give them my name."

"And that didn't strike you as strange?"

Leroy sighed. "I figured whatever it was couldn't be legal, if that's what you're asking, but I didn't think they'd kill him over it. Especially not like this. What kind of people do something like that?"

"The evil kind, and apparently, they're in Mudbug. Are you

sure you're telling me everything you know? I don't want to walk up on another crime scene like the one at Duke's."

Leroy's eyes widened. "I swear to you, I don't know nothing else about it. You don't think they'll come after me, do you—since I'm friends with Duke and all?"

"I don't know. They tossed the cabin, so it looks to me like they wanted something Duke had. If they didn't find it and think you know where it is, they might come after you."

"I gotta get outta here!" Leroy tried to swing his legs over the bed, but Colt grabbed his shoulders and held them in place.

"You're not going anywhere until tomorrow morning. I've asked the state police to put a guard outside your room. He's on his way now, but I don't think anyone will try to bother you here."

"And tomorrow? What about when I leave the hospital? I'm a sitting duck at my cabin."

Leroy's fear was palpable, and Colt couldn't blame him. Even though it went against procedure, he couldn't bring himself to demand the man stay in town. "If you want, you can head straight out of Mudbug, as long as you leave me a way to get in touch with you."

Leroy flopped back on the bed, almost collapsing with relief. "Thank you. I've got an old army buddy in Belle Chasse. I'll call tomorrow and give you all his information."

Colt nodded. "If there's nothing else you can think of, I'm going to get to work and let you get some rest. If you think of anything, call dispatch and have them patch you in to me, okay?"

Leroy nodded.

Colt exited the room and flagged down the harried nurse at the station midway down the hall. "You can sedate him now," he said. "The state police are sending a guard for his room."

The nurse's eyes widened. "Is he dangerous?"

"No, but he might be in danger. And sedated, he'd be easy pickings."

"Oh my! Okay. Is there anything we need to do?"

"Just keep an eye out. Aside from law enforcement and the medical staff, I don't want anyone in his room." He pulled a card from his wallet. "If anyone attempts to see him, call me immediately."

The nurse took the card, her hands shaking slightly and she stuck it in her pocket. "This is my first job after college. I thought as long as I stayed out of big cities, I wouldn't run into this sort of thing."

Colt gave her shoulder a gentle squeeze. "Me too."

He exited the hospital, his mind cataloging everything Leroy had told him. He'd call the shrimp house from his truck, but Colt had no doubt the owner would tell him he hadn't seen thirty-count shrimp in a while. He didn't have concrete proof, but Colt would bet anything Duke was the captain of the sunken shrimp boat of money.

Clearly, the old shrimper had gotten involved with something far beyond his scope and experience, and it had gotten him killed in a most horrific way. But was he killed because he failed to deliver the money? Or for the key? Or for some other reason entirely?

And Colt was still no closer to knowing where the money came from and what it was to be used for than he had been the day before. So many avenues to investigate, and so far, they only provided more questions.

Jadyn paced the length of the sheriff's department for at least the hundredth time. Unfortunately, it only took her ten steps to do so didn't expend a bit of the negative energy boiling inside of her. She paused long enough to glare once more at the daytime dispatcher, Shirley, who immediately averted her eyes, pretending that her supply drawer needed rearranging. It was the fifth time she'd rearranged the file drawer since Jadyn had shown up.

When the front door swung open and Colt walked in, Jadyn exploded. "Where the hell have you been? Why weren't you answering my calls?"

Colt stopped in his tracks and glanced at Shirley, who raised her eyebrows and gave him an almost imperceptible shake of her head.

"I've been doing my job," he replied, "if it's any of your business."

"You know good and well it's my business, given that your job and my job currently happen to be the same thing."

Colt walked by her and pulled a bottle of water from a small refrigerator next to a filing cabinet. "I don't know how you do your job, but when I'm questioning a witness, I don't take phone calls."

She narrowed her eyes at him. "What witness?"

"Leroy Pendarvis."

Jadyn clenched her hands trying to control her ever-increasing frustration. "Why wasn't I included in that interview?"

"I already told you that this mess is now my jurisdiction. I get to decide your level of involvement. If you have a problem with that, I'm happy to relieve you from the case altogether."

"Ha. Well, that might be hard to do since someone tried to kill me this afternoon."

Chapter Fourteen

Colt's eyes widened. "Someone what?"

"Tried to kill me. He called your dispatcher with a phony poaching complaint to get me on the bayou where he took several shots at me. It's a miracle I'm still alive."

"You're sure it couldn't have been an accident—kids playing with their daddy's gun or someone adjusting their sights?"

"Unless he 'accidentally' shot at me at from a tree, aiming at two different locations, and using a silencer, then yeah, I'm positive it was intentional."

Colt looked over at Shirley who stared back at him, her eyes wide. "Okay, let's back up so I can get this all straight. Shirley, you took a call reporting a poacher?"

Shirley nodded. "He said he'd seen someone poaching alligators on Johnson's Bayou."

"In broad daylight?" Colt asked. "On the second-busiest channel in Mudbug?"

Shirley had the good sense to look contrite. "With everything else going on, I guess I didn't stop to think about that, or I might have known he was lying."

"Did you recognize the voice?" Colt asked.

"No. It sounded like it was a cell phone, though, all scratchy and cutting out."

"Why didn't you run a trace?"

Jadyn threw her hands in the air. "Exactly my question."

"I called for a trace," Shirley said, "but they told me they were backed up with a missing-persons investigation and it would take them a couple of hours to get back to me."

"Bullshit," Colt said and grabbed the phone off her desk. He dialed a number and as soon as they answered, proceeded to tear into the person who answered so hard that it made Jadyn feel just a tiny bit better.

"I mean right now," Colt said. "Not five minutes from now. Not even one. In fact, I'm going to stay on the line while you do it."

Jadyn perched on a desk and waited as Colt clenched the phone, staring out the window over the bayou. A minute later, he started talking again.

"You checked it twice? You're absolutely sure? Send that report to me. Thanks."

He hung up the phone, a grim look on his face. "The phone call came from Duke Leger's cell phone."

Jadyn shook her head. "Looks like I'm part of your investigation, whether you want me to be or not."

"As a target, which means you shouldn't be investigating any of this."

"So you're telling me if you were in my position, you'd cut and run or hide out in your house until I told you it was safe to come out?"

He ran one hand through his hair and blew out a breath.

"Thought so," she said. "So we both agree I'm not leaving and I'm not butting out. This got very personal today."

"Which is exactly why you *should* leave and butt out," he argued.

"But since we've already discussed that I'm not, then I expect you to include me when you're going to do things like interview witnesses. You would expect the same from me if the situation were reversed."

Colt sighed. "Shit."

"Yep."

"Did you see anything? Any sign of another boat or something that we could work off of?"

Jadyn shook her head. "The only boats I saw had people fishing."

"Anyone you recognized?"

"Just that guy from the bar the other night."

Colt narrowed his eyes. "Junior?"

"No, the nicer one. Bart." She frowned, trying to process the scene in her mind, assigning time stamps to each occurrence. Would Bart have had time to fire at her, then get to his boat, chase her down, and accost her minutes later?

"Where did you see him?"

"I thought the throttle was sticking, so I stopped about halfway back to town to check it. He pulled up and asked if I was having trouble. Apparently, I'd upset some fishermen with the speed of my escape. You don't think…"

Colt threw his hands in the air. "I don't know what to think anymore. If you'd told me a week ago that Duke's life would end this way, I would have called you crazy, but suddenly, nothing seems too far-fetched."

"Yeah, I guess so. So are you going to tell me what Leroy said?"

"Unfortunately, it wasn't much," he said and relayed his conversation with Leroy.

"And you're sure he's telling the truth?"

"He's too scared to lie, but I think that Duke was the money-boat captain."

"Really?" Jadyn listened as he explained about the thirty-count shrimp and his subsequent call to the shrimp house that completely negated Duke's claim to Leroy.

"So the only person who could have given us information is dead." She sighed. "What about the key?"

"I haven't had time to check into it. Probably won't until tomorrow."

"But you'll tell me what you find."

He looked aggrieved, but nodded. "I'll tell you what I find, but I'm not promising you involvement with everything I do. The reality is, you're not only a stranger here but a woman. People aren't going to speak freely with you. I refuse to jeopardize this investigation just to keep from hurting your feelings."

She felt a flush run up her neck and onto her face. "Is that what you think this is—some girly attempt to force the big man to acknowledge my needs? You've got some nerve. Someone tried to kill me today. Someone I don't know and may have never even come in contact with. The only *feeling* I'm worried about is feeling alive."

"I didn't mean—"

She held up a hand to stop him. "Maybe you should spend less time figuring out how to avoid me and more time trying to find out why someone wants to kill me in the first place. After all, I'm a stranger here, right?"

She stalked past him, not even bothering to speak to Shirley as she walked out of the sheriff's department, slamming the door shut behind her. She was halfway down the street to the hotel when a voice sounded behind her.

"Ms. St. James?"

She whirled around, every inch of her body still tingling with anger, and with one look at the man who'd called to her, she suddenly felt stupid.

"Hello, Father," she said. She had never met the man, but his robe and collar left her no doubt as to his station.

He was in his midfifties, with silver and black hair and pale skin that made her wonder if he always donned the robes before stepping outside. He smiled and extended his hand. "I'm Father Abraham."

"Seriously?" she asked, and before she could help herself, a childhood song about Abraham started running through her mind.

He laughed. "You know the song. It was a favorite of mine too. Some of my fondest memories of my grandmother were her singing that song to me, which is why I picked the name."

"I'm sorry. I didn't mean to sound insulting."

"Not at all. It's quite a common reaction." Father Abraham's smile turned to a frown. "I understand you were at Duke Leger's home this morning?"

"Yes, but I can't talk about an ongoing investigation."

"Of course. I would never ask you to violate a confidence. There have been rumors, of course, that he's deceased. In a small town, it's to be expected with this sort of thing, but I just wondered if you had any idea how long it will take the coroner to release the body. Duke's father is one of my oldest parishioners, and not in the best of health. He visited me this afternoon at church and has worked himself into quite a state about making the funeral arrangements."

Father Abraham gave her an apologetic look. "Given that there's been no official release of information, I tried to reason with him, but when you're battling age and dementia, it's often a losing proposition."

"I understand. I wish I could help you, Father, but I honestly have no idea how long the body will be held. Sheriff Bertrand may be able to give you a better idea."

"I see, so the sheriff is in charge of the investigation? I thought since it happened in the swamp that perhaps that fell in your line of work."

"It only does if it happens in the game preserve."

Father Abraham nodded. "I apologize for my mistake. The inner workings of law enforcement departments aren't something I'm overly familiar with."

"No apology needed. Sometimes the lines are so blurred they're confusing to law enforcement agencies as well. I'm assisting Sheriff Bertrand, as any respectable game warden would, but he'll probably be the one to get the answers you're looking for."

"I understand. Thank you so much for your time, Ms. St. James. I hope to see you at service next week."

Jadyn forced a smile and a nod but didn't reply. Years of private schooling had left her with little desire to spend time closed up with people who would yell at her for her clothes, lifestyle choices, and friends. On the other hand, Father Abraham had seemed nice. Surely he didn't yell at people and make them feel worse about themselves.

Given her current situation, she should probably give church attendance some thought. The last thing she wanted was for her first appearance in church to be in a coffin. Maybe a visit and a serious session of praying were in order.

Maybe since Helena knew God directly, she should ask her to call in some favors.

Colt poked his pinkie finger in the hole at the bottom of the game warden boat. He'd hoped she'd been mistaken—that she'd been confused about the shots and that the explanation was simple and nonlethal—but he'd bet his annual salary that she was dead right. This was definitely a bullet hole from a high-powered rifle, and based on the trajectory, it had been made from a location significantly above the boat. On Johnson's Bayou, that meant a tree.

Shit.

He should have stopped her from leaving the sheriff's office before he'd taken down all of the details on the shooting, but he'd screwed up and pushed her too far...let his own ego get in the way of good common sense. Now, she was too angry to be a good witness, even for her own attempted murder.

He'd watched her out the front window of the sheriff's department, first stopped by Father Abraham, who'd paid him a visit after speaking to her. Then she continued on toward the hotel. Surely no one would have the audacity to take a shot at her on Main Street, but then, he wouldn't have figured Johnson's Bayou as a good choice to pull that stunt either. Why not pick one of the isolated bayous with narrow channels that made speed in a boat next to impossible? The shooter could have sat in a lawn chair, smoking a cigar, drinking a beer, and still made that shot.

He slammed one hand on the side of the boat and cursed. So many things were happening and they all seemed to be related, but none of them made sense. Why would someone want to kill Jadyn? She hadn't even been in Mudbug a week. If that call hadn't come from Duke's cell phone, Colt would have thought one of the idiots trying to fetch money from the pond had been the shooter—trying to get a little revenge for her shooting down the bags of money and possibly trying to drive her out of town.

But Duke's cell phone eliminated that possibility.

It was a miscalculation on the killer's part. Was the suggestion of Johnson's Bayou another as well? Or was the answer as simple as the killer wasn't from Mudbug and therefore didn't know the minor bayou channels or the residents well enough to know the things he could take advantage of?

He climbed out of the boat and looked down the bayou.

What in the world had blown into this sleepy little town? In the past three days, everything he'd known previously had been swept away and replaced by something ugly, the very thing he'd never expected to find here.

Jadyn St. James only added fuel to the fire. Sorting out this mess would be hard enough without her to consider, but conducting the investigation without her wasn't an option. Whoever had taken shots at her thought she knew something so important that it was worth killing her for. But what? Jadyn didn't seem to have any idea what the cause could be and he believed her. Unfortunately, he didn't have a clue what the impetus could be either.

To add insult to injury, he felt guilty for the way he'd spoken to her in the sheriff's department. When he'd first arrived, he'd been annoyed with her attitude—expecting him to answer to her—but then she'd told him about the shooting, and he realized her demands were an attempt to regain control. He'd been there before, and it was a crappy place to exist.

He sighed. The absolute last thing he needed was a damaged, frightened woman on his conscience. Unfortunately, the only solution he had for keeping her safe was keeping her close, and Jadyn was a whole lot of temptation to have at his elbow every minute of every day.

She'd surprised him with the way she handled the crime scene this morning, especially when he considered that the coroner passed out cold and he spent every day with death. Then she'd located the odd key hidden in the backyard, and rounded out her afternoon by narrowly avoiding death herself.

She had brains, beauty, and spunk but most importantly, she had heart.

A quadruple threat. Something he was in no way prepared to handle. Suddenly, his old job in New Orleans looked easier.

Chapter Fifteen

Jadyn blew straight past Mildred and went to her room. She knew the hotel owner was worried—could see it all over her face when she walked inside the hotel—but Jadyn couldn't handle talking to anyone else right now. Her mind was too frazzled, her body weakened to the point of exhaustion. She was tired, frustrated, and angry. But the worst thing was she was scared.

Plenty of things in her past had caused her discomfort, but few had caused the kind of raw fear she'd felt today. In fact, only one such incident existed and she'd spent a good portion of her life trying to forget it. It wasn't the way she liked to remember her father. But today, everything about that day had flooded back—the helplessness, the terror that her life could end at that moment.

When she'd chosen her profession, she'd known that it came with risks, but she'd never imagined the risks would be this great and certainly not occurring in such a short span of time. The job in Mudbug had seemed the perfect solution. Never would she have believed such horrible things could happen in this tiny, seemingly quiet town. She'd had other opportunities, but she'd taken the one she thought was the best fit. The one that gave her the opportunity to know Maryse, the family she'd never been allowed to spend time with.

It had seemed perfect.

She should have known better.

She shrugged off her clothes and stepped into the steamy shower, then grabbed her loofah and gel and started to scrub as if the exfoliate could strip all the negative thoughts and energy from her body. Ten minutes later, her skin tingled and didn't contain a single spot of dry skin. Between the hot water and the scrubbing, she emerged from the shower with a medium-red hue from head to toe.

But for the first time since she'd stepped inside Duke's cabin that morning, she felt clean and fresh. Her mind had cleared some but it hadn't helped her put all the moving pieces together. The picture was still blurry and disconnected, but at least now she knew for sure it wasn't her foggy thinking. The bottom line was, none of the things she knew made sense.

She threw on clothes and headed downstairs. Mildred would fret like a worried mother until Jadyn talked to her. It was an odd feeling for Jadyn, having an older woman looking out for her, but it was sorta nice in a slightly intrusive way. She supposed that's how most daughters felt about their own mothers.

Mildred was in her office, staring at her computer screen, but the floating beach screensaver gave away her lack of activity. She looked up as soon as Jadyn entered the room, and Jadyn could see the worry lines on her face.

"I hear you've had an eventful day," Mildred said.

Jadyn sighed and slid into a chair in front of the desk. "Helena told you."

Mildred nodded. "She burst in here a couple of hours ago, ranting about deer hunting, shootings, and almost dying several times. It took me thirty minutes and all of my good chocolate to calm her down enough to get the story out of her."

"So you know everything?"

Mildred put her hands in the air. "I know everything from Helena's point of view. I was hoping for a more logical, lucid description from a sane person." She gave Jadyn a small smile.

"I bet. Although part of me is disappointed that all the good chocolates are gone. I could have used some myself."

Jadyn took a deep breath and began to recount her day to Mildred. The older woman's expression changed from horrified to exasperated then horrified again, but aside from a few gasps, she never interrupted. When Jadyn finished, she turned around and poured two shots of scotch from a bottle on her credenza.

Her hands shook slightly as she pushed the glass across the desk to Jadyn, then she tilted the glass back and downed the entire serving in one gulp. Jadyn sipped the strong liquid and grimaced. She was a real lightweight when it came to drinking.

"You have to do it all at once," Mildred said, pointing at the glass.

Jadyn wasn't the least bit convinced, but she lifted the glass again and poured the entire serving of scotch into her mouth, swallowing it before it could register. Her throat burned as it went down and her eyes started to water. She coughed twice, hoping she hadn't damaged her throat or burned a hole in her stomach lining.

Mildred laughed. "Give it some time to work. Then you'll be happy you did it." She reached into a small refrigerator next to the credenza and pulled out two bottles of water. "Chase it with this."

"Thanks," Jadyn managed before opening the water and downing a huge gulp, the cold liquid mollifying her ravaged throat. As she took a second drink, a feeling of warmth began to wash over her and she leaned back in the chair.

Mildred looked over at her and smiled. "That should take the edge off, but it's not enough to put you out. You were so hopped up when you came in, I thought you were going to jump right out of your skin. The shower helped you some, but you still had that wild look in your eyes when you came into my office."

"I feel better now," Jadyn said and frowned. Was this why her mother spent most of her life holding a glass of liquor? Was she not as happy as she'd have people believe and trying to take the edge off her choices?

Jadyn shook her head. Her mother's issues had no place in Jadyn's life, especially now. "Did Helena get the story right?"

Mildred nodded. "Her rendition was a lot more dramatic than yours, but essentially, she said the same thing. I was hoping she'd exaggerated the worst of it, but apparently this didn't need embellishment to be a nightmare."

"No. It's all pretty grim. And confusing. Do you have any thoughts on Duke?"

"Not a one. He was a crotchety old bastard. Fond of drinking and fishing. Not at all fond of women. But I can't imagine him getting tied up in something that ended like this. Small-time trouble, sure, but minor offenses don't end this way."

"No, they don't. He told Leroy that he was going to retire off this side job—what does that mean in Mudbug?"

Mildred shrugged. "For someone like Duke, not much. He owned his cabin and land outright. Had an old truck, a shrimp boat, and a bass boat that all run fine. Aside from beer, cigarettes, and the occasional jaunt to New Orleans for a night of gambling, I don't think he did much else."

"So we probably aren't talking a lot of money to most people."

"I doubt it."

Jadyn frowned. "In a way, that makes sense that he'd be on the lower end of the pay scale. Based on what I've heard, he lacked the experience to be a criminal mastermind."

Mildred nodded. "And the intelligence. But clearly, he had something they wanted."

"The key." Helena's voice sounded above Jadyn and a

second later, she dropped out of the ceiling and into the chair beside her, squealing like a five-year-old the whole way down.

Mildred glared at her. "Is that why the bed in your room is broken?"

"Maybe?" Helena said, looking a bit guilty.

"Despite being a ghost," Mildred said, "you're no lightweight. And until you can control going solid, no more dropping through ceilings. It's not like I can call my insurance company and file a claim."

"Fine. This chair isn't comfortable anyway."

"That chair is perfectly fine for sitting." Mildred let out an exasperated sigh, then looked back at Jadyn. "So what did the key look like?"

"It was heavy," Jadyn said, "so probably iron. It was black and honestly...well, I hate to say it, but it looked like those keys you see in horror movies."

Mildred nodded. "Can you draw a reasonable representation?"

"I think so." Jadyn took the pad of paper and pencil that Mildred pushed across the desk and started to draw.

"What do you think?" Jadyn showed the drawing to Helena.

"That looks about right, but I think it was fatter at the top."

"Yeah, I think you're right." Jadyn shaded in another layer around the top of the key, then passed the notebook to Mildred. "That's it as best as I can remember."

Mildred took the notebook and frowned. "This looks familiar. Hmm." Suddenly she snapped her fingers and beamed. "It looks like the key that opens the gate to Mudbug Cemetery."

"Seriously?" Jadyn asked. "Why would someone commit murder over a key to the cemetery?"

"I'm not saying it *is* the key to the cemetery," Mildred said. "I'm saying it looks like it."

"The cemetery on the edge of town, right?" Jadyn asked. "Is

there a caretaker—someone who would have noticed anything odd?"

"Sure. Earl has been the caretaker there since he was a boy." Mildred frowned.

"What's wrong?" Jadyn asked.

"Ha!" Helena perked up. "She's wondering if Earl would have noticed anything odd because Earl himself is odd."

Mildred nodded. "I hate to admit it, but she's right. He's an odd duck. Kids have always been scared of him, even when he was a kid."

"He totally looks like the Crypt Keeper," Helena threw in.

"Great," Jadyn said. "The perfect person to manage Mudbug's dead."

"Not my family," Helena said.

"What do you mean?" Mildred asked.

"My family has a private cemetery about fifteen miles outside of town."

Mildred frowned. "I attended your father's funeral, and I'm certain he was buried in Mudbug Cemetery."

"Sure," Helena agreed. "But everyone before him is in the family cemetery. My father said the rest of the family was a bunch of useless assholes who had squandered a good portion of his inheritance, and he had no intention of spending the afterlife in their company."

"That sounds like your father," Mildred agreed.

"Yep," Helena agreed. "He even put a clause in his will that stated if he wasn't buried in Mudbug Cemetery, he was allowed to sue the coroner posthumously."

"And you were buried in Mudbug Cemetery, too," Mildred said.

"I was the first time," Helena replied.

"What do you mean 'the first time'?" Mildred asked.

"My estate has a clause that if my body has to be moved for any reason, it was to be cremated instead of reburied. I figure if they can't get it right the first time, I'm not going back into a hole. I have a touch of claustrophobia, anyway."

Mildred stared. "So an empty casket went back into the ground after the exhumation?"

Helena nodded.

"I know I'm going to regret asking this," Mildred said, "but where are your ashes?"

Helena smiled. "They were distributed in a secret place of significant importance to me."

Mildred's eyes widened and Jadyn cringed, all sorts of bad possibilities running through her mind.

"What place?" Mildred asked.

"Well if I told you," Helena said, "then it wouldn't be a secret."

Jadyn turned to Helena and interrupted before Mildred got more flustered. "Does your family cemetery use a key like that?"

"I don't know," Helena said. "I've only been there once when I was a kid. That was the day my father insisted on spitting on Grandfather's grave. I was a little freaked out by the whole thing. I don't remember much else but my father ranting and the spitting."

Jadyn wondered briefly what the hell kind of people Helena had descended from, but pushed the thought aside. She'd have plenty of time to delve into Helena's family-of-origin issues with Mildred as soon as the man trying to kill her was behind bars.

"If a key like the one I found opens your family cemetery," Jadyn continued, "where could we find one?"

"That's a good question," Helena said. "It wasn't in my house, so I guess the attorney has it."

"Wheeler?" Mildred asked. "The attorney in New Orleans?"

Helena nodded.

"Crap," Mildred said, then sighed. "He's not likely to give me a key just because I ask."

"Can't we just climb over the fence?" Jadyn asked.

"No way," Helena said. "One of the few things I do remember is looking up at those giant spikes. I swear they were taller than trees."

"It doesn't matter," Mildred said. "We're just guessing it's a key to a cemetery gate, but it could be a key to any old gate."

"True," Jadyn said but instinctively, she knew they were on the right track. "But I still think it's worth looking into."

Mildred nodded. "Do you want me to give Colt a call and see if he will bring the key to the cemetery?"

"No!" The word came out harsher than Jadyn intended.

Mildred raised an eyebrow. "Is there a problem between you and Colt?"

"You could say that," Jadyn said and gave Mildred the CliffsNotes version of their conversation.

Mildred's expression cleared in understanding. "I knew you were mad about something when you stomped upstairs earlier. Scared and frustrated, but also mad. I wondered if Colt was at the bottom of it."

"He's at the bottom all right," Jadyn agreed.

"Well, if he's got the key, I don't see how we can leave him out. It's not like we can stroll in there and take it out of his desk."

"I can," Helena said.

"Absolutely not," Mildred said.

Jadyn looked at Helena, then back at Mildred. It was wrong and she knew it, but part of her relished the thought of solving the case and proving to Colt that she was just as capable as he was.

"Colt said he won't have time to look into the key until tomorrow," Jadyn pointed out, "and who knows what could happen in that span of time."

Helena nodded. "You could be sleeping with the fishes by tomorrow, or even worse, stuck here with me."

Mildred blanched and Jadyn knew they'd made a chink in her armor.

"She *is* getting better at picking things up," Jadyn said.

"You're just saying that," Mildred argued, "and you're also suggesting we steal evidence from the sheriff. Is that really the way you want to end your career?"

"No, but I don't want to end my career in a coffin, either."

Mildred sighed and Jadyn held in a cheer. The battle was almost won.

"I'm not saying we should do nothing," Mildred said finally. "I just think if you gave Colt a chance, you'd find him supportive."

"So if your life was in danger, you'd let some chauvinistic male stick you in a corner and feed you information about your own safety as he saw fit?"

"You know," Helena interjected, "I have to say that's pretty crappy, and I'm rarely opposed to letting someone else do all the work."

"Trust me," Mildred said, "the feminist in me is screaming, and she's a loud bitch, but the bottom line is it's too risky. Look what happened today in broad daylight and on a heavily traveled channel. Why go deep into the swamp and make his job even easier?"

Jadyn leaned forward. "What if I told you I didn't have to be at risk at all?"

Mildred narrowed her eyes at her. "How?"

"You're assuming he's watching me—waiting for another opportunity?"

"Yes."

"But he doesn't even have to know I've left the hotel. Your

car is in the garage. I can hide in the back until we're out of town. He'll think I'm still in my room."

"That could work," Helena agreed. "And I can keep watch and see if he sneaks into the hotel to kill her."

"You're coming with us," Jadyn said.

"No way!" Helena shook her head.

"How are we supposed to find the cemetery?"

"I'll draw you a map. I'll draw it in color even, but I'm not going with you."

Jadyn threw her hands up in exasperation. "Why the hell not?"

"Dead people creep me out."

"You're kidding me." She looked over at Mildred. "Is she kidding?"

"You would think so, but I doubt it," Mildred said.

"It's not up for discussion," Jadyn said to Helena. "This is all your fault, and you will do your part to fix it."

Helena crossed her arms and huffed. "Fine. I'll take you there, but I'm not going inside."

Jadyn jumped up from her seat. "Then let's go steal that key."

Mildred stroked the bottle of scotch. "Wait here for me. I have a feeling I'm going to need you when I get back."

Chapter Sixteen

Jadyn paused on the sidewalk just before the sheriff's department and looked over at Helena. "Are you ready?"

"Yeah, yeah. We're just stealing a key, not doing brain surgery. How hard can it be?"

Jadyn held in a sigh. "The office isn't empty, remember? Even though Sheriff Bertrand is gone, the dispatcher is there. You can't just burst in and start flinging things around, or you'll give the woman a heart attack."

"I know. I know. I have to make sure you have her distracted before I move things. We've covered it a million times."

Despite good common sense yelling at her to abandon this somewhat sketchy long shot of a plan, Jadyn continued to the sheriff's department and walked inside, Helena hurrying in beside her. Shirley gave her an apprehensive look, but Jadyn couldn't really blame her. She hadn't exactly been easy to deal with when she'd been there before.

"Is Sheriff Bertrand here?" Jadyn asked, knowing full well that Colt had driven away ten minutes before.

"No, but I can call him if it's an emergency."

"I don't want to interrupt him. Is he going to be gone long?" Jadyn turned around and pretended to look out the window while waving Helena toward Colt's office at the back of the building.

"He said he'd be back in thirty minutes or so."

Jadyn turned back around, watching as Helena disappeared through the back wall. "Is it all right if I wait for him?"

Shirley's eyes widened a bit. "Sure," she said, but the hesitation in her voice told Jadyn she wasn't sure of anything.

Jadyn walked toward the back of the building, then stopped and pretended to peer outside again. The glass on Colt's office door was frosted, so she couldn't see inside. She hoped Helena wasn't having trouble touching things. If so, this entire excursion would be a complete waste of time.

Suddenly Helena's voice boomed out from the closed office, but the screeching opera of this morning had been replaced with rap. Sort of rap. Jadyn cringed and started back toward the front of the building, hoping that more distance between her and the sound would make it better, but with every step, her optimism decreased.

"So the weather seems nice right now," Jadyn said, trying to drown out Helena by talking. "Does it get a lot hotter by the end of summer?"

Shirley nodded. "Gets another good ten degrees hotter on average, but it's the humidity that makes you run for air-conditioning."

"I have noticed the humidity is a lot worse here than in north Louisiana. I guess it's the proximity to the water."

Good God, St. James, can you sound more banal?

The singing got louder and Jadyn looked over as Helena walked out of Colt's office. She looked at Jadyn and shook her head. Crap. Jadyn had already cased the rest of the tiny office and the only likely place Colt had stored the evidence was a filing cabinet against the back wall. Unfortunately, Shirley had a clear view of that filing cabinet from her desk and the keys to the cabinet hung on a hook behind her.

"Any other ideas?" Helena asked as she walked up beside

Jadyn.

"The filing cabinet," Jadyn whispered.

"Pardon me?" Shirley said.

"Sorry," Jadyn said and smiled. "Just clearing my throat. I think I have a touch of allergies here."

"How can I get in that filing cabinet with her looking?" Helena asked.

Jadyn turned around and faced the window again. "We need to get her outside long enough for you to get in the cabinet."

"Oh, that's easy."

Before Jadyn could say a word, Helena walked through the front wall of the sheriff's department and disappeared. Jadyn prayed whatever Helena had in mind didn't cause more trouble than they already had. She stepped up to the front window and looked out at Main Street, just in time to see Helena slip inside a old sedan in the parking area across the street.

Oh no.

A couple of seconds later, the car started and Helena pulled straight out of the parking lot and onto Main, then cut the engine off. Main Street sloped slightly downhill so the car continued to roll down the center of the street. As the car passed the barbershop, two men ran out of the building and started yelling as they hurried down the street after the car.

"Oh my God," Jadyn said. "There's an old brown Cadillac rolling down Main Street with no driver." She pushed open the door and rushed outside. It was too late to call Helena off. She might as well play along.

Shirley rushed outside behind her and they both stared as the Cadillac rolled past. A second later, Helena popped out of the side of the car and rolled to a stop in the middle of the street.

"That's my car!" Shirley wailed and hurried down the street after the Cadillac, which was now picking up speed.

Jadyn stared at Helena, her concern growing with every

second that the woman remained motionless. She walked over to the ghost and whispered, "Helena?"

"What? Oh!" The ghost jumped up from the street. "I think I knocked myself out. How is that possible?"

"We'll discuss it later," Jadyn said. "Go check that filing cabinet. The keys are on the peg behind Shirley's desk. I've got to help chase that car or I'll look suspicious."

Jadyn took off at a jog down the street, hoping Helena understood her rushed instructions. She caught up with Shirley half a block away, where the woman was bent over panting.

"Are you all right?" she said as she slowed.

Shirley waved a hand. "Get my car."

Jadyn picked up speed and raced down Main Street, passing the two men from the barbershop and drawing abreast of the Cadillac just before Main Street made a hard ninety-degree turn, running parallel with the bayou. She grabbed the door handle, praying Helena had left it unlocked, and yanked the door open. As Jadyn jumped inside, the car rolled onto the grassy bank of the bayou. She jammed her foot down on the brake as hard as she could. The brakes squealed in protest and a wave of panic came over her as the water grew closer by the second.

She pumped the brakes, but it was no use. Apparently, brakes were not one of the items Shirley felt she needed to maintain. Jadyn opened the door ready to jump and as a last-ditch effort, engaged the emergency brake. The car lurched to a stop, slamming her head into the steering wheel, and she staggered out just as a crowd of people ran up.

"Are you all right?" one of the men from the barbershop asked.

"I think so," she replied.

The man looked at her forehead. "You're going to have a good shiner there tomorrow."

She reached up and felt the knot that was already beginning to form. "Probably so."

"We could hear the brakes grinding all the way up the street. How did you stop it?"

"Emergency brake."

The man nodded as Shirley ran up, panting. "How could this happen?" she wheezed.

The man poked his head inside. "The car's in neutral instead of park. And you should fix your brakes, Shirley. You could have killed our new game warden." The man clapped Jadyn on the back and grinned. "It was just like one of them Hollywood movies, you jumping in that runaway car. Heck, you chasing this car and shooting up those bags of money are probably the most interesting things that's happened around here in months."

"Glad to oblige," Jadyn said and forced a smile. Clearly the details of Duke's death hadn't made all the gossip circles yet. Her recent exploits were going to pale in comparison to that tidbit.

"The tide's coming in!" a man at the edge of the bank shouted. "We need to get the car back now or it's gonna be floating."

"The keys are under the floor mat," Shirley said.

The man shook his head and sighed.

"If you guys have it from here," Jadyn said, "I going to head back to the hotel and put some ice on this bump."

She didn't even wait for an answer before starting up the street toward the hotel, making sure she stayed on the opposite side of the street from the sheriff's department and in clear view of the people who'd stepped outside to see what all the commotion was about. Helena hurried across the street as she approached, a big grin on her face.

"I got it!" she yelled.

"Thank God," Jadyn mumbled under her breath, relieved

that all of this hadn't been for nothing.

She smiled and nodded as residents congratulated her on her car rescue, but pushed past them to the hotel as quickly as she could, Helena jogging behind her and yelling at her to slow down the entire way. It seemed to take forever, but finally, she made it to the hotel and hurried to Mildred's office.

Mildred was on her cell phone and hung up when she saw Jadyn come in. "Please tell me that Helena did not drive Shirley's car down Main Street."

"Not exactly," Jadyn said. "Are you ready to do this? I want to make sure there's at least a little daylight given where we're going."

"Ha!" Helena shouted. "Dead people scare you too."

"I know at least one who does," Jadyn said.

Mildred sighed and grabbed her car keys. "Let's get this over with."

Colt pulled open the filing cabinet and felt in the back for the envelope with the key. Flashing it around Mudbug wasn't a good idea given what happened to Duke, but he knew a locksmith in New Orleans who had helped him on a couple of cases. He figured he'd take a picture and send it to him and see if he had any ideas.

His hand touched the cold bottom of the cabinet and he frowned, certain this was the drawer he'd left the key in. He pulled all the folders tightly to the front and peered over the edge into the drawer, but the bottom was empty. A trickle of worry ran through him as he opened the remaining three drawers and searched them.

No key.

He turned to look at Shirley, his blood starting to boil. "Didn't you say Jadyn was here earlier?"

Shirley nodded. "Said she wanted to talk to you. Why? What's wrong?"

"The key I put in the filing cabinet is missing."

Shirley's eyes widened. "You don't think..."

"That's exactly what I think. She wasn't happy that I took the key as evidence, but I never thought she'd stoop this low."

Shirley bit her lower lip then spoke, her voice hesitant. "But I don't see how it could have been her."

"Why not? She was here when your car took a trip down Main Street, right? She could have easily snagged the key when you ran outside."

Shirley shook her head. "She ran outside before I did. And she's the one who saved my car. I pulled into the parking lot just as she was walking back—on the other side of the street. She went straight into the hotel after that, and I came in here. Been here ever since."

"You're sure she couldn't have taken it?"

"Unless she can be in two places at once, I don't see how." Shirley gave him a disapproving look. "I know the girl's a little high-strung and on the aggravating side of what I prefer to listen to, but after seeing that scene at Duke's she did get shot at. And she risked a dip in the bayou to save this old lady's Cadillac. You may want to cut her some slack."

Colt tried to clamp down on his ever-increasing frustration. He already felt bad about the way he'd handled Jadyn that afternoon. He didn't need someone else pointing out his less-than-stellar reaction. "Well, if she didn't take it, who did?"

"I suppose anyone could have taken the opportunity to slip inside while we were all running down the street. I feel really bad about this, Colt."

Colt stared across the street at Shirley's Cadillac. "Have you ever had trouble with your car before?"

"Not at all. I've had that car almost fifteen years and hardly ever a problem. Certainly nothing like this. Why?"

"Just thinking out loud," he said.

Her eyes widened. "You think someone could have pushed my car into the street to get me out of the building?"

"Well, your car has never taken a jaunt by itself before and the one time it does, the key is missing. The odds of the perpetrator just happening down the sidewalk at the exact moment that your car pulled a Christine are pretty slim."

Shirley's hand flew up to cover her mouth. "That means the killer was in this office, right here in this space. Oh God, I feel faint."

"Don't go getting all dramatic."

"Colt Bertrand! After what happened to Duke, you have the nerve to accuse me of dramatics? I'm beginning to understand why our new game warden is so frustrated by you."

He held in a sigh. "I'm just saying, if he'd wanted to hurt you, he wouldn't have staged the incident with the car to get you out of the building."

"So you're saying that a cold-blooded murderer cared about me so much that he decided not to stroll into the sheriff's department in broad daylight and shoot me at my desk before stealing the key. Yeah, I can see how that would have been the better option."

Colt closed his eyes and counted to ten.

"No," he said when he opened his eyes. "I'm saying that if he'd wanted to kill someone, he would have waited until midnight and shot Eugenia at her desk before stealing the key."

Shirley paled. "Oh, well then why not do that? As horrible as it is, it seems easier than what he did."

He drummed his fingers on the desk, a million options

rolling through his mind. "I don't know. Maybe he needs the key before tonight."

"Why?"

"If I knew the answer to that, I'd be well on my way to solving this case." He blew out a breath. "You've got your pistol, right?"

Shirley pointed to the desk. "In my purse, as always."

"Take it out of your purse. Put it somewhere you can easily reach in a matter of seconds."

Shirley's eyes widened. "You don't think he'll come back?"

"I doubt it, but I want you to be ready if he does." He grabbed his keys off Shirley's desk. "I'm going out for a while. Lock the door behind me. Until further notice, anyone who needs something can knock."

He left the sheriff's department and strode off in the direction of the hotel. Jadyn probably hadn't had enough time to cool down, but that didn't matter. He needed every detail he could get out of her about the shooting and about the incident with Shirley's car.

Maryse was behind the lobby desk when he walked in the hotel. He gave her a nod. "Good to see you, Maryse," he said. "How's Luc doing?"

"He's fine," Maryse said with a cheerful smile. "The DEA manages to interrupt our dinner at least three nights a week, but that's just more ammunition for my argument about not learning to cook."

He nodded. "I remember those days well. I thought I'd never make it through a sit-down meal again. Hey, I don't mean to be short, but I really need to talk to Jadyn. Is she upstairs?"

"I don't think so. Mildred said she was working."

Colt frowned. "Can I talk to Mildred?"

"Sorry. She went shopping for hotel supplies. That's why I'm covering the front desk."

Colt reached inside his jeans pocket and pulled out his cell phone. He dialed Jadyn's number, but it only took a second for the call to flip straight to voice mail. He disconnected without leaving a message and dialed Mildred's number, but it rang until voice mail finally kicked in.

"Mildred's not answering her phone," Colt said. "Any idea why?"

Maryse frowned. "It's pretty loud at the warehouse. If she's got it in the bottom of that giant purse of hers, she may not hear it ringing. Is something wrong?"

"No," Colt reassured her before she launched into panic mode. "I just need to go over some things with Jadyn and was hoping Mildred knew what area of the swamp she was headed to."

"I wish I could help. If I hear from either one of them, I'll have them give you a call."

"Great. Thanks." He headed out of the hotel, waving one hand over his shoulder as he closed the door behind him. Something was wrong. He was sure of it. Just as certain as he was that Maryse didn't know anything about it, which made the situation very interesting. The brainy botanist was one of the most intelligent people he'd ever met, but she sucked completely at lying.

Whatever Mildred and Jadyn were up to, they hadn't bothered to fill Maryse in on it. Otherwise, she would have started to panic when he couldn't reach them. And Mildred not telling Maryse the juicy details was odd.

So odd he wondered what the hotel owner was up to.

But something else was bothering him that he couldn't quite put his finger on…something about the boat. They hadn't found any identifying marks and one shrimp boat pretty much looked the same as another, but something about it seemed off. Something besides the obvious.

He started back to the sheriff's department, then changed direction and headed for the garage. Maybe another look at the boat would make something click.

Chapter Seventeen

Maryse frowned as Colt left the hotel. He'd tried to act nonchalant, but Maryse had seen that tension in Luc's shoulders and neck enough to know that something was wrong. When Mildred called her this afternoon, she'd thought it a bit strange that the hotel owner needed to go shopping when Maryse knew she'd been the week before. She'd hauled at least ten boxes into the storeroom of the hotel.

Mildred rarely took a shopping trip outside of the one day a month she had allocated. Sure, things like hurricanes might disrupt the normal schedule, but that wasn't the case now. And then there was the feeling...that strange feeling she'd had all day that something was off. She'd thought it had something to do with her current lab experiment, but that had actually proven a success for a change.

The "Back in 15 Minutes" sign was on the front desk when she'd arrived, and Mildred was already gone. Everything had seemed in order as she'd driven down Main Street, but she couldn't shake the niggle of fear in the back of her mind. Fear that she had no basis for.

She drummed her fingers on the counter and chided herself for not getting out of her lab more. When she got involved with her experiments, the entire world could vanish and she'd walk out without knowing a thing. Something was going on with Jadyn. She could feel it in her bones, but the very person who usually kept her informed was either so engrossed in a toilet paper sale that she couldn't hear her cell phone or she was knee-deep in something she had no business wading into.

Before she could change her mind, Maryse put the "Back in 30 minutes" sign on the front desk and hurried across the street to Bill's. The evening crowd wouldn't start filtering in for a bit, so it ought to be fairly empty. If anyone besides Mildred knew the local gossip, it would be Bill.

She stopped short in front of the door to the bar, unable to force her arms up to push the door open. Her hands were clammy and her fingers ached from clenching them as she'd walked across the street.

It's just a building.

She started to run back across the street and forget the whole thing, but then she remembered that look on Colt's face when he hadn't been able to reach Mildred on the phone. What if Mildred was in danger? For all intents and purposes, Mildred was her mother. If she could walk inside that bar for anyone but herself, it would be Mildred.

Taking a deep breath, she pushed open the door and stepped inside. Bill was wiping down the counter and looked momentarily surprised to see her. He quickly recovered, then smiled and waved her over. "You've picked the best time to come in…before the average IQ of the place gets significantly lower."

She forced a smile, knowing that's what he was trying to get her to do. "Maybe I should stick around for a while then, and raise the average a bit."

He shook his head. "I'm afraid the odds are stacked against you. Do you want something to drink? I got a new wine the ladies seem to like. Said it tastes fruity."

"No, thanks." She pulled herself up on a stool and glanced

around the bar. The only occupants were a couple of old fishermen sitting in the far corner. "I know this is going to sound crazy, but is something wrong in Mudbug?"

Bill frowned. "That's a bit of a loaded question given everything that's happened today."

Maryse's pulse quickened. "That's the problem. I've been in my lab all day—cell phone turned off, no television. I stopped by the hotel, and everything looks like normal, but something feels wrong."

Bill nodded. "Like the air is filled with a negative charge."

Maryse stared. "Yeah, that's it exactly. So I'm not imagining it."

"I'm afraid not. You sure you don't want that drink?"

"Yeah, maybe I should," Maryse said. Being inside the bar was stressful enough, but she already knew that whatever Bill was about to tell her, it was going to make sitting in the bar seem like a stroll in the park.

Bill served her a double shot of scotch then started to talk about the rumors flying around town about Duke and the way he'd died. The longer he talked, the bigger sips Maryse took of the scotch. When he finally finished, the glass was empty.

"I can't believe it," Maryse said. "Of all the horrible things that have happened in this town, that has to be the worst. You're sure this hasn't been blown out of proportion?"

Bill nodded and poured himself a scotch while giving Maryse another shot. "I thought the same thing at first, but my cousin works for the coroner and she confirmed it. Said the coroner passed out cold at Duke's house and Colt threw cold water on him to wake him up. Said when he got back to the office, he was so pale it looked like all the blood had left his body."

"Wow." Maryse was completely out of words. If Duke's death had affected the coroner that harshly, then it must have been as bad as the rumors said.

"So you want to tell me why you came in here for the local gossip instead of asking Mildred?"

"She's not at the hotel. I'm supposed to be covering the desk while she's out shopping, but I couldn't stand that overwhelming feeling that something huge was happening and I was in the dark. I don't know when Mildred will be back, and I didn't want to wait for answers."

Maryse left out the part where Mildred wasn't answering her phone and Jadyn was MIA. The longer she thought about those two things in relation to Colt's visit and what Bill had told her, the more she was convinced that Mildred hadn't gone shopping at all.

She only hoped that whatever Mildred had gotten involved in, it didn't put her at risk of ending up like Duke.

Marty was closing the garage bays when Colt walked up and pulled down the remaining open door.

"You look like a man doing some heavy thinking," Marty observed. "What's on your mind?"

"Too many things to mention, and I couldn't talk about most of them even if I wanted to."

Marty nodded. "Rumor mill's running. I got a good idea what's eating at you. Anything I can do to help?"

"Maybe. We didn't find anything yesterday when we searched the boat, but I can't shake the feeling that I missed something."

"You want to take another look?"

"If you don't mind."

"'Course not." He waved Colt to the office door and they

stepped inside the garage.

"Do you have time to look with me?" Colt asked.

Marty shrugged. "I got the time…just don't know how helpful I'll be. I'm not trained like a detective or nothing."

"No, but you know all the boats in this area."

"That's true enough." He headed to the back bay where the boat was stored.

"What can you tell me about the boat?" Colt asked.

Marty walked the length of it and looked underneath, then straightened back up. "It's an older model—looks like seventies construction. Pretty good maintenance, though, except for a hard hit on the front left. My guess is a stump."

"Is that what made it sink?"

"Yes and no. The original impact looks to be a couple years old, and it would have taken on water after that but it wouldn't have been anything a bilge pump couldn't handle. But if the boat was twisted by the storm, that would have been enough to widen the crack or split it further than it was to begin with."

"Any idea at all who this might belong to?"

Marty shook his head. "Heck, most of the boats in Mudbug were built in the seventies. People here can't afford newer models and there's no need as long as the old one is serviceable. Most of the younger shrimpers got their boats handed down from their fathers."

"I don't suppose you'd recognize an engine if you worked on it?"

"Probably, but I haven't worked on a shrimp boat in years. The locals all handle their own engine work. Sometimes they'll swing by here for me to change a propeller. It's easier since I got the lift at the dock. Saves them trailering the boat to work on it."

Marty stepped around to the back of the boat and frowned.

"Do you recognize the propeller?" Colt asked.

"Yeah, I've done two of 'em just this week, but that's not

what I'm looking at."

Colt stepped beside him and stared at the back of the boat. "What then?"

"The paint doesn't match. I mean, it's all white, but look at the paint on the top of the hull versus the bottom."

Colt looked closely at the paint. "You're right. The bottom is faded. The top looks like it was done recently?"

Marty nodded. "There's only one reason I can think of to paint just the top of the hull."

"To cover the name of the boat."

"Yes, sir."

"You have a grill around back, right?"

"Yeah…"

"Charcoal or gas?"

Marty drew himself up straight. "No self-respecting Cajun grills with gas."

Colt smiled. "Great. I'll be right back." He hurried out the back door of the garage and grabbed a piece of charcoal from the edge of the grill. The center pieces would collapse too easily, but this one should work fine.

When he came back inside, Marty looked at the charcoal in his hands and raised his eyebrows. "Should I even ask what you're going to do with that?"

"You can watch," Colt said and started lightly rubbing the charcoal along the top edge of the boat. "Whoever covered the name didn't sand this down first. Some of the lines left by the previous lettering have created ridges in the paint. I'm hoping this charcoal will expose enough so that we can read the name."

Marty grinned and stepped closer to the boat. "For a minute there, I thought you had gone crazy and was going to ask me to make you supper, but this is right smart."

"We'll see," Colt said, praying that enough of the lettering showed.

When he got to the far edge of the boat, he took several steps back and looked. Marty stepped back with him and narrowed his eyes.

"Is that a *p*?" Marty asked, pointing to the first letter.

"It looks like it. Maybe *p* then *r*, but I can't make out the next one."

"Is that one big word or more than one, you think?"

Colt frowned. "Probably more than one, unless it's a name." He didn't bother to say that the reason for his assessment was the unlikelihood of a Mudbug shrimper christening his boat with a four-syllable name.

"That's an *f*," Marty said. "In fact, that looks like 'fish' to me."

Something clicked in Colt's mind. "Pro Fisherman."

"Yeah!" Marty said, getting excited. "I think you got it." Then his smile disappeared. "That's Junior's daddy's old boat."

"I know," Colt said. "I thought his daddy retired."

Marty nodded. "Several years ago, as a matter of fact. Bad knees."

"Did he sell the boat?"

"No. Far as I know, he gave it to Junior. He already had his own, of course, but when shrimp's running hot, he'd let someone run this boat for a cut of profit."

Colt sighed. Everything had come full circle right back to Junior.

"Marty, let's keep this between you and me for now."

"No problem. I'll get a rag and wipe that charcoal off before I head home."

"Thanks," Colt said and left the garage.

Had he underestimated Junior Thibodeaux? Was all that bumble and bluster a convenient cover for intelligence and cunning? He blew out a breath. Jeez, he didn't think so, but he'd seen stranger things before.

He started his truck and pulled away from the garage. Apparently, he needed to have yet another conversation with Junior. The disgruntled shrimper lived in a shotgun house a couple of blocks off Main Street, so a couple of minutes later, Colt pulled into his drive behind his truck. He tried the front door, but no one answered, so he stepped around behind the house to the garage.

The main garage door was down, but the side door was unlocked. He stuck his head in and yelled, but given that the lights were off, he didn't expect an answer. When he returned to the front of the house, he tried the front door one more time before leaving, but finally decided that either Junior wasn't home or he was so drunk he didn't hear Colt knocking. Most likely, he headed to Bill's for happy hour.

Colt hopped into his truck and drove back to Main Street. First he'd check the bar for Junior, then he'd see if Jadyn had returned to the hotel. After that, he was going home for a hot shower and a cold beer.

It had been an extraordinarily long day.

Chapter Eighteen

Mildred clenched the steering wheel so tightly, Jadyn could see her knuckles whitening.

"You're sure this is the right way?" Mildred asked again.

"No, I'm not sure," Helena said. "The last time I was here was over fifty years ago. I can't remember shit I did yesterday. How am I supposed to be sure about something that old?"

"I can remember everything I did yesterday," Jadyn grumbled from the backseat. They'd already been driving around in the swamp for over an hour and had wound up on at least ten dead ends, none of which had ended at Helena's family cemetery. Jadyn was starting to wonder if Helena had imagined that entire scene from her childhood.

"Try that way," Helena said and pointed at an overgrown path to the right.

Mildred gave a long-suffering sigh and steered her car onto the narrow path. "This is the last one. If we don't find the cemetery here, you're going to return that key to the sheriff's filing cabinet and Jadyn is going to tell him what it might unlock."

Mildred gave both Helena and Jadyn a stern look. "Are we clear on that?"

"Yes, ma'am," Jadyn said. At this point, she was out of arguments and as frustrated with the lack of progress as Mildred. Even Helena appeared more frazzled than usual.

The trees that lined the path seemed to encroach farther

onto the makeshift road, cutting out most of the fading sunlight. At any moment, Jadyn expected Mildred to put the car in reverse and start backing out of swamp, but as they rounded a corner, Mildred slammed on the brakes.

"Holy crap!" Mildred cried as the car slid a couple of inches on the gravel and dirt and stopped right in front of a huge iron gate.

"That came up out of nowhere," Mildred exclaimed, still clutching the steering wheel.

Jadyn peered up at the massive iron fence and wondered just how long it had taken to erect it. Helena hadn't been joking when she said there was no way over it without a crane. The fence was at least fifteen feet tall with each post spaced approximately four inches apart and with a giant spike on the top. One wrong move up there, and you'd be impaled.

She climbed out of the car and pulled the key out of her pocket. Mildred climbed out and stood next to her, an anxious look on her face.

"Here goes nothing," Jadyn said and slid the key into the ancient lock.

She held her breath as she tried to turn the key, but it didn't budge. Figuring it had been forever since the lock had been used, she twisted harder, but to no avail. The breath she'd been holding came out as a sigh and she looked over at Mildred and shook her head.

Mildred's shoulders slumped. "Well, we knew it was a long shot. I'm afraid you're going to have to get Colt's help on this. I'm still sure I'm onto something about the type of lock that key opens. It just isn't at this location."

"You're probably right." Jadyn struggled to control her disappointment. "Still, since we're already here, I'd like to take a look around the perimeter, if that's okay."

Mildred glanced up at the increasingly dim sky. "We can't take very long. The sunlight will be gone completely in about thirty minutes. I don't want to try to find our way out of here in the dark."

Jadyn nodded, completely agreeing with Mildred's unease. They'd made so many turns and backtracks that the way back to Mudbug wasn't exactly obvious. The last thing she wanted was to be stuck in the swamp all night in a car, and certainly not with Helena, who she was certain wouldn't give them even a moment's peace.

Jadyn opened the driver's door and peered in at Helena. "The key didn't work but I want to take a look around the perimeter while we're here. Just in case there's another entrance that isn't visible from the road. Do you want to come with us?"

"No way. I'm not getting any closer to that place than this car seat."

"You'll be here all alone."

Helena looked momentarily conflicted, but fear won out and she shook her head. "I'll just practice changing clothes. I've been watching *Project Runway*."

Before her mind could begin to process the potential horror, Jadyn closed the car door and set out into the swamp to the left of the gate, Mildred creeping behind her. The brush was thick and scratched her bare arms.

"I should have brought a long-sleeved shirt," Jadyn said, looking back at Mildred. "You don't have to come with me. No sense in both of us getting scratched to hell."

"I'd rather be out here with you, the bugs, brambles, and potential spooks than sitting in the car with Helena."

Jadyn had no valid argument for Mildred's statement, so she gave her a nod and continued pushing her way through the brush until the fence made a ninety-degree turn to the right. "I guess this is one end of the cemetery."

She peered down the top of the fence line, but it disappeared into the cypress trees twenty feet from where they stood. "It doesn't look like anyone has passed this way recently."

Mildred nodded. "From the looks of the undergrowth, it's been decades."

"Let's check in the other direction, then get out of here before the light fades completely."

"Good idea."

They tromped back through the swamp toward the gate and were about twenty yards away when they heard Helena scream bloody murder. Jadyn pulled the nine-millimeter from her waistband and ran through the brush, afraid to even think about what was happening.

She burst out of the trees and onto the path and skidded to a stop. Helena was outside of the car, running around it and screaming as loudly as possible, which was disconcerting, but that wasn't what had Jadyn staring.

Helena's speed was currently hindered by a dress that appeared to be constructed completely of interwoven lettuce. She looked like the Jolly Green Giant, minus the jolly part. As she sped past Jadyn, a piece of her dress flew off and smacked Jadyn in the face. She grabbed the piece and gave it a closer look. Yep, definitely lettuce.

"What the hell is she doing?" Mildred stopped beside Jadyn, panting.

Jadyn shook her head and waited until Helena rounded the car for another pass. "Stop!" she yelled and stepped in front of the wall of green.

Helena bounced to a stop, losing enough of her dress to make a decent salad, and looked around, her eyes wide. "Do you see him? Is he gone?"

Jadyn's grip tightened on her pistol and she scanned the

brush. "Where did you see him? What did he look like?"

Helena gave her an exasperated look. "I saw him in the car, of course. He slid right through the door and into the driver's seat. Has to be a relative. All the men in my family have these enormous foreheads and practically no hair."

Jadyn dropped her arm down, feeling the tension leave her body. "A ghost? All that screaming and running over another ghost?"

Helena glared. "I told you ghosts give me the creeps, but you had to haul me out here anyway. Where, I might add, not only was I terrified by a ghost but one of my father's family. That's even worse."

Jadyn grimaced as a piece of lettuce fell off Helena's top, exposing far too much of her ample white chest, and looked over at Mildred, who looked as exasperated as she felt.

"What in the world are you wearing?" Mildred asked.

"It's my grocery store challenge dress," Helena said. "This one is dual purpose. I can wear it out for a night on the town, then eat it with blue cheese dressing for a midnight snack."

"That's gross," Mildred said. "And you're not wearing it in my car. It's like you're doing a striptease without even trying. Put on something made of cotton or I'm leaving you here with your family."

"You're a real disappointment when it comes to fashion," Helena griped. "I suppose you think I should dress like you."

"That would be fabulous," Mildred said.

"Fine." Helena waved a hand and a second later, she was clad in blue jeans, polo shirt, and tennis shoes that exactly matched Mildred's outfit. She shot a final glare at both of them before stomping around the car and getting in the passenger seat.

Jadyn and Mildred looked at each other before shaking their heads and climbing into the car. With no room to turn around, Mildred began to inch her car backward down the path. Helena reached inside her polo shirt, pulled out a slice of lettuce and started munching on it.

"You didn't say anything about undergarments," Helena said.

Mildred looked over at her in dismay. "I'm never eating a salad again."

Helena grinned. "You should see what I did with the croutons."

Before they got back into Mudbug and with much grousing on Helena's part, Jadyn changed seats with the ghost. Mildred had pointed out that this way, if anyone had been looking for Jadyn, she could say she'd gone shopping with Mildred. The fact that they were returning with absolutely no items whatsoever was a dead giveaway that they were lying, but Mildred didn't figure anyone would have the nerve to ask her to produce receipts.

She was wrong.

The second they entered the back of the hotel from the garage, Maryse stepped into the hall from the front lobby and glared at them. Jadyn didn't know her cousin well, but it didn't require familiarity to know Maryse was royally pissed.

"I knew it," she said. She walked up to Mildred and shook her head. "You lied to me."

Mildred didn't even bother trying to mask the guilty look. "I couldn't tell you the truth."

"Why not?"

"Because if I had, you would have told me it was a ridiculous idea and I shouldn't do it?"

"So?"

"You would have been right," Mildred said sheepishly.

"After the earful I got from Bill this evening, I have no doubt. Is there a good reason why none of you bothered to tell me what was going on? Or does that fall under the 'I would have interjected common sense into your lives' category as well?"

"Well…" Jadyn began, but didn't really have a good argument to back their position.

"That's what I thought," Maryse said. "You may be interested to know that Colt stopped by here looking for both of you, and he thought it was strange that neither of you were answering your phones. You might be able to explain things to me, and one day, I might forgive you for putting me in this position, but you can't give Colt the real explanation—not if it involves Helena eating her bra strap."

Maryse spun around, grabbed her purse from behind the counter, and stalked out of the hotel.

Jadyn winced as the hotel door slammed shut. "How mad is she?"

Mildred sighed. "Pretty mad. She'll get over it, but as Maryse is an introvert, she can hold a grudge longer than most."

A pang of guilt knotted Jadyn's stomach. This was all her fault. She'd driven a wedge between the two women who'd been nothing but helpful and nice to her. "I'm sorry," she said, but the words didn't sound like near enough.

Mildred patted Jadyn's shoulder. "It will be all right. She's upset about a lot of things, not just our disappearing act. I'll talk to her tomorrow."

"Hello!" Colt's voice sounded from the front door and they looked down the hallway and into the lobby as he walked inside. "Good. You're back."

"Here goes nothing," Jadyn said under her breath and strode up front, Mildred and Helena in tow.

"What's up?" Jadyn asked, trying to sound nonchalant.

"What's up is that I've been trying to reach you for hours

and couldn't. I find it strange that you pitched a fit to be part of this investigation but the second I try to contact you about it, you're nowhere to be found."

"I needed some fresh air," Jadyn said. "Mildred was going shopping, so I went with her. I thought it might take my mind off things."

Colt raised one eyebrow. "Someone tried to kill you, and I'm supposed to believe that you went shopping to make yourself feel better?"

"I don't care what you believe," Jadyn said, sticking to her lie. "I was with Mildred the entire time, or do you plan on calling her a liar as well?"

Colt stared at Mildred for several uncomfortable seconds. "I have no doubt Mildred can lie and do it quite effectively. You make the mistake of thinking that just because I know people, I trust everything they say."

"Ha!" Helena laughed and jumped up onto the lobby counter, now munching on a carrot stick. Jadyn tried not to think about where it might have been.

Mildred drew herself up straight and gave Colt a stern look. "I can appreciate the difficulty of the job you have to do, but your tone is bordering on disrespect, young man. I'm certain your mother raised you better."

Colt nodded. "Yes, but my mother never saw what Jadyn and I did today. See, an intelligent person would take one took at that and think, 'If I'm in any danger at all, maybe I should stay put and be highly visible to law enforcement.'"

"I *am* law enforcement," Jadyn said, "and I see myself clearly, thank you."

"Uh-huh," Colt said. "So if you were shopping, you won't mind showing me some receipts."

Crap. Jadyn raced to come up with an explanation that

made sense, but nothing remotely sane came to mind.

"We didn't buy anything," Mildred said. "I just went shopping for the hotel last week. I didn't need more supplies. I lied to Jadyn that I did so that she would come with me. I didn't think it was good for her to hole up in her hotel room, dwelling on the things that happened today."

"And you thought she'd be safer shopping?" Colt asked.

"We were in a warehouse with hundreds of other people," Mildred argued. "No one in their right mind would attempt something in that kind of crowd."

Colt narrowed his eyes at Mildred. "Do you really think that whoever did that to Duke is in his right mind?"

Mildred paled a bit. "Fine, you've made your point, Colt. What do you want?"

"Jadyn...and it's going to take a while."

"Whoohoo!" Helena hooted. "He could take all the time he wanted with me!"

It took all Jadyn's self-control to lock her gaze on Colt and prevent herself from attempting to backhand Helena off the counter.

"I'm sure Mildred will let us use her office," Jadyn said.

"No thanks," Colt said. "It's past quitting time and what I have to say is best served with a beer. Besides, I'm hoping to run into someone at the bar."

"Who?" Jadyn asked.

"I'll tell you all about it when I have a beer."

"Fine, then let's get going." Jadyn shot a what-the-hell look at Mildred as she followed Colt across the lobby. Mildred shrugged and shook her head, apparently as in the dark as Jadyn was. Helena, who was now pulling grapes out of her shirt, seemed to be the only one unaffected by all the tension in the room.

Colt was completely silent as they crossed the street and

entered the bar. Bill waved as he saw them come in and winked at Jadyn. She smiled at him and followed Colt around the counter to the back corner, away from the other patrons. Bill came right over.

"I know you can't talk about it," Bill said, "but I heard what kind of day you're having. Anything you want is on me."

"Thanks, Bill," Colt said. "Just a beer for me."

"Same for me," Jadyn said.

Bill popped the caps off two beers and slid them across the counter. "If there's anything else I can do…"

"Thanks," Colt said.

Bill gave them a nod and headed across the bar to serve up more drinks. Colt took a drink of his beer, then stared across the room at the wall, still not speaking.

"So who are you hoping to see in here?" Jadyn asked, unable to stand the strained silence any longer.

"Junior."

"My favorite person. What's he done this time?" she asked as she took a drink of beer.

"The money boat belonged to him."

She plunked the bottle down on the counter so hard, beer sloshed out of the top and onto her hand. "What? How? That boat had no identifiers on it."

"Not that we saw," Colt said and told her about the recent painting on the back and his experiment with charcoal.

Jadyn slumped back on the stool. "I still can't believe anyone would hire him for something like this…petty stuff, sure, but that was a lot of money."

"I agree, but I'm pretty sure it's Junior's boat."

"I suppose you've already been by his house?"

"Yep, three times now, and that's the interesting thing. His truck is there, but he's either not home or he's sitting in the dark and not answering. And I haven't been able to run him down anywhere in town, nor has anyone seen him since yesterday."

"You think he's missing?"

"If he is, he's not the only thing."

Jadyn felt her back tighten and she cringed, certain she knew what was coming. "What do you mean?"

"The key is missing."

Chapter Nineteen

Jadyn forced a look of surprise and hoped it was good enough for Colt to buy it. "I thought you took it to the sheriff's department."

"I did, and locked it in my filing cabinet."

"Then how could someone take it?"

"I'm going to take a guess that the incident with Shirley's car was staged to get you out of the building."

"Wow. In broad daylight, right there in the middle of town? That's brazen."

"Yes, it is. Shirley said you were in the office at the time and rescued her car. I want you to tell me everything that happened."

Intense relief washed over Jadyn as she realized Colt didn't suspect her of stealing the key. As ridiculous as Helena's plan had been, it had actually worked. "Sure," she said. "I got to the sheriff's department maybe ten minutes before the car incident, looking for you. Shirley said you'd be back in thirty so I decided to hang around."

"Why did you want to see me?"

She raised one eyebrow. "You know why," she said, taking full advantage of his earlier boorish behavior.

"Oh." He took another sip of his beer. "So tell me about the car."

"I was looking out the front window, hoping I'd see you returning, and that's when I saw the car rolling down the street.

Two men from the barbershop dashed into the street after it, so I ran outside and joined the chase."

"And you didn't see anyone go into the building?"

"How could I? I was running down the street, in the opposite direction, chasing a runaway car. Someone could have stampeded elephants down Main Street and I wouldn't have known."

Colt sighed. "Shirley said as much, but I guess I was hoping for a long shot."

"You didn't have time to look into the key, did you?"

"Not even a minute. That was on my list for tomorrow, but it looks like the opportunity is gone."

Jadyn frowned. Leave it to Colt to go looking for the key a day early. She'd hoped they could get the key back in place before he noticed it was missing, but now things were a bit more complicated. If the key just popped back up in the drawer, Colt would know someone was playing him. But no way could she keep visiting cemeteries looking for a match. At this point, she was obstructing the investigation, not furthering it.

"I asked Mildred about it," Jadyn said. "I drew a picture as best I could remember. I wish I would have thought to take a picture before you took it."

"Me too. Did Mildred have any thoughts?"

"Yeah, she said it looked like the key the cemetery caretaker has that unlocks the front gate."

Colt perked up a bit. "You know, I think she's right."

"But why would Duke hide a key to a cemetery?"

"I don't know. I suppose someone could be trafficking cadavers, but I'm pretty sure Earl would have noticed if people were missing."

"Mildred said Earl's a bit...um, strange?"

"Yeah, that would be one way to describe him."

"Maybe we should talk to him."

Colt glanced around the bar and nodded. "Might as well do it now. I don't think Junior's going to show and if we hurry, we can catch Earl before it's too late for calling on people."

"Does he live in town?"

"You could say that. He lives in a house in the middle of the cemetery."

Great.

Jadyn waved at Bill as they made their way out of the bar and glanced at her watch as they stepped outside. Almost nine o'clock and the sun had disappeared over the swamp, casting downtown in a dim glow of patchy moonlight and the weak streetlamps Helena complained about. The last thing Jadyn wanted to do was visit a cemetery in the dark, but then, the entire day had been filled with the last thing she ever wanted to do. What possible difference could one more thing make?

They'd just made it across the street when Helena rushed out of the hotel wall and fell into step beside them. Jadyn clenched her jaw and shot daggers at Helena, who was changed back into the full lettuce dress and was beginning to wilt.

"Save your dirty looks for Mildred," Helena complained. "She's the one making me follow you."

Jadyn took a deep breath and blew it out, praying that Helena didn't go solid or steal a car or any of the million other things she was capable of. They walked in silence to the cemetery, Jadyn hoping the entire way that the main gate would be locked up for the night and they'd have to come back in daylight hours, preferably without Helena. Unfortunately, the gate was still standing wide open when they approached.

"Oh, hell no!" Helena yelled. "No one said you were going to the cemetery."

"If he hasn't locked up yet, where would he be?" Jadyn asked.

Colt shrugged. "I have no idea."

Helena crossed her arms across her chest. "Probably mixing spells or cooking small children in that haunted cemetery house of his."

"Maybe this isn't such a good idea," Jadyn said, the thought of accidentally being locked inside the cemetery leaping to the forefront of her mind. "We should probably come back tomorrow."

"Damn straight," Helena agreed.

"Maybe you're right," Colt said, then his frown cleared and he got an excited look on his face. "But what if Earl has seen something?"

"Earl hasn't seen anything in a decade but the backside of one hundred and two," Helena shouted.

Jadyn cut her eyes at Helena then looked back at Colt. "Then he'll be able to tell us tomorrow same as tonight."

"But it may be too late," Colt said.

"How do you figure?" Jadyn asked.

"If the key is important enough to steal from the sheriff's department then it must be hiding something big, right?"

"That's the theory."

"I figure if he stole the key, he's going to collect whatever is stashed as soon as possible."

Jadyn held in a groan. Given the circumstances, she could see exactly where Colt was headed, and she couldn't blame him. If the situation were reversed, she'd think the same thing—that such a bold move as stealing the key from the sheriff's department in broad daylight meant a fixed timetable.

"If the stash is in the cemetery," Colt continued, "then we may be able to catch him when he shows up for it."

"You see what you started," Helena said. "I told you it was a bad idea to steal that key."

Jadyn clenched her hands at her sides. Stealing the key had been Helena's idea, not hers, but since she was the only living body that could be held responsible, it was a moot point.

She racked her brain for any reason to shoot down Colt's plan, but given his incomplete scope of knowledge, what he suggested was exactly what they ought to do. If she backed out, she'd look cowardly and suspicious, and she couldn't afford either. But she had to come up with some logical reason to change his plan; otherwise, she saw a long night of wandering around the cemetery in her future.

"Okay," she said, "but let's head straight to Earl's house and wait for him if he's not there. Combing the cemetery is not a smart thing for me right now given that someone's gunning for me."

The excitement fled from Colt's face. "Damn it. I should have thought about that. I'm really sorry. I didn't mean to sound so callous."

Great. Now you've made him feel bad and you're the one lying.

"You're just trying to catch this guy," Jadyn said.

"Yeah, but I can't put you at risk that way. I'll walk you back to the hotel then come back to talk to Earl myself."

"Damn skippy," Helena agreed.

Jadyn held in a sigh, all plans for a hot shower and a fluffy bed sailing out the window, but her next move might seal Colt's opinion of her as a law enforcement officer. "So that you can be the only one at risk? I'm not leaving you to do this alone. We're both safer with backup, and I want this guy as badly as you do. The last thing I want to do is spend every minute of the day looking over my shoulder."

"What's wrong with looking over your shoulder?" Helena argued. "You're young and in good shape. Take up yoga or something. You young people are so lazy."

Colt stared at her for a while, and she could tell his mind

was warring with the option for backup, which was desperately needed, and the white-knight syndrome of keeping the fair maiden safe.

"Okay," he said finally. "We go straight to Earl's house and talk to him. If he hasn't seen anything out of the ordinary, then we head home."

"And if he's seen something?"

"We'll decide how to handle it based on what he's seen."

Jadyn nodded and walked through the entrance behind Colt.

"I'm not going in there," Helena said as she stomped to a stop at the entry.

Jadyn waved at Helena behind her back and fell into step beside Colt as he started down a path right through the center of the cemetery. Whatever they might find inside the gates couldn't be as bad as the vegetable-clad ghost lurking just outside of them. Unfortunately, it didn't take long for Jadyn to change her mind on that one.

At first, the cemetery grounds were fairly open, but the farther toward the back they walked, the closer the trees grew together, making the path even dimmer. Despite the annoyance level, Jadyn found herself wishing Helena had come along. She was beyond obnoxious, but she was also an extra set of eyes that the bad guy couldn't see.

Finally, the trees came so close together that they blocked off most of the moonlight. She was just about to call a halt to the entire charade and insist they turn back when Colt pointed to a dim glimmer about twenty yards through the trees.

"That must be coming from the house," he said.

"Great. Now let's hope he's home."

They increased their pace and seconds later, Colt knocked on the front door of the tiny house. He'd barely lowered his hand when the door flew open and the oldest man Jadyn had ever seen in her life glared out at them.

To say he was skin and bones was an understatement. Skin hung loose on his gaunt face, and combined with his sunken eyes and wild silver hair that hung down his back. Good God, that "Crypt Keeper" description had been dead on. No wonder kids were scared of him. Hell, she was scared of him.

"Whadda ya want?" he barked out at them.

Colt must have figured he'd have better luck going the official route, because he pulled out his badge and showed it to Earl. "I'm Sheriff Bertrand and this is Jadyn St. James, the game warden. We're investigating a crime and thought you might be able to help us."

"You're letting the air out and bugs in," he said and waved them inside.

Colt motioned to Jadyn and she hesitated for a second before stepping inside. Colt had barely cleared the door before Earl slammed it shut. Jadyn glanced around the room that served as kitchenette, breakfast area, and living room and was surprised to see that it looked completely normal. Then she chastised herself for letting Helena's ranting get to her. Earl was probably a perfectly normal man who just looked scary as hell.

"I was just getting ready to close up the cemetery for the night," Earl said. "Wouldn't want any of the spirits getting out."

Okay, maybe not perfectly normal.

Colt frowned. "We were wondering if you'd seen anything out of the ordinary in the cemetery."

Earl looked confused. "'Course I have. It's full of dead people. You think they're up to anything normal?"

Colt's eyes widened. "I, uh…well, I guess I thought since they were dead they weren't up to anything at all."

Earl shook his head. "You young people don't know anything."

Colt glanced at Jadyn and she shrugged. A week ago, she

would have thought Earl was crazy as a loon, but a week ago, she hadn't met Helena.

"Okay," Colt said, "so have you seen anything outside of the ordinary stuff?"

"Like what?"

"More visitors to the cemetery, or maybe people you don't know. Basically, more activity, possibly at night?"

Earl narrowed his eyes. "You think there's funny business going on in the cemetery? That's ridiculous. And no, I haven't seen no strangers wandering around here, no illegal drug deals, no prostitution…although that one might be interesting."

Colt frowned. "Do you mind showing us the key to the front gate?"

Earl let out a long-suffering sigh, pulled open a drawer in the kitchen, and dragged out a ring of keys with several large black iron ones like the one she'd found at Duke. He held the ring up and pointed to a key on the end. "This one's to the gate."

"Are the rest of them spares?"

"Why would I keep my spares on the same ring as the original? If I lost one, I'd lose them all. The rest open crypts."

Jadyn sucked in a breath. It made perfect sense. A crypt was the perfect hiding spot for illegal merchandise.

"How many crypts are in this cemetery?" Jadyn asked.

"Six, but most of 'em hadn't been used in years 'cept for me doing a regular check. Four of the families ain't got no living relatives in Mudbug and haven't in years."

"And you haven't noticed anything out of the ordinary around the crypts?" Colt asked.

"No. Should I?"

Colt pointed to the ring of keys. "Can I take a closer look at those?"

Earl handed him the ring and Colt motioned to her. "These

are all slightly different on the top. Do you recognize the key you found?"

Jadyn studied the keys, then pointed to one with a wide top that dipped in the middle, almost forming a heart. "I think it looked like that one, but I can't be certain."

Colt held up the key. "Which crypt does this open?"

Earl squinted. "That's to the Monroe family crypt."

"Do you have a map of the cemetery? Can you show me where the crypt is located?"

Earl threw his hands in the air. "Why on earth would I have a map? I've lived here since I was born. I'm pretty sure I can find everything."

"I need to see this crypt tonight. Can you point me in the right direction? And if you have some flashlights we could borrow, that would be great."

"Don't got any use for flashlights. Kerosene lanterns is what my daddy used and that's fine by me. The Monroe crypt is about fifty yards directly behind my house. Just stay on the path. It's the one with a heart and twisted vines on the door."

"Sounds easy enough. If you have two lanterns you can spare, that would be great."

"Don't know as I can spare 'em, but if you don't bring 'em back, I guess I know where to find you."

As Colt slipped the Monroe crypt key off the ring, Earl opened a coat closet in the living room and pulled out two lanterns. "I keep 'em filled."

"Thanks." Colt took the lanterns and headed out the door. "You can stay here if you're not okay with this," he said as he handed her a lantern.

"Stay here with the Crypt Keeper? Pass."

Colt chuckled. "I kept trying to figure out who he looked like. You nailed it."

"You mean I nailed it." Helena's voice sounded behind

Jadyn. "I never get credit for anything around here."

Jadyn clenched her jaw to keep from answering. She could think of all sorts of things Helena got credit for, and none of them were good.

"I got bored at the gate, and I didn't see any spooks, so I decided to come inside. So where are we going?" Helena asked, as if Jadyn could just pop out a reply. Unfortunately, Jadyn knew Helena wouldn't shut up until she had an answer.

"Do you think we'll find something at the Monroe family crypt?" Jadyn asked, hoping Helena would catch the hint.

"I hope so," Colt said.

"A crypt?" Helena's voice rose several octaves. "Have you lost your mind?"

It was a loaded question, so just as well that Jadyn couldn't answer it. Instead, she tried to wave Helena away when Colt was scanning the brush to his right.

"Oh, hell no!" Helena protested. "I can't see in the dark and you've dragged me into the pit of hell back here. I might get lost and kidnapped by spooks. I could be held here against my will for centuries, forced to cook and perform sexual favors."

Jadyn held in a sigh. It was quite possible that she'd finally met someone even more high-maintenance than her own mother, and with a much more vivid imagination.

"That must be it." Colt held up his lantern, casting a dim glow on the marble facing. "A heart with a twisted vine."

Jadyn stepped up to the crypt and lifted her lantern up to increase visibility. "The keyhole is lower down on the right. A piece of vine is starting to grow over it."

Colt pushed the vine out of the way and turned the key in the hole. It stuck for a moment, then Jadyn heard a click and the giant marble door began to creak open. They both took hesitant steps inside the doorway, holding their lanterns in front of them.

"I'm not going in there!" Helena shouted from the opening. It was all Jadyn could do to keep from shouting back "good."

The center walkway of the crypt was fairly large—probably twelve feet wide and thirty feet long. The walls were lined with engraved plaques, indicating who resided behind them. Otherwise, the crypt was empty.

Jadyn stepped closer to one of the plaques and gave it a little shove. It didn't budge. "You don't think anyone went to the trouble..."

"Of hiding something inside the walls? I wouldn't think so. If we're right, this was only temporary storage for whatever that boatload of money was purchasing. It's not like someone was sequestering the family jewels or a treasure map."

"Then I guess we got nothing," Jadyn said.

Colt blew out a breath. "Looks like. Sorry I wasted your time."

"It wasn't a waste of time. I think we're on the right track, just the wrong cemetery."

"This is the only cemetery in Mudbug."

The information about Helena's family cemetery was on the tip of her tongue, and she really wanted to let it out, but knew that she couldn't. Not yet. Tomorrow she could claim she asked Mildred, and the hotel owner knew about the other cemetery. But there was no good reason for Jadyn to have that knowledge now.

"Then we'll start looking in nearby towns," Jadyn said.

"I suppose so," Colt said, sounding as frustrated as she felt. "Let's get out of here."

"You don't have to ask me twice."

She stepped outside of the crypt and something whizzed by her ear. For a split second, she thought the rumor about south Louisiana mosquitoes having to file flight paths with the FAA wasn't an exaggeration, but when the bullet struck the side of the crypt and sent tiny shards of concrete scattering, she bolted back inside, dropping her lantern and almost shoving a startled Colt to the ground.

Chapter Twenty

"The shooter," Jadyn managed before another bullet ricocheted off the inside wall of the crypt.

Colt pushed her to the far side of the crypt, grabbed the edge of the door, and started pulling it closed. Jadyn tried to get her initial panic under control, but the thought of being trapped inside the crypt was sending it into overdrive.

"Lordy! Lordy!" Helena, who'd dashed inside the crypt with Jadyn, started running around in circles, waving her hands in the air. "He's locking us in with the dead people."

Jadyn gestured to the frantic ghost to get her attention then pointed to the outside, hoping Helena got the hint. The ghost stopped running and wrinkled her brow.

"You want me to go outside with the killer? Are you insane?"

Jadyn glared at Helena and pointed outside again, desperately wishing she could talk to the ghost. "We need a diversion so that we can make a run for it," she told Colt, hoping Helena would take the hint. "Otherwise, we're stuck in here until daylight."

Helena sucked in a breath. "Oh no! I'm not staying in here all night. I'll go goose him with a twig or something."

The ghost walked through the crypt door and a second later, Jadyn heard the sound of glass breaking.

"Damn it!" Helena ranted. "Who left a lantern right outside of the door? I've stubbed my toe and set the cemetery on fire."

The image of her and Colt trapped in what could essentially become a smoker flashed across her mind, and she struggled to force herself to stay put. *Give Helena time to do something.* What, she had no idea. If the ghost had gone solid and kicked the lamp, they were already operating at a deficit.

"I can hear him. He's right outside," Colt said as he stood in front of Jadyn and pointed his pistol directly at the door.

Jadyn said a silent prayer as smoke began to filter through the crack Colt had left in the crypt door. Oh, someone was right outside, all right, but it wasn't the killer.

Helena stuck her head through the door. "Someone's moving around about twenty feet up in the trees. I'm going total ghost on this one." A second later, her head was covered with a white sheet, only two openings for her eyes showing through. She disappeared on the other side of the crypt and Jadyn wondered if Helena could make the white sheet visible to the shooter. If a ghost in a cemetery didn't scare him away, she wasn't sure what would.

"This piece of wood will do for a weapon." Jadyn could hear Helena talking to herself outside the crypt. "If I can just get it out of the ground. It's stuck. Help! I'm falling!"

As the sound of the dull thud echoed back at them, Jadyn cringed.

"The stick's on fire!" Helena yelled and a second later, Jadyn could hear the ghost running away from the crypt.

Colt peeked out a crack in the door. "There's some dead brush on fire just outside the crypt. The smoke may be enough to provide cover. I want you to crawl out of the crypt and go to your left. I'll cover you from the doorway, then head right as soon as you're clear and try to draw him off that way."

"No, it's too risky."

"So is sitting here and dying of smoke inhalation or worse."

Because he was right, Jadyn dropped to her hands and knees and crawled to the door. Colt killed the lantern and eased the crypt door open enough for her to exit. A stack of dead brush three feet in front of the crypt was the source of the fire, which leaped up about two feet in height. Fortunately, the surrounding foliage was green so unless the wind picked up, there was little chance of the fire spreading.

She paused a couple of seconds, then the brush popped and sent off a pillar of black smoke. Jadyn took advantage of the additional camouflage and scampered out of the crypt and into the nearby tree line. Pausing only a second to catch her breath, she peered around the tree trunk, then rose from the ground and started darting from tree to tree, working her way away from the crypt.

Every second that passed without the sound of gunfire, her hope grew stronger, and she hoped Colt was out of the crypt and on his way out of the cemetery as well. Just as she was going to traverse a small clearing, she heard the sound of running feet. She barely had time to duck behind a tree when a man came running past her, holding a pistol.

He wore a dark hooded sweatshirt with the hood pulled up, so Jadyn couldn't make out any discerning detail except that he was average height and weight. And he was definitely in a hurry. A couple of seconds later, she knew why.

Helena Henry burst out from the tree line, running after the man and still wearing the white sheet, except she'd added an accessory. Clutched in her hands was an old wooden cross, flames shooting off of it.

"My hands are on fire!" Helena yelled as she ran past.

Jadyn stared, drop-jawed. It was a page out of a Southern nightmare. Being chased by a burning cross was definitely enough to make someone flee, even someone packing a gun, but Jadyn had the added benefit of seeing the whole package, which was far more disturbing.

She could have stopped Helena and told her to drop the cross. It seemed an obvious solution, but in her panicked state, it apparently hadn't crossed Helena's mind. Jadyn was beginning to understand just how detrimental Helena's propensity for panicking could be. She didn't think for a moment that the cross could actually burn her hands, but she did wonder about the mental strain that it might place on an already frantic mind.

Figuring the shooter was long gone, she picked up her pace, heading for Earl's cabin. With any luck, Helena would be long gone, the cross extinguished, and Colt wouldn't catch a glimpse of any of it.

With any luck.

Colt opened Earl's truck door and stepped out, then waited for Jadyn to exit. "Thanks for the ride," he said to the surly caretaker, who waved a hand in dismissal and barely waited for Colt to shut the passenger door before throwing the truck into reverse and screeching back down Main Street.

The caretaker was probably still pissed that not only hadn't they come back with the lanterns, but one was broken. The whole shooting and fire incident hadn't seemed to concern him at all. But the lanterns were a big deal. Colt didn't even attempt to understand the man's rationale.

Before they even reached the hotel door, Mildred threw it open and gave them an anxious look. "Was that Earl? Is everything all right? Did something happen?"

"We're fine," Jadyn reassured her.

"I'm going to head home," Colt said. "We can talk about all this tomorrow, when I've had some time to mull it over."

Mildred disappeared back inside the hotel. "That's fine," Jadyn said, her exhaustion apparent in her voice.

As she started to turn toward the door, he placed his hand on her shoulder. "Hey, I just want to say I'm sorry. I should never have put you in that position. If something had happened to you…"

"But it didn't, and please don't apologize. You were just doing your job. So was I."

She gave him a small smile before slipping inside the hotel. He heard the deadbolt slide into place a second later. He stared at the door for several seconds as guilt, fear, and responsibility warred inside of him. Finally, he blew out a breath and hurried across the street to his truck.

He didn't want to think about how his heart had clenched when he'd realized how much danger they were in. Didn't want to dwell on the fact that the thing that had scared him most was something bad happening to Jadyn. And even worse, didn't want to consider how much it would hurt him if something did.

As he drove down Main Street, he knuckles whitened on the steering wheel and cursed. They were on the right track with the key…he was certain. But had the shooter been in the cemetery retrieving his goods and simply taken the opportunity to kill them because it happened to present itself, or had he followed them to the cemetery, hoping to eliminate them before they got too close to his secret?

Surely if he risked stealing the key from the sheriff's department in broad daylight, it meant he needed to move the product soon. Was one of the other crypts the hiding place for whatever Duke had died for? He banged one hand on the steering wheel, so angry over the theft of the key that he could barely see straight. That key could have broken this case wide open, and it had been stolen from right under his nose.

Tomorrow, he'd pay another visit to Earl. Even though

none of the other crypt keys looked like the one from Duke's, he still wanted to take a look inside all of the crypts in Mudbug cemetery. Then he'd call around and see if any other towns had recent issues in their cemeteries. Maybe he'd get lucky.

He sure hoped so. In his opinion, he was long overdue.

The shooter watched from the alley as the sheriff pulled away from downtown Mudbug and headed down the highway into the swamp. His problem had just multiplied, and his failed attempt to eliminate the woman on the bayou that afternoon had been a pointless risk, although a well-calculated one. He'd seen the woman's posture at Duke's cabin when talking to the sheriff and had hoped that her obvious animosity would cause her to keep the key to herself. But clearly, she'd weakened as women usually did and turned the evidence over.

When he'd caught sight of them entering the cemetery, he figured they'd guessed the identity of the key, but he'd been watching closely when the sheriff opened the crypt, and the merchandise he desperately needed to find was nowhere to be seen.

Could the key open more than one crypt? Had his supplier given him the wrong key? Or was something more insidious going on and his supplier was playing him?

Regardless, he needed to find the merchandise and fast. His life depended on it, and quite possibly his sanity. He still wasn't sure what he'd seen that night in the cemetery, but he was determined to convince himself it was all due to the stress he was under. He didn't even want to think about the alternative.

He pulled the hood back on his sweatshirt and sighed. It had been a simple plan. Deliver the money and the supplier would tell him what the key unlocked. Then his transport guy could do his part and get the product to the buyer. But that idiot Duke had totally screwed them when he lost control of the shrimp boat in the storm.

Fortunately, the shooter been smart about the way he'd structured his business. No one—not his suppliers or his customers—had ever met him face-to-face. Because he'd always used expendable middlemen and made all arrangements by untraceable cell phone and money drops, no one was aware of his identity.

The men who'd supplied the merchandise were low-life thugs and didn't have the means to determine who he was, much less find him once he left Louisiana, but the buyer was the type of man who would track someone who crossed him to the ends of the earth. And then he'd make him pay. Look what he'd done to Duke, and that poor bastard hadn't even known what the money was for, much less where the merchandise was hidden. The only way out of this mess was to find the merchandise and get it to the buyer before the buyer figured out who he was. Then he'd take the considerable amount of money he'd amassed and leave Mudbug forever.

Narrowing his eyes at the fading taillights, he cursed himself once more for his greed. Between his meager legitimate earnings and the deals he'd made the last six months, he'd already saved enough money to leave the country and never lift another finger again, but when he'd been offered this job, he hadn't been able to say no. The payout would have been the icing on the cake.

Now, unless he found the merchandise, he was totally screwed.

JANA DELEON

Chapter Twenty-One

An hour before dawn, Jadyn handed Helena the iron key and watched as she tucked it into her jeans pocket. Yesterday had been a brutal day followed by an exhausting night. It had taken Jadyn and Mildred a good hour and half a bottle of scotch to calm Helena down. Jadyn wasn't convinced that the ghost could actually feel the alcohol, but when the first shot seemed to bring her down off the rafters, Mildred kept pouring.

By the time Helena's hysterics were under control, it was well after midnight and Jadyn knew she was already facing a night of tossing and turning before she ever went up to her room. Her mind was too overloaded to stop whirling. Even her body, which was exhausted beyond belief, refused to relax. She'd spent four hours catching ten to twenty minutes of sleep before her alarm went off, and she popped out of bed, anxious to get the first order of business behind her.

"The night dispatcher will be there," Jadyn reminded Helena. "If she sees the filing cabinet open, we'll have a whole new set of problems."

"I know. I know," Helena said. "I wait until you call, then I swipe the filing cabinet key and put the crypt key back in the cabinet."

"But not where you found it, otherwise Colt will know something's up. Slip it inside one of the folders at the back of the drawer. Then maybe he'll think he accidentally dropped it inside."

199

Helena shook her head. "Do you know how stupid that sounds?"

"It sounds more intelligent than telling him I helped a ghost steal the key and it almost got us killed last night."

"There is that," Helena agreed. "Make sure you keep her on the phone long enough. And this is sketchy at best. If she looks that direction when I have the cabinet open…"

"Don't worry. I have an idea about that."

Helena didn't look convinced but she set off down the street to the sheriff's department. As soon as she slipped through the wall, Jadyn picked up her cell phone and dialed the dispatcher.

"This is Jadyn St. James," she said when the dispatcher answered. "I don't suppose Sheriff Bertrand is there, is he?"

"No. I expect I won't see him for a couple of hours, but if there's an emergency, I can get him for you."

"You heard about that trouble with Shirley's car yesterday, right?"

"Of course."

"Well, I was having a cup of coffee on the roof of the hotel and I saw a man I didn't recognize enter the parking lot from the alley. I lost sight of him behind the oak tree. Can you look and see if he's still there?"

"Oh my! Give me a second."

Jadyn heard some rustling and then the dispatcher came back on the line. "The parking lot looks clear from here. Where did you see him?"

"I saw him entering from the back, just past the general store's Dumpster. Do you have a clear view?"

"Pretty clear, except I can't see behind the plumber's van."

"I have a decent view of the van. I don't see anyone behind it. But I can't figure out where he's gone to."

"Should I go outside and look?"

Jadyn deliberated sending the woman outside for a moment, but then Helena popped out of the building and started down the street back to the hotel. "No. That might not be safe. If neither of us can see him, he was probably just walking by. I apologize for bothering you, but given everything that's happened and not knowing all the locals by sight, everything is starting to look suspicious to me."

"I understand, and it's no bother. I'm always telling Colt to err on the side of safety. He doesn't listen, of course, but it's nice to know that at least one law enforcement officer in this town sees how reasonable that is."

"Absolutely. Well, I'll let you get back to work. Thank you for humoring me."

"Anytime, Ms. St. James."

Jadyn slipped her cell phone back in her jeans pocket as Helena walked into the hotel wearing a broad smile.

"I don't know what you told her," Helena said, "but it worked like a charm. She stood right at that front window, staring across the street."

"So the key is back in place?"

Helena nodded. "I dropped it into the second-to-last folder of the second drawer. That should be good, right?"

Jadyn nodded, a wave of relief washing over her. As long as Colt believed he was distracted enough to drop the key into a folder instead of the bottom of the cabinet, as he actually had, they'd be in the clear.

"If you're all done with me for now," Helena said, "I'm going to the bakery to smell the cinnamon rolls."

Jadyn froze. "You're not planning on stealing one, are you?"

"No, I'm not going to steal anything, Goody Two-shoes. I just like the smell of them baking. Maybe I'll get Mildred to buy me one later."

"Why don't you just conjure one up? Wouldn't that be

easier?"

"Oh sure, like it's that easy. If I could conjure stuff up, why would I be hanging around you guys?"

"But you conjure up different outfits all the time."

"But that's all I can do." Helena shrugged. "I don't know why."

Jadyn suddenly realized that Helena was dressed in normal jeans and T-shirt. "Hey, what happened to the grocery store dress? Did you eat it all?"

"I got fruit flies in it running through the cemetery. I need to rethink the concept."

Before Jadyn could formulate a response, Helena left through the wall. Jadyn looked out the window and watched as she crossed the street to the bakery. At least things were starting off good this morning. The key was back in place, and Colt had no reason to suspect it had ever been in her possession.

Now, she just had to figure out a way to get him to find the key, and she could put the crypt key nightmare behind her. In addition, she made a mental note that if Helena thought something was a good idea, it was likely to be far more trouble than it was worth. From now on, she listened to her own instincts and stopped letting emotion enter into her decision-making.

That's a first.

She frowned as the thought entered her mind. Searching her memory, she tried to think of a time when emotion had overridden good common sense during a job decision and she couldn't think of a single time. So why now?

Granted, there were any number of good reasons—a boatload of cash, the circumstances of Duke's death, getting shot at, Helena's appearance, her attraction to Colt.

Hold up!

Where had that last one come from? She wasn't attracted to Colt.

Liar.

She slumped down in a chair in the lobby, a feeling of dismay coursing through her. Colt? She was attracted to white-knight-syndrome, I'm-the-boss Colt? She groaned, trying to understand how this could have happened.

Maybe it's because he saved her life last night…or at least, tried to.

Yeah, that made sense. She'd go with that. It was a temporary state given her precarious position as a target. As soon as this case was solved and well behind her, the attraction she thought she had for Colt would fade away.

At least, that's what she was going to tell herself.

Maryse peeked into the bathroom, making sure the coast was clear before Luc got out of bed.

"You're looking for Helena, aren't you?" Luc's voice sounded behind her, causing her to jump.

"What—no—I was just trying to remember where I left my watch."

He tapped her arm. "On your wrist. But nice try."

"Busted."

Luc gathered her in his arms and kissed her. "You're a horrible liar, but that's probably a good thing. Still, we've got to address this Helena thing. The aggravation is going to interfere with your work, our lives…hell, everyone's lives."

Maryse sighed. "Don't you think I know that? But what are we supposed to do about it? We can't exactly talk to God and ask him to take her back."

"Yes, you can. It's called prayer, and I doubled mine right

after I removed the handcuffs."

"Do you really think that will work?"

"No, but I have another option."

Maryse perked up. "What?"

"We can move."

She shook her head and he held up a hand to stop the barrage he knew was coming.

"I've been with the agency long enough to request a transfer, and with my track record, most offices would be happy to take me. Anywhere in the US."

"This is my home. This is your home. Can you honestly tell me you could up and move without a second thought?"

"I'd have second thoughts and probably thirds, but what I know for certain is that we can't live with Helena Henry forever. God won't have her. If he's smart, Satan's afraid of her. So that leaves her here with us."

He gave her a hug and a kiss on the forehead before releasing her. "Can you handle it forever—not knowing if your life or the life of someone you love is in danger because Helena's around?"

"Your life is in danger all the time," Maryse pointed out.

"It's my job to put my life in danger, and it's a job I'm well-trained for, unlike you. And despite the fact that I've seen some pretty hairy things, I have to be honest with you—Helena scares me far more than any investigation I've ever been on. Drug runners are predictable compared to her."

Maryse sighed. It was hard to find an argument when everything Luc said was accurate.

"We don't have to make a decision now," Luc reassured her, "but it's something I think we should give some serious thought."

She gave him a nod as he grabbed a towel from the rack and strolled into the bathroom. Maryse turned around and stared out the bedroom window into the swamp. Could she really leave Mudbug? It was the only home she'd ever known and despite what others perceived as shortcomings, she really loved it here. Well, she loved it here without Helena.

When she'd been alive, Helena had been the bane of her existence. Who would have thought her death would make things so much worse?

But could she pick up everything and move? Luc's idea had merit—she had to give him credit. Even though she had the ability, Helena was unlikely to follow them away from Mudbug. It was her home too, and where things felt familiar.

She blew out a breath and headed out of the house to her truck. Sabine and Beau returned late last night from their cruise. She needed to get to them and explain the situation before Helena turned up. Luc's proposal was something she'd think about later. But right now, with Jadyn in danger, Maryse couldn't justify leaving. Maybe when things were settled, she'd think it over.

It was only 7:00 a.m. when she pulled into Sabine's driveway. She and Beau had occupied the cramped apartment above her shop in downtown Mudbug for a month before deciding they needed more space. It took another six months to find a contractor and get their cabin constructed, but it had been worth it.

It was set back in the swamp, with a small area cleared for the cabin and a bayou running behind it. The cabin was log construction and blended so well with the surrounding foliage that it looked almost as if the swamp had grown it. It was so well done that it had almost convinced Maryse that she and Luc needed one themselves. Almost.

Despite Maryse's previous home on an isolated island in the bayou, she'd grown fond of living close to downtown…especially as it meant she never had a problem with meals. In a matter of minutes, she had access to the handful of eating establishments in Mudbug as well as Mildred's hotel for her coffee wake-up. A year ago, if someone had told her that she'd be living in town and perfectly happy, she would have had their mental state examined. But then a year ago, she hadn't been with Luc.

Despite the early hour, Maryse could see the light on in Sabine's kitchen. She'd taken a chance that her friend would be restless and unable to sleep after all the traveling, and was happy she'd been correct. She'd been preparing for days for this conversation and didn't want to delay it any longer than necessary.

As she stepped out of her truck and walked toward the cabin, Sabine, still wearing her pajamas, opened the front door and walked out on the porch to give her a hug.

"You must have been reading my mind," Sabine said as she released her. "I was just thinking about how I couldn't wait to see you and catch up on everything. The coffee just finished brewing. Let's pour some and sit on the back deck. It's a beautiful morning."

Sabine smiled and a wave of guilt washed over Maryse for what she was about to do. Their entire lives, Maryse had never seen her friend so happy, so settled. The last thing she wanted to do was bring news that would upset the balance, and that's exactly what she was about to do.

"Sounds great," Maryse said and followed Sabine to the kitchen.

Beau was pouring a cup of coffee into a travel mug as she walked into the kitchen. He popped the top on the mug, then set it down long enough to give Maryse a hug and kiss on the cheek.

"I'm sorry to greet and run," he said, "but I got a call this morning from a long-term client in New Orleans. Her grandson is missing. I'm going to see if there's anything I can do."

"Oh, that's awful," Maryse said. "I hope you find him."

"Me too." He gave Sabine a lingering kiss that made Maryse smile then hurried out of the cabin, waving to Maryse as he went.

"He's so wonderful," Maryse said.

Sabine beamed. "He is. So is Luc."

Maryse nodded. "We are the luckiest women in Mudbug."

"I will agree with you as soon as we both have a cup of coffee and are sitting on that deck."

"You don't have to ask me twice." Maryse grabbed two mugs from Sabine's cabinet and Sabine poured. After a quick dash of sweetener, they both headed outside on the deck and plopped into spacious lawn chairs with thick cushions.

Maryse drank her coffee in silence for several seconds, focusing on the beautiful view of the rising sun glistening on the water of the bayou.

"Now that you've had half a cup of coffee," Sabine said, "are you going to tell me what's wrong?"

Maryse sighed. "How do you do that?"

"Know when something's bothering you? Well, showing up at my doorstep with the chickens is a dead giveaway, but even if you'd arrived at noon, I still would have known from the sound of your voice. You did an excellent job attempting to sound fine, though. I don't think Beau noticed a thing."

"Like that's a big accomplishment. Beau never notices anything when you're in the room." Maryse took a minute to collect her thoughts. Three days of mulling this over—you'd think she would already know what she was going to say, but she'd yet to come up with a good way of delivering the news.

"Helena's back," she said, giving up on a better way to inform Sabine that her pleasant life was now over.

Sabine's eyes widened and her hands started to shake. She placed her mug on the patio table and took a deep breath, then slowly blew it out. Maryse figured twenty years of yoga and meditation were still no match for Helena, but everyone had their own way of dealing with things.

"So many questions," Sabine said, "I guess the big one is 'why?'"

"Yeah, and that's a loaded one."

Maryse recounted Helena's sketchy and brief commentary about her trouble with God. Sabine's eyes grew wider and she shook her head.

"That is so much bad karma," Sabine said when Maryse finished. "I don't even know where to start."

"No doubt. Unfortunately, that's not the worst of it."

"What can be worse than directly pissing off God?"

"My cousin, Jadyn, arrived this week to start the game warden job."

Sabine nodded. "I remember you saying she was coming."

"She can see Helena."

Sabine's hand flew up to cover her mouth. "Oh no," she whispered. "Do you think…"

"That's exactly where my thoughts went, and since someone tried to kill her yesterday, it looks like I was accurate."

"I understand that you don't know Jadyn well, but do you have any idea why someone would want to kill her?"

"Yeah," Maryse said and told Sabine about the boat of money, Duke's murder, and the host of other incredible things that had happened in Mudbug while Sabine had been gone.

"So you think the boat of money is the nexus?" Sabine frowned. "And Jadyn says the boat is connected to Duke's death, which I have to say is the most horrible thing I've ever heard, and I'm sure you went out of your way to make it less horrid than it actually was. If you put all those thing together with Helena's appearance—"

"We got trouble."

"Again."

Maryse nodded, certain she looked as miserable as she felt.

"I don't suppose I have to ask if Helena's being as difficult as ever."

"More than ever," Maryse said. "Mildred and I convinced Jadyn to keep her around as much as possible, but that's a lot to ask of anyone."

"Have her skills improved any?"

"She's more accurate with touching things, but still misses a lot, and even worse, she seems to be 'going solid' more often than before. I thought getting her a prepaid cell phone would be a good idea, because that way she could call for help, assuming she's in cell range."

Sabine's eyes widened. "And you can hear her over a phone?"

"Loud and clear. Unfortunately, she lost the first one in a bar fight, the second to a boating mishap, and the third running through a cemetery." She sighed. "I'm rethinking that plan."

Sabine placed her hand over Maryse's and gave it a squeeze. "We're going to figure this out. We did it before and we can do it again. The important thing is to protect Jadyn."

Maryse's heart warmed at Sabine's words. Her friend was the most generous person she'd ever known. "Then I guess we better get to work."

Chapter Twenty-Two

It took Colt forever to fall asleep, but once he did, he slept like the dead. Overslept like the dead was a more accurate description, so it was close to 8:00 a.m. before he left his house the next morning. He stopped by Junior's house on the way to the sheriff's department. Given the hour, it was possible the man was already shrimping or fishing, but at least his truck would be gone, and Colt would know that Junior was somewhere around Mudbug and could be tracked down later on that day.

As he pulled into the drive, he frowned when he saw Junior's truck in the same place it was the evening before. He hurried up to the house and banged on the door, hoping the shrimper was sleeping off a monumental drunk, but the twinge of bad feeling he'd gotten the day before had now launched into overdrive.

He waited several seconds, listening for any sound of movement inside, but didn't hear so much as a creak of flooring. Reaching out, he checked the door and found it locked, but he was beyond caring. If he was wrong about this, he'd apologize and buy Junior a new door, but if he was right, that apology would be too little too late.

He took a step back, then slammed into the door with his shoulder. Lucky for him, it wasn't the best framing job and the jamb splintered easily, allowing the door to swing open. He scanned the front rooms but when he saw no sign of Junior, he started down the hall. The guest room was currently utilized as storage and showed no signs for alarm so he continued to the master bedroom.

As he pushed the door open, he caught sight of Junior lying in his bed, eyes closed. He stepped next to the bed and put his fingers on Junior's neck, but he knew the man was dead before he ever touched the cold skin.

"Damn it, Junior. Were you involved or simply a liability?"

He pulled out his cell phone and called the coroner, then called Jadyn.

"We've got a problem at Junior's house," he said when she answered.

"He's not…"

"I'm afraid so."

"I'll be there in a minute."

She hung up before he could stop her. There wasn't anything she could do. The coroner would take pictures and he'd be willing to bet he'd find no sign of forced entry. He started with the master bedroom, checking the windows, and worked his way down the hall back to the front of the house. By the time he reached the living room, Jadyn was pulling into the driveway.

"You find anything?" she asked and stopped to look at the front doorframe.

"That's my handiwork," he explained. "I had a bad feeling…"

"I get it. Any other sign of entry?"

"It's all locked up like a drum."

"Any possibility it's natural causes?"

Colt frowned, realizing that thought hadn't actually crossed his mind. "I didn't see any marks on him, and his eyes are closed, but something tells me we're not getting off that easy, especially since we know it was Junior's boat carrying the money."

"His dad's boat," Jadyn corrected. "Do you really think he wrecked the boat, then called everyone on the CB to scoop up the money?"

"No. I still think Duke was the boat captain. But I think it was Junior who put out the CB call about the money."

"Junior had to have recognized the boat that day at the pond."

Colt nodded. "Probably. The fact that he didn't say anything makes me think he either lent Duke the boat or knew he's the one who took it. I figure he put out the call on Marty's channel hoping the men would collect all the money before I heard about it, and the boat would sink low enough in a day or two that no one would check it."

"Why didn't he say anything after Duke turned up dead?"

"Maybe he was going to. Until we have a time of death, we won't know for sure how long he's been dead. Air-conditioning is on. It could be they killed him before he could get to me."

"Or he thought he could get something out of keeping that tidbit to himself."

Colt sighed. "He was stupid enough to try it, that's for sure."

A crunch of tires on gravel echoed through the house and they stepped outside as James climbed out of his car. He grabbed his bag and walked up on the porch.

"Is there anything I need to know?" he asked, hesitantly.

Colt knew exactly what he was referring to. "This one looks normal," he said.

James blew out a breath and some of the blood rushed back into his face. "Thank God. I mean, not that I'm saying it's good he's dead, but..."

"I understand," Colt said. "This way."

James nodded to Jadyn then started down the hallway with Colt.

As soon as they entered the bedroom, James pulled out his

camera and snapped some shots of Junior. Colt saw Jadyn enter the room behind them, but she stayed just inside the doorway, leaned against the wall.

After taking pictures from every angle, James put the camera back in his bag, and started examining Junior's body.

"How long has he been dead?" Colt asked.

"Without an autopsy, it's hard to say for certain, but based on rigor, I'd say he died sometime yesterday around or after noon."

"So while we were processing Duke's house?"

James nodded. "That would be the earliest, but given that the air-conditioning was on, it could have been as late as yesterday evening."

"Can you tell what killed him?"

James frowned. "You mean does it look like foul play? On the surface, I'd have to say no. There's no bruising, no cuts or bullet holes. Nothing that clearly screams poison."

"He's young to die in his sleep, isn't he?" Jadyn asked.

"Well, yes." James sighed. "But Junior didn't exactly lead a healthy lifestyle. He drank half his weight in booze every night and his daddy has heart problems. It's highly likely Junior inherited them."

The paramedics entered the bedroom and James motioned to them to load the body. "I'll let you know as soon as I have something more concrete."

"Thank you," Colt said.

James gave him a nod and followed the paramedics out of the house.

"Natural causes?" Jadyn said. "Two days after his boat was used to commit a crime. That's a hell of a coincidence."

"Yep. A hell of a coincidence."

"You don't think it's natural causes, do you?"

"Do you?"

Jadyn shook her head. "Who all knew that you were looking for Junior yesterday?"

Colt frowned. "Shirley, of course. Marty and Bill."

"Marty's had access to the boat from day one. He could have stripped anything out of it before we did our search."

"Yeah, but Marty's the one who noticed the name was painted over. Why would he point that out if he had something to do with it?"

"Because it was Junior's boat and he knew Junior was already dead?"

He ran one hand through his hair. "Damn it. I suppose it's possible."

"What about the bar? Was anyone else in the bar when you told Bill you were looking for Junior?"

"Your buddies Bart and Tyler."

"They're not my buddies," Jadyn protested. "But they do seem to be around a lot. Are you sure Marty or Bill couldn't be involved?"

Colt threw his hands in the air. "I'm not sure of anything anymore."

Jadyn sighed. "Me either."

Colt's cell phone rang and he pulled it out of his jeans pocket and answered. Several seconds later, he slipped it back in his pocket.

"That was Shirley," he said. "She wants me back at the sheriff's department as soon as possible."

"She didn't say why?" Jadyn said, starting to worry that the body count had risen again.

"No, but she sounded excited, not scared."

"Well, that's good. Right?"

He shrugged. "I think we better see."

It took them ten minutes to nail Junior's front door onto

the frame and put police tape on the front of it. Then they both headed to the sheriff's department. Shirley met them at the door, a huge grin on her face.

"I've been meaning to sort out those old files forever," she said. "I started with the top drawer, which took an hour, and then when I got to the second, look what I found." She held up the iron key.

Jadyn struggled to contain her glee. Shirley had just eliminated one huge problem from her day.

"Wow!" Jadyn said.

Colt's eyes widened. "You're kidding me! It was in there the whole time?"

She nodded. "You must have accidentally dropped it inside a folder instead of in the bottom like you thought, which means the killer wasn't in here stealing it in broad daylight."

"It also means your car seriously needs a service," Colt said.

Shirley frowned. "Yes, I suppose it does. I also got a call from the hospital, and that news is not nearly as good."

"Did something happen to Leroy?" Colt asked.

"He skipped. Walked out sometime early this morning."

"Didn't you have a guard on him?" Jadyn asked.

"Apparently," Shirley said, "he waited until the officer went into the restroom, then made his getaway."

Colt cursed. "I hope he's not as stupid as I suspect he is."

Jadyn blew out a breath. "Well, there's nothing we can do about it now, except hope that the people who got to Duke aren't looking for him."

"It can't come as much of a surprise, really," Shirley said. "The man's entire life has been one bad decision after another. Well, I best get back to my filing." She lifted a stack of files out of the cabinet and headed to her desk.

Colt stared out the window, frowning.

"Are you worried about Leroy?" Jadyn asked.

"I'm worried there's something he didn't tell me, and even more worried that I didn't catch on to that. I'm usually pretty good at judging when someone's hedging an interview."

Jadyn nodded. "Then let's just hope he's smart enough to hide somewhere that he can't be easily found."

"Yep. Well, enough about Leroy—let's talk about the key. I intended to visit Earl again this morning but got sidetracked with Junior. Let's go now."

"Actually," Jadyn said, "I talked to Mildred last night and I think I have a better idea. I don't think anyone would risk hiding merchandise in Mudbug cemetery. It would be too hard to get in and out without being seen, especially given that the only entrance is right off the main street."

Colt frowned. "What did Mildred think?"

"She said that Helena Henry's family had a private cemetery in the swamp." Jadyn reached in her jeans pocket and unfolded a sheet of paper. "She drew me a map—of sorts. It's been years since she's been to the place, but she thought it was in this vicinity."

Colt studied the map. "It's northeast of town and definitely isolated—no homes within ten miles that I'm aware of. She may be onto something. We should check it out."

"Yeah, there's only one problem."

"What?"

"Mildred remembered the cemetery having a huge iron fence with spikes on it. If that key opens a crypt and not the gate, then it sounds like we're not getting in there without the gate key."

Colt blew out a breath. "Who would have the key?"

"Mildred's guess was the estate attorney in New Orleans."

"Which means Hank Henry is likely the only person who could get the key."

Jadyn nodded. "That's what Mildred thought, so she called

him first thing this morning and asked him to check into it. Let me call and see if she's heard anything."

She pulled out her phone and called Mildred, who gave her an update. Smiling, she slipped the phone back in her pocket. "The attorney had the key and Hank picked it up an hour ago. He should be here soon."

"Great." Colt grabbed a key from Shirley's desk and motioned her into his office.

"I don't want Shirley worrying about us any more than she already is," he said as he closed the door behind them. "I didn't tell her about last night. Have you told anyone?"

"No one but Mildred, but she's not going to say anything."

He nodded. "I think the fewer people who know what we're up to the better. We also have to be far more prepared than we were last night. We got lucky. Really lucky. I'm not willing to risk my life and especially yours on luck again."

He unlocked a cabinet on the back wall, pulled out two bulletproof vests, and handed her one. "Before we walk out of this building, I want you wearing that. And I want you to promise me you'll keep it on unless you're showering or sleeping, at least until this is over."

Jadyn took the vest, the weight of it already giving her comfort. "You don't have to ask me twice."

He pulled a shotgun and a small nine-millimeter out and handed those to her as well. "We'll both take shotguns and our regular piece to the cemetery, but I want you to put that smaller nine on your leg for backup." He reached back into the cabinet and pulled out an ankle strap and tossed it to her, then motioned for her to take a seat in one of the chairs in front of his desk.

She sat down and strapped the pistol to her leg, making sure the strap was secure before pulling her jeans over it. Colt placed his vest and shotgun in the middle of the desk, then sat on the end of it, facing her.

"I owe you an apology," he said.

She stared up at him, surprised. "For what?"

"For being condescending when you first arrived, for insinuating you'd be a burden to my investigation, and most importantly, for putting you at risk when it wasn't necessary."

"The risk is part of both our jobs. No apology is necessary."

He smiled. "And the rest."

"The rest is sketchy, but I can see how you might have felt things would be easier without me tagging along."

He shook his head. "I'd love to agree with you and let it go, but then I'd be compounding bad behavior with a lie. The truth is, I didn't want to work closely with you because you remind me of someone I don't really want to remember."

"Oh." It was one of the very few times in her life that Jadyn didn't have anything to say.

"I don't want to get into the dirty details, so I'll just say this—she was a cop, we had a thing, then we didn't any longer."

Jadyn studied his face, trying to gain a deeper understanding than what his words offered. He didn't look sad or angry or even wistful. In fact, if she had to attach any emotion at all to his expression, it would be resignation.

She felt a twinge of jealousy that another woman had meant so much to him that he still harbored feelings for her. What kind of woman inspired a man like Colt to carry a torch long after the flames had been doused with water?

"I'm sorry," Jadyn said finally.

"Don't be. The things about you that remind me of her are the good things."

"Then maybe you should tell me some of the bad ones in case I need to piss you off."

He laughed. "You know, I bet you'd do it, too." He studied her for a moment. "But I don't think you could ever match her evil side. I don't think you have it in you."

Jadyn shook her head. "I can be pretty bitchy, though."

He smiled. "So I've seen. Anyway, long and short of it—the problem is mine, it shouldn't be yours, and I'm going to correct it. How about you?"

"What about me?"

"How are you doing with all this? You seem to be handling some hard-core stuff pretty well, but you're new here and don't have the support system that you would have back home."

"Ha. Like you, I have things I don't want to dwell on, so let's just say I have more support here with people I've known a couple of days than I ever did with those I've had a lifetime with."

His expression shifted, but the pity she'd dreaded seeing wasn't there, just understanding. "My mom always said we can't pick our family," he said, "but we can make our own. I've got some relatives I prefer at a distance and some friends I'd give the shirt off my back. Mildred and Maryse are good women. A bit odd at times, but then it wouldn't be Mudbug without a little oddity."

His words made her heart swell just a bit. In a few sentences, he'd captured what she'd been feeling since she arrived—that this was where she was meant to be, where she fit. That everything about her life prior to Mudbug had been wrong, the people toxic. In Mildred and Maryse, she could have the family she'd always wanted. It may not be traditional, but that didn't matter.

"They are good women. I'm lucky to have them. Lucky to be here."

He sighed. "Maybe not this week. Are you sleeping all right—I mean, given the circumstances? That scene at Duke's...well, let's just say I expected to be scraping you up off the floor like I did the coroner."

"There was a moment or two I thought you might. I'd be lying if I said it didn't haunt me some, but I figure catching the guy who did it will go a long way to curing my problems sleeping."

"Yeah, you're probably right." He rose from the desk and placed his hand on her shoulder and squeezed. "If you ever need to talk, no matter the time, you can call me. I know what it's like to sit alone in the dark, waiting for daylight."

His touch warmed her body even more than his words. Such a simple thing, a hand on her shoulder, and yet every inch of her skin went on high alert. Everything about Colt Bertrand was so right, but yet so risky.

"Thank you," she managed, afraid to say more for fear of what might come out. At least she was at a safe distance, sitting in the chair. If she'd been closer to him, eye to eye, it would have been far harder to stop herself from reaching out to touch him as well.

A knock at the door broke the moment and he released her shoulder as Shirley stuck her head inside. "Hank Henry's here and wants to see you."

"Great. Send him back."

Jadyn rose from her chair, anxious to get her first look at Helena's son and Maryse's ex. According to the Mudbug gossip, Hank's reputation had preceded him for years, but he'd recently turned his life around, settled down with a good woman, and was now expecting a child. Jadyn liked redemption stories and couldn't wait to meet the man who'd actually accomplished it.

A few seconds later, a tall man with an athletic build and a gorgeous smile pushed open the office door and strolled inside. He shook hands with Colt, then turned to her.

"You must be Jadyn," he said. "I know because you've got those same beautiful eyes with the no-nonsense glint as Maryse."

He leaned forward and kissed her on the cheek. "It's a

pleasure to meet you."

Jadyn couldn't help smiling, immediately understanding why Maryse had gone against conventional wisdom and hooked up with the man in front of her. Hank Henry was, quite simply, charming.

"Nice to meet you, too," she said.

He pulled a key out of his pocket and handed it to Colt. "Not so much under these circumstances, though. Mildred gave me the CliffsNotes version of what's going on. I'm happy to help, but you two have got to promise me you will be careful. If anything happened to either of you in that cemetery, I'd never forgive myself."

"We're taking every precaution," Colt reassured him. "Do you know anything about the cemetery? The layout maybe?"

Hank shook his head. "Not a thing. Until Mildred called asking about it, I didn't even know we had a family cemetery. I doubt I've ever set foot in it. If I have, I don't remember. I did ask Wheeler about it though."

"The attorney?" Colt asked.

Hank nodded. "He said it hasn't been used since my great-granddad's time. It's been over forty years since he's seen it but he recalls several crypts. He just has no idea as to location of the crypts or the overall scope and size of the cemetery."

"I'll get this back to you as soon as we're done, maybe over a beer down at Bill's," Colt said.

"I'm going to hold you to that," Hank said and turned to Jadyn. "You keep him out of trouble. He was always in trouble."

"Ha," Colt said. "Given that this is the first time I've seen you in the sheriff's department without wearing cuffs, I think you've got me beat."

Hank grinned. "You were just better at not getting caught. Be safe," he said and exited the office.

Colt looked over at Jadyn and shook his head. "Why do all women get that look on their face when they're in the presence of Hank Henry?"

"Because he's handsome and charming?"

Colt grinned. "Honesty. I liked that."

Jadyn smiled. "He's happily married with a baby on the way. I'm allowed to appreciate him from the bleachers."

"Is that what you call it? Heck, I always thought I was breaking some rule when I found attached women attractive. I didn't realize bleacher admiration was perfectly acceptable."

"It depends on who you're admiring, or more accurately, who you're admiring is attached to."

"Isn't that the truth?" He sobered and took a step closer to her, leaving only inches between them. "Are you sure you want to do this? I can go alone."

She tried not to think about his body so close to hers. Tried not to think about how easy it would be to lean forward, wrap her hands in his unkempt hair, and press her lips to his. Such thoughts had no place between them—not now, not ever if they were to maintain a professional relationship.

"No," she said finally. "It's too dangerous. He may not be working alone."

She could tell by his expression that he knew she was right. Had known before he'd ever said a word, but some part of him required that he give her an out.

She wasn't about to take it.

Maryse waited on the bench outside of the sheriff's department for Hank to exit. As soon as she'd seen him pull into town, she'd hurried down the street, hoping to catch him before he left. For days, she'd been trying to reach him, but they'd never managed to connect. Now, she needed to hurry up and get everything on the table in case Helena spotted him in town.

The wait was excruciating, but finally, he walked out of the sheriff's department. He glanced over at her, then drew up short and smiled. "Maryse!"

She rose from the bench as he walked over and gave her a hug and kiss on the cheek. "I swear I haven't been dodging your calls—it's just that work has been crazy and we're trying to remodel one of the rooms to be a nursery. I was going straight to the hotel from here to see if Mildred knew where to find you."

"Don't worry about it. I know you're busy. How's Lila feeling?"

Hank beamed. "Great. Hasn't been sick a single day and says she feels better than ever."

Maryse shook her head. "She'll probably never have a labor pain and will deliver that baby while simultaneously knitting it a blanket and filing your tax return. The woman is perfect. It's scary."

Hank laughed. "Yeah, I'm going to agree with you, but don't tell Lila I'm scared of her. She'll just add to my chore list."

"It's our secret," Maryse agreed. "Look, I've got something to tell you that you're not going to like, so I'm just going to come right out and say it—your mother's back."

Hank's eyes widened. "What do you mean 'back'?"

"Still dead, but back on earth. In Mudbug, to be exact."

"What the hell is she doing here?"

"She says God has no sense of humor and she pissed him off…I don't know. With Helena it could be anything. Bottom line, it looks like she's here to stay for a while, and she knows Lila is pregnant."

Maryse held up a hand to stop Hank before he yelled. "None of us told her. She claims God let her watch what we were doing, like some really inappropriate reality show."

He ran one hand through his hair. "What the hell am I going to do? I can't have her around all the time. With the business and the baby, we're already stretched to capacity. If you throw Mom in the mix, it's a recipe for an insanity plea."

"Don't I know it, but I don't think you're in as much risk as the rest of us. Helena hasn't learned to fly, or anything equally as onerous, so unless she hitchhikes to New Orleans, or one of us agrees to bring her, she's not going to show up on your doorstep."

Hank relaxed a bit as he processed Maryse's words. "That doesn't sound quite as dire."

"No, but you need to visit her, and if she's still around when the baby comes, you need to establish some sort of visiting schedule. Otherwise, she'll make us all crazy."

"Yeah, you're right." He blew out a breath. "A visiting schedule for my dead mother. This may just be the thing that causes perfect Lila to break rank."

"She wouldn't be the first."

Hank placed his hand on top of Maryse's and squeezed. "I really appreciate you taking this on. I mean, I know Mom doesn't give you much choice, but I feel better knowing you and Mildred will attempt to ride herd over her."

He looked down Main Street, then back at Maryse. "Do you think I'll be able to see her? I mean, I did for a little bit before, but not the whole time she was here."

"That's a good question. Mildred and I can both see her and unfortunately for Luc, he can again."

"Oh wow. I bet he's pissed."

"So much that he's suggesting we move."

"I can't say that I blame him. I don't suppose you know where she is now?"

"She was eating a cinnamon roll with Mildred when I left the hotel."

Hank rose from the bench. "May as well get this over with."

Maryse nodded.

Famous last words.

Chapter Twenty-Three

"Wow!" Colt stared up at the massive iron gate that guarded the old cemetery. "That is some serious ironwork. If this key doesn't open it, we'll have to come back with a bulldozer."

"Sounds like the best idea ever!" Helena boomed from the backseat.

It had been a bit of a fight to get Helena to come with them. Tears were shed, accusations were flung, and finally Mildred put her foot down and told her she wouldn't take her to visit Hank and her grandchild as they'd all agreed upon earlier when Hank was at the hotel and much to his dismay, could see his mother in all her ghostly glory.

Jadyn wasn't convinced having Helena along was worth the trouble, as the ghost had done nothing but complain from the moment she'd sat down in the truck. The fact that Jadyn was the only one who could hear her rantings and completely lacked the ability to respond didn't seem to faze Helena at all. She just kept belting them out.

"Why haven't you ever seen it before?" Jadyn asked as they climbed out of his truck.

He frowned. "I don't know. I guess because it's in the opposite direction of all the best hunting and fishing. No reason to come back here."

"I couldn't agree more," Helena said. "Why don't we leave?"

Jadyn cut her eyes at Helena then looked back at the gate. "I guess there's no shortage of swamp for boys here to tromp around in."

Colt pulled the key Hank gave him from his pocket and stepped in front of the gate. "Here goes nothing," he said as he slid the key in the lock.

He twisted it to the left and it turned effortlessly, then emitted a loud click.

"That was easy," she said.

"Too easy. Someone's been here recently and oiled this lock."

"Not a good sign," Helena said.

It was probably the only accurate thing Helena had said all day. "I can't think of any reason someone would come here," Jadyn said. "Can you?"

He slipped the key back in his pocket and pulled out his pistol. "Not a single one."

"Probably grave robbers," Helena said. "Though if they took any of my family, they probably brought them back. I would."

Jadyn held in a sigh. Oh the irony.

"Let's get the supplies," Colt said. "You have on your vest, right?"

"Yeah," she said as he walked back to his truck and hauled the rifles out, handing one to her. Then he pulled a backpack out of the truck and slung it over one shoulder.

"Ammo?" she asked. She'd been hoping they wouldn't even need what was chambered, much less additional rounds, but he was smart to prepare for the worst.

"Ammo and a CB."

She nodded. "Because our cell phones won't work out here."

"Ha!" Helena hooted. "If you're not calling about speckled trout biting, no one on that CB's going to care."

"Well, let's hope we don't need either." Bart had told Jadyn that law enforcement had their own channel. If things got bad enough to send out a distress signal, she hoped someone was listening.

"That's the plan." He shut the trunk and pulled out his pistol. "You ready?"

Jadyn pulled her pistol out of her waistband and chambered a round. "As ready as I'm getting."

"Then let's do it." He strode to the gate and pulled it open wide enough for them to slip inside. Jadyn looked back at Helena, who was standing on the other side, her arms crossed. She let Colt get ahead of her and motioned to Helena to hurry up. Helena let out a long-suffering sigh, then walked through the gate and into the cemetery.

The center path that led into the cemetery branched off in four different directions about thirty yards in. The cypress trees, which had been thinned out around the main path, grew closer together here, with giant sheets of moss hanging off of them. In spots, the branches touched, forming canopies that completely blocked out the sunlight. Jadyn noticed that the trees got closer as each path progressed, making it look as if you were walking into a cave.

Colt walked back and forth down part of each path, studying the ground. "This one looks like it's had recent traffic, and some sort of cart...wheelbarrow or dolly, maybe."

"Sounds like the place."

He nodded. "Stay close, but try to watch behind for any sign of movement," he said. "And listen. Anything sounds or even feels out of place, you tap me on the shoulder. Otherwise, I want to do this as quietly as possible."

"Got it," she said and fell into step behind him as he started down the trail.

At first Jadyn thought covering the rear would give her

plenty of opportunity to keep an eye on Helena, but it wasn't necessary. The ghost had lagged entering the cemetery but now that they were off down one of the narrow, dim paths, she was practically on top of her. In fact, when Colt stopped short once and Jadyn followed suit, Helena walked right through her.

"Sorry," Helena said and fell into place behind Jadyn again. "Hey, at least I didn't get solid."

Jadyn shook off the chill Helena had caused, not even wanting to think about the possibility of the ghost going solid. The last thing she needed was Colt thinking she was a clumsy idiot who tripped at the drop of a hat—especially while she was carrying two loaded weapons and wearing another on her ankle.

She scanned the cemetery as they walked, surprised at the number of graves contained within it. Helena's family either had been here for a very long time or was much larger in decades past.

"I don't see any crypts," Jadyn whispered.

"No, but I get a glimpse of the tire tracks ever so often. Maybe the crypt is toward the back."

"When Daddy dragged me here to spit on Granddad's grave," Helena said, "he said at one time, the cemetery had been made up only of crypts, but that stupid ancestors had squandered their inheritance and had too many children, diminishing the lineage and the family fortune."

Jadyn shook her head. The more stories she heard about Helena's father, the more she understand why Helena had issues. Briefly she wondered if there was such a thing as counseling for ghosts. Maybe Sabine, the pseudo-exorcist, would know.

They rounded a corner past a huge azalea hedge and Colt pointed. "There."

Jadyn peered around him and saw white marble glinting through the trees. Her pulse ticked up a notch as they picked up pace until they arrived at the cleared area around a huge crypt.

Jadyn ran one hand down the marble wall. "How much money did something like this require back then?"

"A shitload," Helena said. "Why do you think I never had to work?"

"A lot," Colt said. "But I'm less interested in how much the wall is worth and more interested in what might be inside."

He set his backpack on the ground near the crypt, pulled the key from Duke's house out of his pocket, and twisted it in the lock. The thick marble door began to slide open on its own. Colt glanced at Jadyn before pushing the door wide open, allowing the sunlight to enter.

For a couple of seconds, they both stared in shock. This had to be the right place, but the last thing they'd expected to see was coffins, stacked in the middle of the crypt.

"Oh, hell no!" Helena shouted. "That's new dead people. I'm out of here."

Jadyn shot a dirty look at the ghost, who backed up several steps but didn't flee as threatened, then looked over at Colt. "Any thoughts on this one?"

He blew out a breath. "I, uh…no. This wasn't even on the list of things I'd thought of."

He stepped up to the coffins and pushed on one of the lids. "It's sealed."

Jadyn leaned her rifle against the outside wall of the crypt and stepped inside. She ran her hands over the wooden surface. "They look real. You don't think…"

"That there's bodies in them?" He shook his head. "I wish I was certain there weren't, but this entire case has been unlike anything I've ever seen."

She pulled her hand back from the coffin, feeling slightly ill. Behind her, she heard an intake of breath and glanced over to see Helena peeking around the corner of the doorway and into the crypt. She looked as if she would pass out at any moment. "What now?" Jadyn asked.

"I'll call Shirley and tell her to get a flatbed truck and some dollies over here. We can open the caskets up once we get them to the sheriff's department."

"I'm afraid I can't allow that," a familiar voice sounded behind them.

Jadyn spun around and saw the coroner, James, standing just outside of the doorway, a handgun leveled at them.

"Throw your weapons out the door," he said. "Come on now. I know you have pistols in your waistbands."

Jadyn pulled her pistol from her waistband and tossed it out the crypt door, but didn't make a move for the one on her ankle. If James didn't know about it, she might have an advantage. Colt tossed his gun out the door as well, but never took his gaze off James.

"Why?" Colt asked.

"Do you know what the coroner's salary is? Do you know how many years I've stared death in the face, knowing my own was coming and that I'd never get the life I wanted?"

"So you're trafficking...corpses?"

"Heavens no. I'm trying to get away from dead people. Those caskets are full of automatic weapons. I know it seems an odd choice, but it's simple economics, really. It takes only a few arms deals to amass a healthy retirement, and finding the buyers and suppliers was surprisingly easier than I expected. So many interesting things can be found on the Internet."

"You weren't scared you'd get caught?"

"Of course, there was risk, but I had far less than most people. I ship the guns to the New Orleans buyers in caskets. No cop is going to open a sealed coffin without a warrant, and they'd need a damned good reason to get one."

Colt shook his head, his disgust apparent. "How could you kill Duke like that?"

James's eyes widened. "I didn't do that. Why do you think I passed out when I saw him? When the guns weren't delivered as promised, the buyer must have come looking for Duke to collect his weapons."

"But Duke didn't know where they were?"

"Of course not. Even I didn't know where they were. Not until you found them. The seller doesn't provide the location of the merchandise until they receive payment."

"Why didn't Duke give the buyer your name? I can't imagine him dying to protect you."

"I arranged the entire deal by phone. The buyer made the money drop. Duke was supposed to make the delivery, and that was the only role he was to play."

"Then why did he steal the crypt key?"

James shrugged. "I don't know for sure, but when I realized the key was missing, things clicked into place. There's been some vandalism in some of the wealthier families' crypts in New Orleans. A lot of the older generation insisted on being buried with quite a bit of expensive jewelry. Each time the crimes occurred, Duke and Leroy were in New Orleans for one of their casino binges."

"You think he stole the key hoping he could steal jewelry off of dead people?"

"That's my theory. What I know for certain is that Duke was in the coroner's office when I put the key in my desk drawer, and I found his cell phone on my desk after he'd gone. He'd been commissioned to make a coffin for Mr. Elroy Senior, who was too tall to fit in any of the standard offerings."

"That would also explain why Leroy skipped," Jadyn said.

"What about the gate key?" Colt asked. "How were you supposed to retrieve the product without a gate key?"

"My suppliers always remove a panel from the cemetery fence large enough to move the merchandise through. I've never asked how they get the keys to the crypts. I don't think I want to know."

Colt shook his head. "So Duke stole the key from you and buried it in his backyard, not even realizing that you were the middleman and the key was half of the reason he was tortured to death." Colt shook his head. "That's the most ridiculous set of ironically bad choices I have ever heard of."

"Things weren't supposed to happen this way," James said. "I never meant for anyone to die. If Duke had used his own boat instead of borrowing Junior's none of this would have happened. He should have known that boat had problems as long as it's been sitting there."

"Did you really think you could take up with these kind of people and not have something like this happen?"

He sighed. "I guess I did."

"So who killed Junior, and don't even tell me it was natural causes?"

"I imagine Duke did."

Colt shook his head. "That doesn't jibe with time of death."

"Oh, I lied about that. I wanted to give myself an alibi, you see, and what better alibi than being with you?"

"If Junior wasn't part of the plan, then why would Duke kill him?"

"I'm just guessing, of course, but I know Junior didn't tell you it was his boat sunk in the pond. There's only one reason I can think of that he wouldn't have."

"To get money out of Duke for keeping quiet."

James nodded. "They were both too foolish to make good criminals. If everyone sticks to his assigned task and doesn't try to navigate outside of his pay grade, then no one dies."

Jadyn's stomach rolled. "How can you be so callous? You've known those men your entire life."

"And both were fated for lives that ended badly. Their choices precluded any other final chapter. When one spends so much time around death, you begin to understand the logic of it."

"You mean the coldness?"

"I'm not cold, and I'll prove it. I have no intention of killing the two of you, although it would probably be the smarter thing to do. I'm simply not a murderer. Instead, you're going to haul the coffins out of the crypt and then I'm going to lock you inside. When I make it out of the country, I'll call and tell someone where you are. It will be uncomfortable, but you'll live."

He waved his pistol at them. "The two of you should have no trouble lifting the coffins. Go ahead and bring the first one out. And no funny business. It wouldn't take much to change my mind on the murderer thing.

Seeing no other alternative at that moment, Jadyn grabbed one end of a casket and she and Colt hauled it outside, placing it where James indicated. Helena, who'd apparently been shocked into silence for a bit, came alive when they hauled the first coffin out of the crypt and started pacing along beside Jadyn.

"Do you think he'll kill you or just lock you in like he said? I can get help if he just locks you in. What do I do?"

Jadyn's mind raced with a million possibilities, but every possibility attached to Helena came with risks that might outweigh the benefits. And how was she supposed to give instructions to the ghost without Colt thinking she'd lost her mind?

"I wish we'd brought the CB inside," Jadyn said to Colt as they hoisted up the next coffin. "We could send out a distress signal."

Helena perked up. "I can send out a signal." She ran out of the crypt ahead of them, Jadyn staring after her in dismay. The backpack was on the side of the crypt in plain sight. No way could Helena get that pack without James noticing, and even if she could, the likelihood of someone hearing her was slim to none.

As they started out the door with the casket, Helena bent over the backpack. "Stop for a second," she said. "Pretend to stumble or something."

Jadyn glanced over at James and realized that with the way they were currently positioned, the coffin blocked his view of the backpack. She shuffled a bit and pretended to lose her balance.

"You okay?" Colt asked.

"Yeah. I just need to reposition."

"Hurry up," James said. "There will be plenty of time to rest when you're locked in that crypt."

Jadyn shifted her hands a bit on the bottom of the coffin and saw Helena lift the backpack off the ground and disappear into the trees. Thankfully, Colt was too busy watching James to see the activity going on beside him, and as she continued forward with the coffin, she said a quick prayer that James wouldn't notice that the backpack was missing.

And a second that Helena knew how to operate a CB radio.

Maryse had spent an exhausting morning on the bayou, searching for a plant that seemed perfectly content to remain elusive, despite being native to the region. Oysters had moved in on two known locations and the plants had disappeared, causing her to search for a new cultivating spot.

She was just pulling up to the dock at her office when her CB radio blared.

"Help! Someone help! He's got a gun and he's going to kill

them in the cemetery."

Helena!

A wave of dizziness washed over Maryse as Helena's words sank in.

Jadyn!

She bolted over the bow of her boat and jumped into the shallow water of the bank. The thick Louisiana mud sucked her rubber boots down and locked them into place, but it didn't slow her one bit. She simply ran right out of them and kept running up the bank, barreling into a startled Luc, who'd just walked out the back door of her office.

"Helena!" Maryse shouted, breathless from her panic and the dash. "She's on the CB—the sheriff's channel. She said a man is holding them hostage at a cemetery. It must be Colt and Jadyn."

Immediately, Luc launched into action. He called Shirley and verified Colt and Jadyn's location, then called two coworkers who lived close by for backup. It was a testament to Luc's reputation that he asked only that the men meet him in downtown Mudbug in five minutes and come armed, and that's all it took to launch them into action.

"Get back to the CB," Luc told her as he hurried for his truck. "Call me if you hear anything else, but do *not* respond. The perp can't hear Helena, but he would be able to hear you reply."

Crap! She hadn't even thought about that aspect, but Luc was right. She had no idea if Helena was within hearing range of the killer. If Maryse responded, she could make matters much worse.

She ran back down the bank, tromping through the mud and water barefoot, and climbed back into her boat. The CB was silent, and the worst part was, she had no idea whether that was good or bad. Praying for good, she sat in front of the CB and crossed her fingers.

Chapter Twenty-Four

As Colt and Jadyn lowered the last coffin on the ground in front of the crypt, he studied James. The man was clearly on the edge. His hands shook. His skin was pale. Colt had no faith that James would keep his promise and let them live. Even if he did, how long would it take someone to find them? And if the crypt was airtight, how long could they survive once closed inside?

"I'm sorry it has to be this way," James said, looking genuinely distressed, "but it's time to bring this to an end. You won't be in the crypt more than a couple of days."

"I have a better idea," Colt said. "Why don't you turn state's evidence on the supplier and the buyer? I can't make any promises, but if they're running enough product, you could end up walking away from it all."

James's eyes widened. "Don't you remember what they did to Duke? I don't think you have any idea what kind of people you're dealing with."

"Then maybe I should tell him," a man's voice boomed behind James.

James spun around and they all stared as a man walked out from behind the azalea hedge, flanked by two more men holding semiautomatic weapons.

All the blood rushed from James's face. "Marcelo," he whispered.

One of the men with a gun motioned to James to drop his

weapon. He released the pistol as if it were on fire and it hit the hard ground with a thud.

"So you know who I am?" the man in the middle said. "That's good. An appropriate amount of fear makes every business transaction easier for me."

He smiled at James. "Coroner, huh? When I heard the guns would be delivered in coffins, my first thought was the funeral director. I suppose he's lucky I decided to sit here and wait for you to come, right?"

"How did you know…?" James's voice shook.

"It wasn't all that hard. Duke couldn't tell me where my weapons were, but he did know where to find the supplier, so I paid them a visit. They were angry, of course, that the payment had not arrived as scheduled, and were quite surprised to hear what had befallen all my money."

"I was going to make it right," James pleaded. "That's why I was looking for the guns. A new delivery guy is on the way. He was going to bring them all to you."

Marcelo shook his head. "The suppliers were not very nice people. They showed no sympathy for my lost money and insisted I pay again. Such arrogance, and after I'd taken great pains to meet their odd demands of plastic bags and wasted hours to separate the money as instructed. I wasn't pleased."

"You killed them," Colt said.

Marcelo smiled. "Of course, although not at first. I needed to know where my weapons were, after all."

"Clearly they gave you the answer you wanted," Colt said. "Why didn't you take the guns and leave?"

"And let the man who'd made a mess of everything get away with it all? Our coroner friend cost me time and could have cost me my reputation. In this business, reputation is your ticket to keep breathing. I don't take that ticket lightly. My customer was willing to wait another day, but he would be very unhappy if all loose ends weren't handled."

Marcelo pulled a .45 from his jacket. "No sense attracting attention with the semiautomatics. They sound as impressive as they look." He looked back and forth among Jadyn, Colt, and James. "Where to start. Such a dilemma."

Colt felt all the heat leave his body. He knew his options but none of them had even a remote chance of success...not against the firepower in front of him. Rushing Marcelo or making a run for it would both end in certain death, but then so would standing there. Mind made up, he prepared to spring. Maybe he would buy Jadyn enough time to get away.

But before he could launch, Marcelo leveled his gun at Jadyn. "I think if the woman dies first, it will distress both of you more."

"No!" Colt yelled and jumped in front of Jadyn just as Marcelo fired. The bullet caught him square in the chest, sending him backward into Jadyn and knocking them both to the ground.

His chest felt as if it was split in half, his breath completely gone. He blinked, struggling with consciousness, as he heard gunfire again, but different from Marcelo's .45.

Jadyn yelled at him, practically pulling him to his feet. His vision was blurred so he couldn't make out what was happening, but he didn't slow down to work it out. Instead, he stumbled behind Jadyn as she ran around the crypt.

"What the hell is going on?" he asked as they leaned against the backside of the crypt, bullets ricocheting off the marble walls echoing throughout the swamp.

"Someone else started shooting," Jadyn said.

"Who?"

"I don't know. Someone in the trees."

Colt tried to take a deep breath, but he hadn't gotten in even half the air he needed before his chest screamed in pain.

His focus started to return, and he assessed their options.

Unfortunately, they weren't much better than before.

Jadyn cringed as another shower of bullets flew past the edge of the crypt. They couldn't stay here, but would they be able to elude the shooters in the trees?

"They're shooting at me!" Helena yelled from the swamp. "How do you work this thing? It's empty."

Marcelo and his remaining henchmen didn't have a clue where the other shooter was, but when the stray bullet had caught one of Marcelo's bodyguards right in the throat, Jadyn hadn't even hesitated a second to haul Colt up from the ground and run for cover, no doubt in her mind from where the other shot had derived. Colt's backup weapon had been in the backpack with the CB.

"How many are left?" Colt asked.

"I think just two. Marcelo took out James while we were getting away."

"You have your spare, right?"

"Yeah, but only the magazine that's loaded—six rounds."

"Then that will have to do."

"You think we should run for it?

He shook his head and pointed up.

"You want to get on top of the crypt?"

"We can't outrun bullets and they've got a lot. There's two of them, so they can easily flank us. The cypress limbs hang low over the roof and will provide decent cover, and they won't be expecting an attack from above."

"But when you shoot the first one, the other will know where we are."

Colt nodded. "But without moving some distance away from the crypt, he won't have a clear shot at us."

"So this entire plan hinges on you picking off the first guy with one shot and the second as he's running away?"

"Yeah."

"You first. It will be easier on your ribs," she said and bent over, bracing her arms on her knees.

He hesitated a moment, but common sense won out and he stepped on her back, then pulled himself up onto the crypt. As Jadyn jumped up and grabbed the ledge, he turned around and latched onto her wrists, pulling her as she scrambled up the side.

He winced as he pulled her over the edge and she knew the pain had to be excruciating. They crawled across the roof, staying under the canopy of branches and moss, until they could see over the front of the crypt.

Marcelo's guard lay about twenty feet away from the crypt, a pool of blood circling his neck. James was splayed five feet in front of him, more bullet holes than she could count riddling his body, but there was no sign of Marcelo or the other guard.

"Where are they?" Colt whispered.

Shaking her head, she scanned the cemetery for any sign of movement. About the time she was beginning to worry that they had been made, Helena ran out of the trees and straight for the crypt, the two men not far behind.

"Save me!" Helena screamed as she ran, hands in the air, straight toward the crypt, then disappeared beneath them. Marcelo and his guard skidded to a halt in front of the crypt.

"He had to come this way," the guard said.

"Well, I don't see him," Marcelo said, clearly disgusted, "and the other two aren't behind the crypt. They must have made a run for it."

"Help! The door closed behind me," Helena yelled. "I'm locked in here with dead people."

Jadyn's anxiety took another leap. If Helena had gone solid and trapped herself in the crypt, she couldn't be any help to them. Their only hope was if Colt made both shots count.

He leveled her pistol at the guard and she frowned. Her heart wished it was Marcelo he targeted first, but the guard's weapon was a far bigger threat than Marcelo's .45. He took a shallow breath then released it slowly, squeezing the trigger when all the oxygen was out of his lungs.

The shot caught the guard right in the forehead and he dropped like a stone. Colt aimed for the second shot and pulled the trigger, but the gun jammed, giving Marcelo time to grab the guard's gun and disappear into the trees.

"Shit!" Colt said as he cleared the jam and fired two shots at Marcelo as he disappeared into the trees.

"How long until he figures where we are?"

"He already has." Colt pointed to the right where a shadow slipped behind a tree. "If he thinks anything like me, he'll slow down long enough to climb that tree and then he'll have a clear shot."

"Then get him first."

Colt shifted so he could see into the swamp to the right. "Get ready. As soon as I say, jump off the crypt behind us and haul ass for the gate. I'll be right behind you."

Jadyn nodded and crouched under the branches, ready to spring over the edge of the crypt as soon as Colt gave the signal.

"I see the branches moving," Colt said. "Get ready. Come on, you bastard. Show yourself."

A bullet ripped past Jadyn's head and she flattened herself on the crypt. A second later, Colt fired off two shots in rapid succession. "Got him! Run!"

Chapter Twenty-Five

Jadyn sprang for the edge of the crypt, rolled onto her belly, then flipped over the side and dropped to the ground. Before sprinting into the trees, she glanced back long enough to see Colt sliding over the edge of the crypt.

The brush tore at her bare arms and the muscles in her legs burned as she sped through the cemetery. Her sense of direction was usually dead-on, but she couldn't be certain she was headed in the right direction. About fifty yards into the cemetery, Colt caught up with her and motioned for her to veer right.

His breathing was so labored and he was practically dragging his right side, but he pushed on as if ignoring it would make it go away. Jadyn slowed her pace a bit and prayed that he had enough in him to make it to the truck. It seemed like forever, but only minutes later, they dashed through the gate and toward Colt's truck.

Then Marcelo stepped out from behind it, his pistol leveled at them.

Blood ran down his shirt from the bullet wound on his shoulder, and scratches and cuts covered the rest of his bare skin, but he'd had the advantage of running without injured ribs, giving him the edge.

Jadyn's heart plummeted into her feet. This was the end of the line. They were out of bullets, Helena was locked in the crypt, and they had no room to run. Colt looked at her and she could tell he knew it too.

"I'm sorry," he said.

"How romantic," Marcelo said, his finger whitening on the trigger. "The two of you will make a couple of beautiful corpses."

Jadyn almost passed out when the shot came, and it took her a second before she realized she hadn't been hit. She clutched Colt, looking for the wound, but he stared back as her, as shocked as she was. Then they both turned and saw Marcelo lying on the ground, a bullet hole through the center of his forehead.

"That's two you owe me, Bertrand." Luc LeJeune stepped out from behind the truck, holding a smoking gun, two other armed men beside him.

Colt broke out into a huge grin. "Two? I don't think so. It was my bullet that took out that drug dealer at that shipyard in New Orleans."

Luc shook his head. "Forensics couldn't determine whose gun fired that shot. As the officer with jurisdiction, I'm taking credit."

Jadyn felt her knees go weak and she staggered backward a couple of steps to lean against the fence. She'd thought she was dead. Thought both of them were dead. Instead, they were both standing there, and Colt was cracking jokes with Luc like they'd spent the afternoon watching football.

"Are you all right?" Luc asked.

Colt whirled around and hurried over to her. "Jadyn?"

She took a deep breath and blew it out. "I think I'm just so relieved that I'm ready to collapse."

Colt smiled. "That's the adrenaline leaving your body."

"Yeah, well, it could have waited until I got back to the hotel."

All the men laughed.

"You'll be a little achy," Luc said, "and you'll probably have a fantastic headache for a while."

She stood up straight and smiled. "Compared to what could have happened, a fantastic headache sounds like a trip to Disneyland."

Colt looked over at Luc. "Why are you here?"

"I thought that was obvious," Luc said. "I'm saving your ass."

Colt grinned. "I mean, how did you know?"

"Maryse heard a distress call on the CB about shooting in the cemetery," Luc explained. "She had a bad feeling about it, so I checked with Shirley and found out you two were here." He pointed at the two men beside him. "Steve and Ryan are on assignment in the area, so I asked them to back me, just in case."

"I can't tell you how much we appreciate it. Who made the distress call?"

Luc shook his head. "Maryse didn't recognize the voice."

Jadyn held in a smile. Luc was a damned good liar.

"Maybe it was the other shooter?" Colt said.

Luc narrowed his eyes. "What other shooter?"

"Jadyn said a shot came from someone behind us in the trees. It took out one of Marcelo's guys and that's when we bolted. My vision was too blurred to see anything."

Luc nodded and turned to Jadyn. "Did you see the other shooter?"

Jadyn froze for a moment, trying to come up with a clever way of answering the question as she wasn't near as good a liar as Luc. "There was no person back there that I could see."

Luc looked momentarily confused at her choice of words, then his eyes widened slightly, and she knew he'd caught on to what had happened. "It was probably a local," he said. "Someone who wanted to help but doesn't want to be involved. That sort of thing happens more than you'd think, especially in these bayou towns."

"Well, I hope karma comes back on him in a big way," Colt said.

Jadyn coughed. Oh, karma had come back on the shooter all right. Just not in the way Colt thought it would.

"So what's the story here?" Luc asked.

Colt waved down the path to the crypt. "You'd have to see it to believe it."

As they stepped into the clearing at the crypt, Steve whistled, taking in the three dead men and the pile of caskets. "This is some twisted shit."

Luc bent over James's body. "Is that the coroner?"

"Yeah, I'm afraid so," Colt replied. "He was the middleman."

Luc shook his head in disbelief. "Were they trafficking bodies?"

"No," Colt said. "Guns."

"Damn." Ryan looked a bit sad. "Seems like we're always doing the ATF's job for them."

Luc scanned the clearing, then looked over at Jadyn, and she knew he was looking for Helena. She inclined her head toward the crypt just as Helena's voice wafted to them.

"Help! I'm going to suffocate. It's dark and I'm locked in here with dead people. I'm claustrophobic, for Christ's sake. That's why I was cremated and spread."

Luc rubbed his chin and Jadyn could tell he was trying not to laugh. "So the guns are in the coffins and they were stored in the crypt. And the coroner was the middleman for all this carnage."

Colt nodded. "Hard to believe. I've known the man my entire life."

"Luc!" Helena sounded again. "Is that you? Get me out of here. I promise I'll never try to see you naked again. I'll even close my eyes when you walk into a room."

Luc coughed. "The job always sucks worse when you know the perp," he said and pulled out a sat phone. "The state police can secure the area, and I'll call a buddy of mine with the ATF. We can wait here for the state. Jadyn, why don't you get this man to the hospital?"

"Absolutely," she said.

"I'm fine," Colt protested.

"Dude, I know broken ribs when I see them," Luc said. "Everyone loves a hero. No one loves a martyr. Go get them wrapped before the shock wears off."

Colt hesitated before answering and Jadyn could tell he was weighing the desire for painkillers against perceived responsibility. "You're sure?"

"Positive," Luc said. "Just leave the keys to the crypt and the gate with me. The cops are going to want both."

"I love you, Luc!" Helena shouted. "You're a God."

As they started to leave, Jadyn stopped in front of Luc, hesitated for a second, then threw her arms around him. "Thank you," she said.

Steve and Ryan whistled.

"Don't let Maryse know about that," Steve teased, "or she'll have your hide."

Luc smiled as Jadyn released him. "Jadyn is Maryse's cousin. I think she'll be okay with it."

Ryan raised his eyebrows and gave Jadyn a hard look. "Cousin, huh?" he said to Luc as they headed to the crypt. "Is she single?"

Jadyn waved at the men and started down the path back to the gate. She walked slowly, allowing Colt to progress at a stride that was less aggravating to his ribs. When they got to the truck, she opened the door and he climbed in the passenger's seat, his face contorting in pain as he pulled himself onto the seat.

"Are you all right?" she asked.

He smiled. "I feel like I've been hit in the chest by a space shuttle, but other than that, it's turning out to be one of the best days of my life."

She nodded, understanding exactly what he was saying. Never had she been so frightened, so certain that her life was over. Now, every intake of breath seemed a huge gift.

He put his hand on the side of her face. "You saved my life."

Her heart began to pound in her temples as warmth ran through every inch of her. "You took a bullet for me," she said. "It would have been rude to leave you there."

He looked at her a moment longer, his indecision clear. Then he laughed and dropped his hand. "Welcome to Mudbug, St. James."

Jadyn smiled and closed the passenger door. He'd said the same thing to her the first time he'd met her, but this time, she could tell he meant it. It wasn't the ending she'd thought she was going to get, but apparently Colt had decided he wanted her to stick around.

That would do. For now.

Chapter Twenty-Six

"Bring more potato chips," Beau called from the deck as he pulled a stack of hamburger patties from the grill and handed them to Luc, who placed them on the patio table. The smell of onions and pepper wafted by Jadyn's nose and her mouth watered.

Sabine and Maryse walked out of the house carrying potato chips and a huge pan of baked beans. Mildred refilled everyone's iced tea and they all took a seat at the patio table. Jadyn looked around the table and couldn't help smiling.

It was a beautiful Saturday with a nice breeze wafting across the deck. The past week had been a whirlwind of interviews with the state police and the ATF, but it had resulted in more arrests in the arms trafficking ring. Luc, always the practical one, said it wouldn't make a difference in the big scheme of things as another criminal would simply step into the vacated slots, but then he'd smiled and said something about job security.

Colt had been thrilled with the additional arrests that the ATF made, but Jadyn could tell that the entire thing still weighed heavily on him. So many times that week, she'd started to talk to him about it, but she had no idea what to say. Colt settled back into talk about work and regular Mudbug happenings, and Jadyn decided that's the way he wanted it, so she let it go.

After Luc rescued her from the crypt, Helena had gone straight to her hotel room and refused to come out for three days.

Mildred sent up bath salts and candles every day, and Sabine came by every afternoon to counsel the ghost on releasing the stress she was harboring. Several times, Jadyn thought about exactly what was going on in Helena's room and questioned their group sanity. Finally, the ghost had emerged refreshed and insisting on visiting Hank. Mildred had arranged the visit and taken her to New Orleans the day before.

Mildred cleared her throat. "Before we eat, I'd just like to take a moment to thank God for bringing you all into my life and keeping you safe. And a special thanks for the newest addition to our family." She reached across the table to give Jadyn's hand a squeeze.

Jadyn's heart swelled as the others cheered and clinked their plastic cups together. She'd thought she was coming to Mudbug for a job.

But she'd gotten a family.

The End

For new release notification, to participate in a monthly $100 egift card drawing, and more, sign up for my newsletter:

http://janadeleon.com/newsletter-sign-up/

JANA DELEON

The Author:

Jana DeLeon grew up among the bayous and 'gators of southwest Louisiana. She's never stumbled across a mystery like one of her heroines but is still hopeful. She lives in Dallas, Texas with a menagerie of animals and not a single ghost.

Visit Jana at:

Website: http://janadeleon.com
Facebook: http://www.facebook.com/JanaDeLeonAuthor/
Twitter: @JanaDeLeon

JANA DELEON

Books by Jana DeLeon:

Rumble on the Bayou

Unlucky

The Ghost-in-Law Series:

Trouble in Mudbug
Mischief in Mudbug
Showdown in Mudbug
Resurrection in Mudbug
The Helena Diaries—Trouble in Mudbug (Novella)

The Miss Fortune Series:

Louisiana Longshot
Lethal Bayou Beauty

CPSIA information can be obtained
at www.ICGtesting.com
Printed in the USA
LVHW052138101119
636891LV00009B/120/P

9 781490 490564